# WARRIOR'S POSSESSION

## MEDIEVAL WARRIOR'S LEGENDS BOOK 1

### BY GIANNA SIMONE

warrior's possession

Rosavin Publishing
Contact: rosavinpub@optonline.net

Warrior's Possession
Copyright © 2016 Gianna Simone

ISBN: 978-0692675410
ASIN: B01AYF21PC

Cover Design: Gianna Simone

# also by gianna simone

**Medieval Warrior's Legends**
Warrior's Vengeance – Book 2
Warrior's Wrath – Book 3

**The Norsemen Sagas**
Norseman's Revenge – Book 1
Norseman's Deception – Book 2

**The Bayou Magiste Chronicles**
Claimed by the Devil – Book 1
Claimed by the Mage – Book 2
Claimed by the Enchanter – Book 3
Claimed by the Zyndevine – Book 4

# PRAISE FOR GIANNA SIMONE:

**Warrior's Vengeance**

**The Romance Reviews:** The plot is so captivating that the reader feels compelled to know more. The story, the development and the end are, to put it mildly, peculiar and original. This is my first Gianna Simone novel and I must say, she did a great job.

**Goodreads:** Impressive and totally hot bodice ripper!

**Warrior's Wrath**

**BDSM Book Reviews:** This story combines the richness of the 14th century history, meshed along with the stories of betrayal and the stories of love. There is a sweetness of Aeron as she is immersed in a sexual education she never knew existed.

**Goodreads: The menage scenes were H.O.T.!** Ms. Simone really does well with the heat and creativity of the triangle in action.

**Warrior's Possession**

**BDSM Book Reviews:** Gillian is keeping secrets and Royce will use everything in his sexual arsenal to make her tell him all of them. A BDSM bodice ripper… if you enjoy spanking, bondage, subduing and sexual interrogation you'll have plenty to enjoy.

**The Romance Reviews:** As a period piece, I was impressed with the author's research into all aspects of the story (language, clothing, food, activities, etc.). And in typical period fashion, Lady Gillian is treated more as an object to be controlled than a partner. Something she wants nothing to do with. Well, mostly. For the Panther has a knack for turning his lady inside out. The sex scenes and the BDSM scenes are scintillating as it's easy to imagine your own skin warming under the Earl's capable hand.

## Claimed by the Devil

**BDSM Book Reviews:** Five Paddles! The story leads you on an emotional rollercoaster, but it is well worth the ride. As Helene and Devlin get older their past is ever present, but Devlin works at gaining what he desires. Devlin fed into Helene's needs giving her what she wanted. Sex is here, often and hot, well written and intense.

**You Gotta Read Reviews:** This is one intense and hot story that grabbed my attention from the start and would not let go. While we are treated to the romance between Helene and Devlin we also get to find out about their lives outside of the bedroom, which include both friends and enemies. I loved watching the attraction between the two become so much more. Helen blooms with the help of Devlin and his love.

## Claimed by the Mage

**The Romance Reviews:** Gianna Simone does an

excellent job with Aiden's seduction of Lily. He reads her well and understands, most of the time, when to push and when to give. He takes care not to overpower or frighten away his healer as he carefully reveals her submissive side to her. My favorite parts of the book are those moments when he uses everything at his disposal to make love to her, and magic can allow for some sinfully erotic maneuverings.

## Claimed by the Enchanter

**BDSM Book Reviews:** The author did a wonderful job of contrasting Regine's need to control and be dominated. She also showed how much trust plays into a relationship. Once Cameron and Regine get together, the sparks fly. The chemistry between the two is intense and the scenes between the two, and later with David, are very hot.

**Coffee Time Romance:** Claimed by the Enchanter is published by a suitably named publisher, because it is a sizzler of a story. The struggle between self-perception and self-awareness is strong and the emotions it invokes mirrors the struggle between who a person thinks they are, and who they are afraid to be. The internal struggle was as strong as the struggle to solve the mystery. I absolutely fell right into the story and lived as the characters lived with every emotion magnified. I am happy to say I am a new fan of Ms. Simone and look forward to reading more from this talented artist.

## Claimed by the Zyndevine

**BDSM Book Reviews:** This is a fast moving magical story with many twists and turns. I enjoyed this book with its feisty characters, spells and hexes, evil forces and new lands. The romance was inevitable and the sex was hot. Even though BDSM was the main element to all romantic encounters, the prominent feel for me was one of true love conquers all. If you like magic, fantasy and happy endings this is the story for you.

## wed on the king's command, she finds an unexpected passion!

Upon her father's death, Lady Gillian Marlowe is ordered by King Edward I to wed Royce Langley, the Earl of Montchester. Worried she is being offered up as little more than a sacrifice in a political game, Gillian is surprised to find herself intrigued by her arrogant and infuriating husband.

Tasked with ridding the border along Wales of rebels who seek to unseat the king, Royce finds subterfuge and secrets everywhere, even with his beautiful wife. Though he only agreed to the marriage because of the king's order, he finds himself both fascinated and incensed by Gillian at every turn. She tries his patience, defies his orders and places herself in danger. To keep her in line, he spanks her, binds her to his bed and dominates and torments her, not only to ensure her submission, but also to coerce her into revealing her secrets. But even that is not enough to subdue her stubborn determination to stand beside him and defend her home and people.

Discovering his wife enjoys the same dark pleasures Royce does stirs more confusion. He has sworn never to fall for a woman's wiles, but his wife captivates him in ways he never expected and she stirs a desire deeper than any he has ever known. Trusting her is another matter, as he fears Gillian may bring about his downfall with her continued secrets, which he views as an attempt to undermine his authority.

The rebel attacks increase and danger lurks everywhere. Gillian falls under suspicion as the traitor, despite her vows of loyalty. Royce must overcome his mistrust and find a way to maintain his possession of Gillian as they battle the enemies both within and without, if there is any hope for them to save each other.

## FEATURING A KINKY TWIST ON HISTORY!

### INCLUDES MALE DOMINATION, BONDAGE, SPANKING AND SO MUCH MORE!

# chapter one

*Autumn, 1283*
*Wickshire, England, near the Wales border*

He had arrived.

In the chaos and sorrow of the last few days, Lady Gillian Marlowe had almost forgotten. Standing just outside the mews, she surveyed the courtyard unnoticed. Weary travelers accepted assistance from bustling servants. Her gaze moved to the red and black pennant fluttering in the breeze, its image seared into her mind. The panther, black as night, white claws and teeth bared, reminded her of her fate. The Earl of Montchester, commonly called the Panther, now stood somewhere amidst the dirty, sweaty soldiers of the king's army. Her bridegroom.

Which one was the earl? The idea of flight briefly entered her thoughts, but she quickly dismissed it. Should she act on the cowardly impulse, she would endanger everyone at Lyndon.

The wedding was planned, her fate sealed. The last weeks had passed too quickly. The suddenness of her father's illness and death had pushed thoughts of her wedding right out of her head. Trying to save him had taken precedence over ensuring the harvest was complete, the stores readied for both the celebration and the long winter ahead. 'Twould make no difference. She prayed her marriage would bring more wealth to the small village.

Once again, the thought of fleeing entered her mind. She couldn't, no matter how tempting the idea. The survival of her home and village depended on her. She was Lyndon's only hope, now that her father lay buried in the cemetery behind the chapel.

Glancing down at her drab gray kirtle, she grimaced. The only cure for her heavy heart had been taking Ares out to the valley beyond the trees. The solitude and her concentration on her hawk helped mourn her loss. She wished she knew where Simon had disappeared to. He usually accompanied her, but she'd felt an urgency to get beyond the keep walls that she didn't look very hard to find him.

At the very least, she should have planned better and gone earlier. She would have returned ere now, with time to change her clothing. The hastily borrowed shift belonged to one of the maids, as she'd had no desire to be tied into one of her own gowns. No wimple covered her head. 'Twould be a disgrace to greet the earl in such attire. She stepped into the courtyard. Could she reach the keep unnoticed?

She ignored the way several knights stopped in their conversation to watch her pass. Having grown up among her father's men, she knew well what those stares meant. Her face heated. With suddenly shaking hands, she smoothed the dress. She stopped short, dismayed to see her stepmother approaching. Fury clouded Anne's green eyes as she reached Gillian.

"'Where have you been? Your father is barely cold in the ground and already you're gallivanting among the soldiers like a harlot!"

Gillian had no chance of being unnoticed now, thanks to Anne's cruel shouts. Ignoring the turned heads and quieting of voices, she clenched her fingers, surprised at the power of her urge to hit the other woman.

"I need no reminding of my duty from the likes of you."

"What would the Earl of Montchester say to have his bride greet him looking as you do?" The reminder irked Gillian. Anne was likely right in that. But she would never give her stepmother the satisfaction.

"'Tis not for you to judge."

Damn the woman, 'twas if she deliberately stalled, so Gillian would have no choice but to greet the earl in such a state. The shrew, while not much older than Gillian herself, went out of her way to make Gillian's life miserable.

Those days would soon come to an end. She lifted her

chin.

"You no longer have any power here. Lyndon will soon belong to the earl, and I will have him banish you."

The sudden sting of Anne's striking hand startled her. She balled her fists, prepared to strike back.

\*\*\*

From his position near the stables, Royce Langley, Earl of Montchester, watched the servant girl making her way through his men. The sudden wave of desire that flickered to life stunned him with its intensity. Never had he reacted so strongly to the mere sight of a woman. His first thoughts about any female were usually of distrust. But something about this slender young servant intrigued him.

Her hair, black as a raven's wing, hung down her back in ebony waves and he imagined tangling his hands in the luxurious mane and drawing her full lips to his own. A thousand other seductive images of her rose to the fore of his thoughts and he shifted, his cock awakening in a most uncomfortable way.

A screeching voice pulled him from his wayward thoughts. He turned his attention to the elegantly dressed woman's approach. Her nose wrinkled in distaste as she gingerly picked her way through the bailey to stand before the girl. Heated words passed between them, though Royce could not hear. However, the sharp sound of her hand connecting with the girl's cheek reached him clearly. Anger, already close at hand due to the troublesome journey, surged through him. Tossing his gauntlets to his squire, he headed toward the two women.

"The girl did naught," he said when he reached them.

He noted the way the girl's hands curled into fists. Had she been about to return the blow? 'Twould seem he intervened just in time to save her from a worse fate than a mere slap.

"'Tis disgraceful the way she flaunts herself among the men." The red-haired woman sneered, folding her arms.

"I assure you, she attempted nothing unseemly. I... noticed her on her way to the keep. She spoke with no one."

Apparently, his gaze reflected his anger, for the other woman paled and stepped back under his scrutiny.

"She should be inside. There is much to be done."

Her wariness quickly faded while she studied him more closely. He recognized the moment her fear vanished, replaced with appreciation. Revulsion rolled his stomach. Could this viper be his intended? He prayed not, but who else could she be? Edward had told him his bride was comely, a highborn lady, exactly what this woman appeared to be. A troubling sensation knotted his stomach. He had no wish to wed, but marriage was necessary in order to gain more lands and have an heir. Edward needed him here, near the Welsh border, to ensure no further uprisings. How would he endure with such a shrew for a wife?

He looked down at the servant girl, her violet eyes wide and focused intently on him. Her head tilted back, revealing the sensuous column of her neck and he found himself longing to lay his mouth against her skin. When his gaze settled on her alluring lips, the lips he had imagined kissing only moments ago, the desire rose quicker than he was ready. With a barely concealed groan, he looked away, lest his cock start to do his thinking for him.

At the sound of a voice from the keep's entrance, movement in his vision's periphery gave him pause.

"Lady Gillian, you are needed."

He turned. A growing sense of astonishment and relief accompanied realization. His intended was the servant girl! He shook his head when Lady Gillian strode proudly toward the door. He couldn't tear his gaze away. Drab though her dress may be, she held herself as if she wore a gown of rich velvet.

She paused in the doorway and turned. A slight smile curved her lips. Had she read his thoughts? He grinned. Perhaps this marriage would not be so bad after all.

"That girl is naught but trouble."

The words cut rudely into his thoughts. His fury once

again returned, stronger this time, and mingled with a fierce protectiveness. This woman had dared slap his betrothed! How he contained his need to strike her in retaliation he'd never know.

"Who are you to strike the mistress of this castle?" He forced the words through clenched teeth.

"She is not mistress." The woman's eyes narrowed, focused on the keep doors. With a slender finger, she tapped her chest. "I am mistress. I am the Baron's widow. She is merely his daughter, who will soon be out of my hair when she weds."

*Jesu*, did the woman have no idea to whom she spoke? He remained silent as he studied her. Many might call her beautiful, but the hatred in her eyes turned her into a crone, to his thinking. She turned once more to face him, her scowl softening into a smile.

"I have worked hard to prepare the keep for the earl's arrival," she said. "I will not allow Lady Gillian's abhorrent behavior to ruin everything."

Clearly, the baroness remained oblivious to his identity. Royce chose not to reveal himself just yet. "Have you?"

"Aye. She is forever wandering the hills and forests while there is work to be done. Glad I will be when the wedding is over and the earl returns to Montchester."

"Are you sure he will not remain here?"

"Why would he remain? This place is so far from London. And as small as it is, certainly not worth much effort."

"You forget, my lady, the Welsh threat. With your husband dead, shouldn't you be worried for your safety?"

Royce had received the message of the baron's death the day before their departure. The news had lent an urgency to the journey, raising questions that needed answers. He tried to ignore the fact his wedding would also now occur much sooner than he'd planned. On the morrow at the latest.

"Nay. We've not been bothered for years. Many of the

servants and villagers are of Welsh blood. And Lyndon has a fine garrison. I have no fear."

Her arrogant tone bordered on boastful. She didn't appear to be troubled by her husband's death. Combined with her lack of concern, he wondered if she was simply a fool. He would find out soon enough. Burke, the captain of his troops, approached. The baroness' gaze now settled on the other man. Clear appreciation grew in her green eyes, as well as a hint of excitement. She would bear watching.

Burke paid her no notice as he neared. "My lord? Is aught amiss?"

A gasp escaped the baroness. It seemed she now realized his identity. She immediately bowed her head. Never once taking his angry gaze from her, Royce issued instructions to his captain.

"Naught I can't handle. Find the stableman and have the horses seen to. Have the men set up camp in the bailey. Our hostess will see me inside. Meet me there."

He turned back to the woman, who nodded, her eyes once more veiled in wariness as she turned to the steps. Some unknown warning poked at him. This woman required close scrutiny. Putting his suspicions aside for the moment, Royce followed, glad to get out of the wind. Once inside, he ignored her and went to the fire burning in the hearth. He warmed his hands. Between the gathering at Shrewsbury, the preparation for his nuptials and the trip here, he'd had no chance to pause. Now, he allowed himself to relax his tired body in a comfortable chair. All around him, the keep was alive with activity, no doubt in preparation for the king's impending arrival. And Royce's own wedding.

The order to leave Shrewsbury, with Parliament about to convene to decide the matter of the Welsh prince's punishment, had not been received well. Especially since the order also included a decree he wed the baron's daughter. With the baron now dead, under suspicious circumstances, there was not enough time to have the girl brought to Shrewsbury.

The excursion to Wickshire and Lyndon Castle had been disastrous from the moment they set out, and the journey, which should have lasted a day at most, had turned into three. All he wanted now as a tall mug of ale, a hearty meal and a soft bed. Thoughts of sharing it with his intended took him on an imaginary journey that again had his cock hardening like an untrained squire.

"My lord, forgive my earlier words. I meant no disrespect."

Royce looked up at his hostess, who stood before him, her expression a picture of humility and chagrin. His anger had faded a little and he had no wish to stir more turmoil at the moment. "What is your name?"

"I am Anne, Baroness of Lyndon, my lord. With my husband dead, I am in charge, should you require anything."

Royce nodded. He didn't tell her the truth, preferring instead to watch her. He'd announce that he already owned Lyndon, wed or not, during the meal. Anne moved away and he heaved a deep breath. Something about her set off a multitude of warnings. The simple annoyance he'd first thought her to be could prove dangerously wrong. He would discuss strategy for handling her with Burke.

He stood, folding his arms behind his back and took some time to survey his surroundings. He needed to be as familiar with Lyndon as with Montchester, as much of his time in the coming months, mayhap years, would be spent here. With the Welsh situation still unresolved, rumors of a small band of rebels not far from Lyndon worried him.

His gaze roamed the hall, pleased to find the castle well-kept and clean. Fresh rushes, scented with herbs covered the floor. Flickering torches cast a warm light across the room, revealing the staircase that wound up the far wall. The layout of the keep must be learned this very eve. Servants hastily prepared tables for the evening meal. His stomach rumbled, reminding him he had eaten nothing since breaking his fast that morn. After supper, he and his soldiers would question every one of the servants. Men needed to be tasked with securing the keep and grounds ere the king arrived. Then Royce would turn his attention to the surrounding forests.

Despite the severity of the state of affairs in the region, he found his thoughts once more turned to his betrothed. Her image seemed to hover before him, violet eyes staring, filled with curiosity. He recalled her knowing smile when he realized her true status. While he trusted no woman, his bride was obviously innocent, and so very young. Still, he sensed in her a maturity and a capability that spurred his curiosity. He hoped the idea proved true. For the first time, he found himself anticipating the upcoming wedding.

***

Gillian closed the door to her father's chamber and leaned against it. The astonishment on the face of the dark-haired man when she'd responded to the call made her smile again. He'd thought her nothing but a servant, and she supposed 'twas exactly as Anne planned it.

Gillian sobered as she wondered which man would be her groom. She found herself hoping 'twould be the man with the golden eyes. She'd seen appreciation in his gaze, and found herself oddly thrilled by it. If only she would be so lucky. The earl was likely a much older man, balding, and paunchy from lazing at court.

She savored the brief warmth of the recollection of the way the gold-eyed man's gaze had moved over her, almost hungry in its intensity. Just as quickly, she forced it aside. More important matters needed her attention.

On unsteady legs, she made her way to the empty bed. Had it really been a week since he'd passed? It seemed much longer. A sob escaped her and she fell on the bed, letting free the sorrow she'd kept composed through the long days of preparing and then burying her father. Strong hands on her shoulders jerked her from her weeping. She looked up into Simon's dark eyes.

Her brother, though never claimed. William's bastard son. She threw herself into his arms, sobbing anew.

When she had no tears left, she pulled free of his tight

embrace. His eyes were wet as well, and she gave a soft smile.

"I miss him so much already."

Simon nodded. "I know. And we'll prove she did it."

"I pray you're right. She has to pay. If only the earl had gotten here sooner."

"It doesn't matter. Lyndon is already his."

Gillian gaped at her brother. "How can that be? I am not wed yet!"

"The night before... William gave me several messages to send. One was a reply to the king agreeing to give over the lands of Lyndon and Wickshire immediately."

Gillian sank back onto the bed. Her home was already taken from her, before she'd even been sacrificed. The room seemed to tilt and she clutched at the blanket to steady herself. Her father dead, her home already in the possession of another... her life had been torn asunder in a few short days.

"Gilly, everything will be fine, you'll see."

"Everything's changing. I..." She stood, pacing the chamber, trying not to look at the empty bed. She needed to prepare the room for the earl. The thought of another man sleeping in her father's bed almost set her to weeping anew. She strode to the door and yanked it open, intending to call for the steward.

Instead, Anne stood in the doorframe. Gillian backed up, alarmed by the unholy light in the other woman's eyes.

"You'll be gone soon." Anne stepped into the room, her gaze settling on Simon. "I should have known I'd find you here. Your days of cavorting with this slut are soon over. I doubt the earl will allow you to even remain here at all."

"Shut your lying mouth!" Gillian shouted. She grabbed Anne's arm and spun the woman to face her. "You did this, you killed my father, and I will prove it. I am not going anywhere. You are!"

Anne jerked free. "You spoiled brat. At every turn you undermined me. Me! The lady of this keep. You are chattel, to be bargained away. Except I now have the perfect weapon to ensure this all remains in my possession."

She rubbed her hand over her belly and gave a broad triumphant grin. "I carry the baron's son."

"Liar!" Gillian lunged at her stepmother, but Simon held her back.

"'Tis true. I am with child."

Realization set in amid flashing memories of conversations. So much made sense now.

"Now I know what Papa meant that night, before he became ill." Gillian smiled. The knowledge she possessed would soon humble the viper.

"What did he say?"

"He petitioned the king to set aside a contract. I believe he meant his marriage contract." She grinned at the anger pinching Anne's face.

"'Tis you who lies."

"Nay, he knew. He knew the whispers were true. You carried on an affair with a man from the village. The child is not my father's. It's your lover's!" Gillian folded her arms. "No matter though. Lyndon has already been awarded to the earl."

She turned her back; satisfied Anne's latest scheme had failed. If only Gillian could have prevented the other plan from succeeding.

***

Gillian's declaration carried out of the room. Royce smiled and paused in the doorway. Though small, this castle in the Marches increased not just his holdings, but his power. He was one of a handful of men the king truly trusted. Giving Lyndon and its daughter to Royce proclaimed that to all. With no other heirs of the baron, none could usurp Royce as the next Baron Lyndon.

He stepped into the room and froze. His betrothed embraced another man. Jealousy stunned him with the force it rose. His angry gaze settled on Anne. Outrage whitened her already chalky face. The hairs on the back of his neck prickled. One hand went to the hilt of his sword, while the other hovered near the weapon in his belt.

Anne crept closer to the pair holding each other. Her hand disappeared into her skirts and removed a dagger. She raised her arm, prepared to strike. With lightning quick reflexes, Royce grabbed her wrist, halting her. Anne howled in fury.

Gillian spun about and his gaze flicked between her and the struggling woman he held captive. Air crackled, the tension a net ensnaring everyone. Anne fought against Royce's grip. With ease, he plucked the bejeweled knife from her slender hand and tossed it aside.

"You've gone too far!"

He sensed Gillian's eyes on him, but paid her no mind. His fury with the woman before him consumed every thought.

"You will pay for this treachery. The king himself will judge you."

Anne swung at him with her free hand, but he captured her fist and pinned both behind her back.

"My lord, I merely defended myself!"

Anne's ridiculous claim fueled Royce's already raging anger. It took all of his control to refrain from slaying the woman where she stood.

"Curb your lying tongue. I saw everything."

The ice in his voice brought fear to Anne's eyes.

"You have ruined everything!" Anne shrieked at Gillian. She struggled mightily against Royce's grip, to no avail.

With Anne somewhat subdued, Royce turned his attention to his betrothed, who stood motionless before another man. One hand on her throat, she backed closer to the bed. He almost smelled her panic. Good. He glared at the man behind her, whose hands rested possessively on Gillian's shoulders. Royce fought the urge to release his prisoner and instead slice at the man's hands.

Once more, he focused on his bride. Wariness deepened her eyes to a dark plum. Or was it guilt? Yet, when her lips parted to take in air, he had to look away to quell the sudden rush of lust. His annoyance that her mere presence could make him so foolish took over at the same moment Anne struggled once more. Despite her small stature, Royce found it difficult to maintain his grip. He squeezed hard on her wrists until she stopped squirming, crying in pain.

He called for his men, his gaze once again returning to Gillian. Three soldiers ran into the chamber.

"Take her!"

Two moved forward, each taking one of Anne's arms. She fought against them, until the third gave his assistance. Outnumbered, unable to break free, she held her head defiantly as she stood before him. Royce tore a strip from his surcoat and bound her wrists. She screamed and kicked, but he took her jaw in his hand, squeezing her cheeks with his fingers so she quieted.

"If you continue, I will truss you like a fowl." He released her and turned to Gillian. "Where can she be kept?"

"There are chambers below. The steward has the keys."

"Take her there and lock her in until the king arrives."

Once Anne had been led from the room, Royce turned back to his betrothed. No longer did he bother to hide his anger. He glared at the man behind her as he took several steps closer. "Unhand the lady."

The other man's hesitation almost undid the fury threatening to take control. The red haze clouding his vision cleared when the man did as ordered.

"What is going on here?"

Gillian lifted her chin. "I am clearing the room for you, my lord."

Her voice held the proper tone of respect, yet he detected resentment. He realized they had yet to be introduced, though she clearly realized who he was by now.

"And him?" He jerked his thumb in the other man's direction.

"This is Simon. One of my guards."

The explanation soothed him somewhat, but the affection in Simon's gaze unnerved him. There was more here than a lady and her guard. Or did he overreact to something innocent? Another situation that would require further inspection.

"You are no longer needed here. I can protect my betrothed."

The guard nodded and leaned down to whisper something into Gillian's ear. She nodded and gave him a warm smile before he turned and strode out of the room.

The envy poking his ribs startled Royce. He shouldn't be jealous, he should be angry at the thought of his wife betraying him. Before she was even his wife. The possessive feelings were uncomfortable, unfamiliar and most certainly unwanted. He folded his arms. Despite his anger, he couldn't help being impressed with the way she held her head and back straight, never cowering away from him. Few dared stand up to him this way. His respect for her strengthened.

"You will no longer need a personal guard once we are wed. I will assign him to other duties."

"Nay, you cannot!"

"Pray tell, my lady, why not?"

"Because... he is more than my guard. He has helped me with the household for a long time."

"You have a steward. You can work with him."

She shook her head, her lips pressed together in a tight line of panicked annoyance.

"'Tis not enough. I need Simon."

He said nothing, imagining all sorts of reasons why his betrothed would need another man. "We wed on the morrow."

She gaped at him, eyes wide. "But I thought we were to wait for the king."

He shook his head. "There is no time, now that your father is... has passed. Though 'tis true I own all of Lyndon, we cannot afford any weakness in the holding. You and I must seal the contract by wedding immediately."

"Have you spoken with Father Anselm yet?"

"Nay, I will see to it during the meal. Finish what you

must and join me below stairs."

He turned and strode out of the room, not daring to look in her direction. She stirred things in him he wasn't sure he liked. At the same time, he wanted her, and didn't want to wait more than another night to possess her. His fascination with her could be dangerous if he didn't take care.

Yet, the image of her boldly watching while he subdued her stepmother tormented him. He still didn't know what he saw in her eyes. Curiosity or something else? She hadn't reacted to the attempt on her life like the vain, simpering women he knew at court, the women who wanted naught but the riches a man could bring them. She had watched everything closely, not once screaming or swooning to the floor. She showed no fear. Until her gaze met his.

A glimmer of satisfaction at alarming her still hovered in his thoughts. The calculation in her eyes unnerved him. He shouldn't be surprised; she was a woman, and could surely play the games of manipulation to her advantage. The reasons why he wanted no wife reminded him to use caution. Was he trapped to spend his life worrying whether she would turn away from him, longing for only the material possessions and position at court he would bring her?

\*\*\*

Gillian collapsed onto the bed, her relief at being alone overpowering. She thought about her earlier hopes. They'd been granted. Somehow, those hopes seemed a cruel taunt now.

He'd handled Anne with no care for her comfort. Surely he wouldn't have done so if he'd known of her condition. Gillian's bitter laugh echoed in the chamber. Whether 'twas true or not, the man she was to marry wouldn't have cared at all. Like any other man.

They cared for naught but the alliance of a powerful marriage. The lands and authority 'twould bring. With the exception of her father, she'd yet to meet any man who cared for the woman he wed rather than her lands.

She would not be treated thus. She knew this keep as well as anyone, mayhap even better. No one could protect it as she could. She would show her husband she would not be a wife he could dismiss, perhaps even banishing her to a far estate, while he drove her people and her lands into ruin.

As much as he frightened her, she vowed not to allow him see her fear. The Panther would not take her down.

Still, questions taunted her. How would she survive marriage to such a brutal man?

# chapter two

Gillian stood at the bottom of the stairs surveying the raucous scene in the great hall. So many men. When was the last time Lyndon had hosted such a horde? The rumble of voices mingled, no single conversation clear from even this short distance.

Near the head of the table, the earl stood in conversation with Father Anselm. The village priest nodded as they spoke, and both men then broke out into laughter. Gillian's breath caught in her throat.

Never had she seen a more handsome sight than the earl's tawny eyes twinkling with humor. His lips curved, revealing even white teeth. Even from her position across the hall, the faintest hint of dimples in his now clean-shaven cheeks caught her eye. Until now, he'd only scowled, his eyes flashing with anger. Seeing his smile tempered her wariness.

As if sensing her gaze upon him, he turned. Her awareness of the cacophony around her faded. 'Twas as if he held her captive with his golden gaze, which seemed to delve into her soul. A curious look replaced the humor in his face.

A hand on her arm startled her. She turned, realizing she had been holding her breath. Simon scowled, and drew her into the corner.

"What happened?"

"Nothing." She glanced toward the earl. His smile had vanished. Her gut knotted.

"Then what's wrong?" he asked.

She gazed sadly at him for a moment. "Everything is... changing. I'm worried for you. He says he will set you on another detail."

"Don't fret. 'Tis not a problem, and I understand. You'll be his wife."

"I'm afraid he might send you away. Or me. I... want to tell him who you really are. You're more than just a knight in the garrison. You're –"

His fingers on her mouth silenced her.

"Tell no one. We will be fine Gilly, both of us. You'll see."

"Tell no one what?"

At the sound of the earl's voice, Gillian stiffened. She turned. The hard lines of his face revealed no emotion, yet she sensed his tightly leashed fury. He glared momentarily at their clasped hands before turning to Simon.

"I've already explained to Lady Gillian you are no longer needed as her guard. Did she not inform you?"

"Forgive me, my lord, if I still harbor the need to ensure her safety. I've done so for a very long time."

Gillian held her breath at the hint of resentment in Simon's voice.

"Yes, well, no longer. Seat yourself at the lower table with the other men at arms. See my captain in the morn for your new duties."

Gillian opened her mouth, but her brother nudged her toe, signaling her silence.

"Yes, sir. My lady, if you will excuse me." Simon bowed again and turned on his heel. "Who is he to you?"

Her eyes widened at his question. Though his tone was bland, his eyes held a glimmer of mistrust. Was the fierce Panther jealous of Simon? Were he not scowling openly at her now, she might laugh.

"He is my guard, my lord." She would say nothing more as long as Simon wished it so. For now. She would not keep this secret forever.

One dark brow arched and she knew he did not believe the half-truth. But he remained silent, merely offered her his arm to escort her to the head of the table.

\*\*\*

The still night air offered welcome relief after the oppressive heat and noise of the great hall. The men of Lyndon and Montchester had devoured every morsel of food laid out before them, leaving Gillian to wonder whether anything would be left in the stores for the wedding feast. Tonight, the earl sat in the lord's chair, Gillian beside him. It proclaimed so much that at this point, the wedding was little more than a formality. Royce's presence had encompassed the hall, leaving no doubt who was in possession of the land.

Throughout the long meal, she had answered his questions about Lyndon, but those had been few. The worst part was sharing a trencher. Their hands had brushed several times, and by the time the meal ended, Gillian's nervousness had reached a level she'd not known before. He'd watched her intently all evening, adding to the unbalanced sensations. Keeping her hands steady had been a monumental task.

All her life, she'd been surrounded by her father's men. Never had any affected her this way. His very nearness made her heart race, her palms sweat, her stomach flutter. She attributed the reactions to fear, but the underlying thread of dark pleasure lured her. How would she survive a marriage to him if she could barely control these unfamiliar feelings whenever he was close?

What kind of man was he, truly? When he had held Anne in his iron grip, fury had emanated from him as though Gillian might be able to reach out and touch it. She'd never witnessed such intense rage before. She prayed he never directed his anger at her.

A footfall in the bailey drew her from her musings and she turned. As if she had conjured him with her thoughts, the Panther stood behind her, silhouetted in the moon's glow. The light glinted off his dark hair. His position obscured his face but she felt his gaze upon her. Again. She pressed her damp palms against her gown.

"You should not be alone out here." He stepped closer. "'Tis not safe."

"This is my home. No one would dare to try to enter with the sentinels on duty."

"Lyndon is close to the Welsh border. There is always

danger."

"So you've said. But the Welsh have been subdued. They won't bother us."

"Listen to me. Lady Anne might very well be involved with a Welshman. A traitor in our midst will prove disastrous. Unless you have a particular reason for feeling so confident?"

He stepped closer still, only inches away. So close she now saw every stone-like feature in his face. Her heart pounded in a crazy, erratic rhythm. At the hint of accusation in his words, she found herself almost too angry to respond. Amid the tangle of sensations, a hint of warning sprouted. She ignored it.

"Do you accuse me of being a traitor?" She made no effort to hide the hostility in her voice. He tilted his head and she found herself caught by his golden eyes. He gave a soft chuckle. "Nay, but I wonder if you are truly so naïve."

"Not naïve, my lord. Safe."

He shifted again, and his eyes seemed to bore into her. Perhaps 'twas a trick of the moonlight that made him seem even more imposing. Clad entirely in black, he loomed over her, yet she did not find him threatening.

Instead, an odd fascination with the way his tunic stretched across broad shoulders drew her focus. What would it feel like enclosed in those arms, protected against the wall of his chest?

Bah! 'Twas the words of bards she imagined now. Foolish girl! Shaking her head, she forced herself to respond.

"I often walk here after dinner. I've never seen anything amiss. Not for years now."

"Bandits are not always visible and they don't always endlessly lay siege. Perhaps they lay in wait in the forests."

"For all this time? Why hide in the forest? They would have attacked long ere now if so."

"They're cunning. The right moment is key to winning a siege."

Gillian didn't like the direction this discussion took. "And how do they determine that? Wait for years and then strike? It makes no sense. Not to me."

"You do not understand the political maneuvers being waged."

"So they wait for the right time. How will they know when to strike?"

"A signal from inside the walls is most likely." He folded his arms.

"Now I think I understand. Do you say, my lord, I am giving a signal to attack my home?"

"Are you?"

Spine stiffened with indignation, she lifted her chin.

"How dare you! I would not betray my king. More importantly, I would not betray my people. If you believe that, you are a fool."

"I am no fool, my lady." Tightly leashed anger wove through his words.

"And I am no traitor." She made no attempt to conceal the ice coating her words, despite the tremor of alarm threading through her veins.

An awkward silence hung between them. She bit her lip, startled when he shut his eyes and turned away, his shoulders rising with a deep breath.

"Nay. Still, you should not be alone."

She glanced around the bailey. Several soldiers gathered near the stables. Extra guards had been set along the ramparts and at the gates. In actuality, she was not alone, though she doubted he would be pleased should she point that out. But Gillian wanted to be alone, needed to get away from him. She had much to think on, and couldn't concentrate with him so near.

"My lord, I have tasks to attend. If you will..."

"I shall join you."

When he reached for her, she backed up a step. *Jesu!* Judging from the tight set of his jaw, she had just reinforced his suspicions.

"You must have other business more important than I."

"Nothing is more important than my bride. Ease my worries for your safety, demoiselle, and allow me to escort you."

Though he claimed concern, his words clearly held a command. Did he think she planned a clandestine meeting with Welsh rebels? He had no reason to worry about not gaining Lyndon.

'Twas already his. He only came because the king ordered it. For some reason, the realization stung. Deep inside, she wanted him to care for her, even a little. The urge to deny him hung on the edge of her tongue. She held it back.

Refusing him would raise his suspicions further, so she silently allowed him to take her arm and escort her to the mews.

"Your father enjoyed hawking?"

"The hawks aren't my father's."

"Then who hunts with them?"

"I do."

She restrained the grin that threatened at his look of surprise. She opened the gate and ducked into the tiny building. Moonlight streamed through the window, casting a silvery glow.

Most of the falcons slept upon their perches, jesses fastened to prevent a sudden flight should they be startled awake.

"Close the door," she ordered, stepping up to the rows where her dozen birds perched.

She approached Ares, her favorite, and unhooded him. Gillian cooed to the hawk, blowing gently on his face. The merlin watched her with golden eyes so like the earl's. She ruffled the bird's chest feathers.

"'Tis unwise to get so close."

"I have trained him since shortly after he hatched. He has never threatened."

"A fright could cause it."

"Ares knows me. Usually, I wear gauntlets when I handle the birds. I had no time tonight to fetch them."

"Your father allowed this?"

She bit back the sharp retort and took a deep breath before responding.

"Yes. He did. I'm a better falconer than anyone for miles."

'Twas true she had a natural talent for working with the birds. When Walter, the old falconer had passed, Gillian had taken over caring for the birds, though she hadn't been permitted to live in Walter's former quarters beside the mews. Still, she took pride in her skill in training and maintaining Lyndon's birds. She truly loved every moment she spent with her hawks.

"Your father spoiled you."

He leaned against the wall and folded his arms. The movement rekindled her fascination, and a sharp yearning washed over her like a great wave. Her tongue felt as if it were coated in dry wool. Until his words penetrated the haze.

"How dare you! You have known me only a few hours, yet you have already passed judgment."

"My wife won't work in the mews. I'll hire a falconer. You need only concern yourself with matters of the household."

"The mews are part of the household. Therefore, I'm responsible."

The fierce need to prove herself grew stronger. Perhaps he should see just how capable she truly was. Would it change his mind? She honestly had no idea.

"In the morning, I'll take Ares out. Join me. Judge me then."

"Where will you go?"

"Through the forest, to the fields beyond. I can show you..."

"Are you daft, woman? Do you not know the danger – ?"

"I am safe!"

"Safe? How many times must I remind you rebels lurk nearby? You are too tempting a morsel for anyone to ignore should they come upon you."

"I don't go alone. I have my guards."

"Other than Simon, how many?"

"One, sometimes two."

She turned back to Ares, stroking the bird's head as she spoke softly to it.

"Do you know what a band of Welshmen can do to one or two guards? You will be lucky to survive. If you are so lucky, you will soon wish you had died."

Gillian spun around, startling Ares, who squawked in protest and fluttered his wings. She backed away as the bird jabbed out with his beak. Though Ares did not make contact with Gillian's face, 'twas close.

Anger at her betrothed grew fast. He'd caused the tension in the roost. The other birds shifted restlessly, wings fluttering for a few anxious moments in response to Ares' cry. Finally, they calmed, soothed by Gillian's low voice. Carefully, she replaced the hood on Ares's head and stroked the soft feathers once more before letting loose her temper.

"Keep your voice down! You should know better!"

"I seem to lose patience all too easily when you insist on taking such foolish risks."

Gillian narrowed her eyes. The derision in his tone fueled the defiance she struggled to hold at bay.

"With or without guards, I am capable of defending myself."

The corners of his mouth lifted, accompanied by a muffled laugh. His amusement sent her anger soaring. She turned to leave, unwilling to endure any more of his mockery. As she passed, he grabbed her arm.

"You are very much at ease despite the talk of rebels. How can you defend yourself? With your hawks?"

The disdain with which he tossed the words twisted in Gillian's stomach like a rusted knife. Her skill with a bow and arrow was admired by all her father's men. She had trained hard to prove herself worthy of being her father's heir. She would prove it to the earl as well.

"You know nothing of my abilities." She met his gaze, daring him to question her further.

"True, I do not. But I will know everything about you ere long."

The urge to look away grew, but Gillian resisted. She wouldn't cower before him, though she sensed his words held a more subtle meaning, judging from the heat flaming in his eyes.

"Tell me, Lady Gillian, how would you defend yourself against a horde of Welsh rebels on horses? Your pretty jeweled eating dagger may impress your servants and villagers, but 'twill provoke nothing but laughter from a savage band of murderers."

"I can take a man from his horse at fifty paces with a longbow."

The earl nodded. "Very well, suppose you could take out one, perhaps two men before the others, maybe twice as many as your guards, reached you. Your longbow will do no good at close range. Then what, Lady Gillian? Who will save you then?"

The words to respond eluded her. She looked away, silently cursing his triumph.

"You know nothing of warfare and rebel attacks. I can't help wondering again at your confidence in your safety. Perhaps you're involved more than you say. Perhaps you aided the Welsh during this last war."

Gillian met his steady gaze. A shuttered coolness now replaced the earlier heat.

"I would never..."

"Wouldn't you? Your stepmother has a lover, possibly Welsh. Perhaps you do as well. Perhaps 'tis your 'guard'. Perhaps you intended to meet him tonight and that's why you are so anxious to be rid of me."

The sound of her palm cracking against his cheek echoed through the mews. His head turned slightly under the force of the blow. Tension crackled between them, like lightning during a spring storm. Once again, the birds stirred restlessly in response to the turmoil. A wave of fear dimmed her rage as she realized she had struck her future husband. The king's favorite. She held her breath, waiting for the punishment sure to follow.

"Men have died for less than what you dare."

His voice, low and menacing, terrified her more than if he had shouted. His eyes glittered and his fury smelled of brimstone. She trembled, fright making her knees weak, and she might have fallen had he not grabbed her arm. His grip tightened as he jerked her roughly against him. Only the restless movements of the hawks broke the silence.

Gillian tried to pull free, without success. A brief recollection of his coarse treatment of Anne skittered through her jumbled thoughts, and she tugged again. This time, he pulled her still closer, his other hand cupping the back of her head as his mouth suddenly claimed hers with a punishing kiss.

Fear consuming her, once more she tried to pull away, but his fingers bit into her arm and tightened in her hair. His mouth continued its assault, bruising her lips. She stood in his harsh embrace, her hands coming to rest on his chest, waiting for an opportunity to shove at him. Panic taunted her, but she kept it at bay, determined not to show her terror. At that moment, a strange thing happened.

Her body warmed and a strange feathery delight blossomed in her belly. She found herself responding to the demands of his mouth. The kiss softened, just a little, and a hint of pleasure burst into a decadence she'd never imagined. A strange calm came over her as his lips now moved gently over hers. When he drew away, she found herself disappointed.

He raised his head. No longer did she find fury in his gaze. Instead, flames flickered amid something she did not recognize, something alluring. The remnants of fear rapidly faded, replaced by curiosity. She leaned closer, trying to understand the emotion she read. Her breasts tightened, her gown suddenly confining. She'd never had such a physical reaction to a mere stare. Then again, she'd never been kissed like that before. The few pecks one of her father's men had given her had not stirred anything even remotely similar to the powerful sensations taking over her body now.

To her surprise, the expression on his face softened more. He looked as though he might smile. His grip on her arm loosened, but he didn't release her, instead holding her close with a firm yet gentle grip. His fingers moved along the sensitive underside of her arm and she sucked in a breath at the slither of warmth along her spine.

Enthralled by the heated glow in his golden eyes, Gillian didn't resist. Forgotten was her anger over his arrogant words, her fear he'd demand retribution for her actions. Her sole focus remained on the hold of his gaze and the way the closeness made him seem larger, more powerful. New emotions swelled, confusing her, yet exciting her at the same time. Her heart pounded, and beneath her palms, his heart thumped just as vigorously.

He yanked her more fully against him. His fingers on her chin tilted her head back so she looked into his face. Darkened to a deep amber, his intense gaze warmed. Slowly, he lowered his head and Gillian realized he meant to kiss her again. This time she recognized she wanted him to.

His lips brushed softly, once, twice and then again. She remained motionless when he embraced her. The kiss grew more potent, the pressure of his lips increasing. Unlike the last kiss, this one stirred heat slowly, yet steadily until she thought she might combust. Her body slackened and she melted, returning his kiss.

Excitement surged. Her head swirled with dizzying emotions. The tender way he held her, this warrior knight, exhilarated her. She never wanted the kiss to end.

The tip of his tongue brushed against her lips and her eyes flew open in surprise. His golden eyes, so like her hawk's, met hers. Then his tongue brushed against her lips again, parting them and plunging inside to sweep her mouth. Her knees would have buckled had he not held her. She sighed at the blissful stirrings. A sea of clouds surrounded her, blinding her to everything but his captivating kiss.

Her sex tightened when he deepened the kiss further, his hand brushing across her breast. He cupped her flesh and gave a gentle squeeze. A violent quiver swept over her. She wanted more of this tempting, wicked delight.

\*\*\*

Royce rapidly lost his grip on the thread of control as he caressed his betrothed's breast. Even through the bliaut, the feel of her scorched his hand, the press of her hardened nipple tempting him. He pinched lightly, delighted with the quiver that swept over her, even as she so pleasingly responded to his kiss. He repeated the motion and she moaned into his mouth, stirring him beyond what he thought he could bear. His cock hardened at the thought of pulling her dress away so he could see her flesh. Touch her more fully.

To prevent himself from acting on the impulse, he swept his fingers through the velvet of her hair, realizing his earlier fanciful imaginings. It did little to stem the rush of need. Her musky taste tempted him almost beyond his control. He fought the urge to lower her to the ground and take her there in the mews. With a groan, he set her away. When had a woman ever stirred him so much, and so quickly? 'Twas but another danger his bride presented. He turned to face her once more.

Her eyes, darkened to a deep violet, slowly opened to meet his. Her lips still held a soft pucker. He groaned aloud. Damned if he didn't want to toss convention aside and simply take her now. Remembering where they were, he turned to block the sight of her flushed face and swollen lips. This slip of a girl had bewitched him somehow. Mayhap once they were wed, and he'd taken his pleasure, this powerful yearning would subside.

"We must get back. And know this; you are not to wander alone, especially at night, anymore."

"You worry for nothing. And I will not be confined."

"You are my wife and you will obey!"

"Not yet, my lord. And if you don't take care, 'twill never happen."

He grabbed her arm once more. "Do you threaten me?"

She gave him a sly smile. "I can petition the king for a delay."

"There is no time. You will wed me in the morn, if I have to bind you hand and foot."

Her eyes widened, but he found only fury. No fear.

"You wouldn't dare!"

"Aye. Do not test me."

He let go of her arm and she turned away. Royce noticed her hands clenched and held back a smile. Would she dare? Part of him wished she might strike again, for then he'd have more reason to punish her. The thought of taming the fire he sensed in the woman who would be his added to a slowly growing anticipation.

She made a noise, half an outraged growl, half a sob. Without another word, he grabbed her wrist and pulled her across the bailey. When they reached the castle steps, he released her.

"Go inside."

He gave a nod and turned, lost in the turmoil of thought. The sense of entrapment grew along with all the other sensations fighting to overtake the others. He paced in the bailey for several minutes. He needed to put everything but securing the lands aside.

Yet, the recollection of Lady Gillian in his arms, her mouth softening beneath his, remained a constant. His cock stayed half-hard.

The chill of the autumn night soon enabled him to gain control, though did nothing to cool his yearning. Lady Gillian was an intriguing contradiction. One moment she challenged him, sparks in her eyes. Other times, she viewed him with wariness and hesitation. He preferred the sparks. His cheek still tingled from her slap. He gave a wry smile. She would pay for that tomorrow.

He thought about what Burke had told him. And wondered why his bride didn't. Her mother was Welsh, rumored to be a distant cousin of the prince who waited in Shrewsbury for his trial. Was there any chance Lyndon was not loyal to Edward? It might explain Gillian's lack of concern over her safety. If she had shared this herself, he might be inclined to trust her, but since she had not, suspicion remained.

He frowned. He had many ways to lure secrets from prisoners. Mayhap he should approach this marriage in the same way until he absolutely proved she wasn't a traitor. The very real heat between them was a valuable tool, one to wield to gain what he needed. He smiled as he formulated a plan to learn all of his betrothed's secrets. Once she was his wife, he would exercise complete power over her.

Pleased with his solution, he gave a last glance around the bailey. All appeared still. He entered the hall, surveying the combined forces of his and Lyndon's men. There were more than sufficient troops to subdue any rebellion attack. But if the danger came from within, 'twould not matter how many able men he had.

\*\*\*

He kept his step light, not wanting anyone to know of his presence here. Though the chambers on this lower level of the keep went mostly unused, he did not want to take the chance of being seen by anyone other than his lover. His worry for her outweighed his anger at her foolish actions.

When he neared her chamber, her face came into view against the small window in the door.

"'Tis about time," she snapped. "I wondered if you would ever come."

"I had to make sure none knew I was here. The Panther seeks his bride; there is little time before he returns."

"Free me." She reached her hand through the door.

He shook his head. "Nay, 'tis not the right time. Soon, our forces will arrive and you will be brought to safety."

"But the babe..."

"Why did you attack Lyndon's daughter? 'Twas a foolish mistake."

Anne lowered her head. "I'm sorry. I... that girl and her

wedding has ruined all we've planned. My anger overtook me."

The remorse in her tone softened his brusque manner. "But now you are locked away, where you cannot help me. I depended on you and you failed."

"Please, forgive me. The babe has made me ill. I wasn't thinking clearly."

He sighed. He knew her condition made her emotions more uneven than usual. "Here."

He slipped a cloth-wrapped bundle through the small hole. Inside were several pieces of meat, a few tarts and some bread. 'Twas all he could manage to gather without raising suspicion and he hoped it would be enough. He doubted anyone had given her a meal since locking her in here.

"Please let me out."

"Soon, my love, I promise. I must go before anyone grows suspicious of my absence."

"Wait. I've learned something. We've not spoken ere now, so you do not know."

"Know what?"

"There is another who can claim Lyndon for Edward."

His fingers tightened on the bars of the window. Anne reached up and laid her hand against them. Why did he not know of this?

"Tell me."

"My husband has a bastard-born son. He has acknowledged him in a letter to the king, which is to be given to him should anything befall the Panther and his bride."

"It cannot be." This news required changes to his plan and little time to implement them.

Anne nodded. "He gave the letters to a messenger be delivered to the king the night before he passed."

"Who is it?"

"I don't know. I only happened upon this when they were almost finished. They don't know what I've learned."

His eyes narrowed, but he composed himself to see the

panic in her eyes. But he could not so easily put aside his annoyance this time.

"If you knew this, then this makes your actions earlier the more foolish and risky to our endeavors. We could have lost all because of your temper."

"'Tis too late to change things."

He nodded, but his annoyance didn't ebb. "This information is useful. You have done well. I will try to determine who this bastard son is. He must be eliminated. Now."

He leaned over and she put her face close to the window. He brushed his fingers along her lips, savoring her sigh before he drew away.

"You'll be free soon. And we'll be together."

He turned and did not look back until he had climbed the stairs and closed the door behind him.

# Chapter Three

Gillian sat beside her husband, still not sure precisely how she had gotten back to the great hall. She remembered nearly nothing of standing outside the chapel and reciting her vows, and even less of the long mass that followed. All she knew was she had been wed to the king's favorite earl.

The presence of the powerful man beside her took all of her notice. She'd studied him closely, looking for clues to the man he was, but his stony expression revealed nothing. A thousand different emotions ran through her, warning her of his effect on her. Still, nothing solidified enough to dwell on. The shivery excitement lurking in her belly taunted her, as did the frisson of fear that swept along her spine whenever he looked at her. She knew what was to come this eve, and the mixture of anticipation and dread left her with uneasy feelings in her heart.

Servants entered with the first course, trays piled high with mutton, beef and chicken, rabbit and duck, all prepared in rich creamy sauces and steaming from the ovens. Pitchers of spiced wine and ale were served for another of the many toasts sure to follow. Later, even more dishes would be brought out to the assemblage when the feasting continued through the day and into the night.

She wanted to stand up and have the room cleared. Her father had been buried only four days before. To celebrate now seemed wrong. And yet, no one appeared to care.

She glanced down the row of tables. Simon sat with the other men, instead of near her. She missed him. He looked up and caught her eye. The hint of sadness in his gaze told her he possessed similar resentful thoughts toward those around them. She lifted her goblet and took a long drink of wine, hoping 'twould steady the unbalanced sensation.

"Are you anticipating the coming night already?"

Gillian's head snapped up to find her husband gazing at her with amusement. The knowing curve of his smile caused beads of sweat to break out along her brow. She swallowed.

He leaned close, his mouth beside her ear. His lips grazed her ever so lightly as she spoke, his warm breath making her shiver.

"Fear not, my bride; I am as eager as you. Soon enough we shall be alone."

His hand covered hers, sending heat coiling up her arm and throughout her body. She looked away, taking a deep breath to steady her thumping heart. Her hand shook more than ever as she took another long drink of the cool, sweet wine.

\*\*\*

Royce watched his bride closely. He smelled her fear and her excitement. The musk of arousal hovered over her, despite the wariness ever present in her eyes. The contradiction intensified his hunger. He didn't think he could wait much longer, but knew he had to endure at least two courses of the meal Lyndon's cooks had prepared.

He also wanted to find some way out of the traditional bedding ceremony. He would allow Gillian only her maid. How would he keep the other women out? He leaned toward Burke.

"I want no bedding ceremony. Spread the word to the men. I'll inform the women that because of the bride's recent loss, she finds the idea unbearable. They'll have more sympathy if I blame her for the reason."

"Do you fear she isn't pure?"

Royce shrugged. He didn't like thinking about it, but he couldn't forget the sight of Gillian in the arms of her guard. He glanced at her and followed her gaze. Anger burned his throat but he looked away from the stare she shared with Simon.

"Mayhap. I would not have that be known to all. I'm prepared should that be the case." Burke grinned. "I suspect Lyndon's daughter holds many secrets."

"And I intend to get every one out of her. Take care of what I asked."

He leaned back toward Gillian. She still held a stare with Simon. He reached for the goblet in her hand. She faced him, those alluring eyes wide with confusion.

"Have more wine. Then after this next course, seek out your maid."

"But I thought —"

He leaned closer and lowered his voice. "There will be no bedding ceremony. But I will give you until the vespers bells ring to prepare yourself. Be ready for me when I arrive."

"Aye. My lord, how will you keep the others from...?"

He held back a chuckle at the flush creeping into her cheeks. His cock hardened anew and he wondered if he'd survive this next course.

"'Tis being handled. Now eat."

She picked up her spoon and lowered it to the trencher, scooping stewed violets with a dainty and elegant motion. They ate in silence, and somehow the chaos of the room faded away. He supposed she would have liked some romantic gesture, but he found himself too distracted by studying her.

He slipped his hand under the table. She appeared not to notice the movement. He let his fingers brush against the ornate emerald gown. Her shoulders stiffened, but she didn't lift her head. Instead, she selected another piece of goose and bit into it. He admired her manners, her fingers and hand placed just so to conceal her mouth as she ate. She would do well at court.

Impatience left him agitated while he waited for her to finish her meal. She'd barely leaned away from the trencher when he laid his hand firmly on her leg. At the contact, she froze completely. Several seconds passed before she met his gaze.

"Go now, seek your maid."

The pink in her cheeks faded until she appeared almost ashen. He squeezed her leg. She flinched.

"Now." He gave another squeeze then released her.

"Aye, my lord." Her voice shook, near as much as her hands. Still, she rose steadily and made her way toward the stair.

*** 

Gillian tried to slip unnoticed through the hall, but knew she didn't succeed. The eyes of nearly everyone rested on her, making her feel as though she walked across the room naked. She silently thanked her husband for banning the bedding ceremony. She didn't think she'd survive that without being sick.

She caught the eye of one of the maids. The girl appeared envious. Gillian supposed her husband would be considered handsome by most. God's bones, she considered him handsome. More than he should be.

Edith awaited her in the chamber. She hesitated, pleased to see the bedding replaced with the earl's colors. The table and chairs near the hearth had been brought in from the solar, as per her instructions. The room no longer held any sign of her father. She lowered her head, sending his soul a prayer of peace.

"Edith, I... must prepare."

Her maid immediately set to helping Gillian out of her gown and undergarments. When nothing but the chemise remained, Gillian halted the maid.

"That is enough. Can you please undo the ribbons in my hair?"

"Yes, my lady. You are a countess now! Married to an earl. And the king will be here within a sennight. 'Tis the most exciting thing to happen to Lyndon in many years."

Despite her worries over everything Edith gushed over, the maid's excitement was infectious. Mayhap the past weeks of dark days were truly over.

The door flung open. The earl filled the frame. His dark tunic outlined the breadth of his shoulders and her gaze moved over him, her heart once again taking the same uneven rhythm his presence always sparked. He stood there several moments before stepping into the room. He strode around the chamber, perusing the furnishings and the bed. He turned to her and gave an approving nod.

"I am pleased with the room."

"Thank you."

Royce's gaze settled on Edith.

"Leave us."

The maid lowered her head and hurried from the room, closing the door behind her. Royce strode over and slid the bar into place.

The hint of uneasiness bloomed into fear. She was alone with this man, her husband, and no one could save her.

He strode to the table and the pitcher of wine. He picked up one goblet and filled it. All the while, she studied him, noting the way his hair fell around his shoulders, the way his fingers gripped the pitcher. Her gaze moved lower, the sight of his powerful legs encased in hose hinting at his stamina.

The rush of lust that came over her left her breathless. She wanted to look away, but didn't. He turned and held out the goblet.

She shook her head. "Nay, I..."

He stepped closer, forcing her to tilt her head back. He did it apurpose, she knew, to try and intimidate her. She held her ground.

"Drink the wine, 'twill help settle your nerves."

She scowled at him. He liked to give orders. She would obey this night, if only because she must, but if he thought she would submit to his command beyond that, he would have a long wait.

She took the goblet from him and gulped down some of the fruity liquid. He took the cup from her, lest she finish it all.

"Slowly. I don't want you sotted."

He turned the cup and deliberately placed his mouth where hers had been. When he pulled the goblet away, he licked his lips. Her breasts felt heavy and tight, nipples peaking hard. Between her legs, her sex slickened and swelled. No matter what she felt about him, her body clearly appreciated what he hinted he would soon do to her.

He handed the goblet back to her, turning it once more so she would drink again from the same spot. She hesitated a moment, then took another drink. She handed the cup back to him. "Come."

He took her hand and led her to the stand beside the bed. He ran his fingers along the top of her chemise.

"Why do you still wear this?"

"I... there was a draft."

'Twas the truth, though not her real reason.

"I expected my wife to be waiting for me naked in that bed."

She held back the angry words she longed to spit at him. The risk of being beaten, especially on her wedding night, truly worried her.

"You did not say anything other than for me to be ready for you. And I am."

"I think you know exactly what I meant. Mayhap you should be punished for disobeying my orders."

"Nay! You cannot! I did nothing wrong!"

With shaking fingers, she reached for the laces of the chemise and pulled, letting the garment slide down. Baring her before his hungry gaze. She shivered, but not from cold.

He grinned, the wolfish expression sending an oleo of excitement and need, along with a healthy portion of apprehension, slithering along her spine to settle with a low hum deep inside.

He said nothing more, merely grabbed her wrist and hauled her against him. Her naked breasts smashed against him, the fabric of his tunic stimulating her sensitive nipples further. His arms wrapped around her, holding her still while his mouth crashed onto hers.

His fingers swept through her hair, combing it back from her face as he ravaged her mouth, his tongue parting her lips and sweeping inside with hungry urgency. The intimate contact weakened her knees. She leaned into him to keep from falling even as she responded to the heat in his kiss.

Her fingers curled into his shoulders and he shuddered beneath her touch. His tongue tantalized her, made her light-headed. Forgotten were all the conflicting emotions he stirred. All that mattered was the promise of pleasure so intense, she could almost taste it. When he tore his mouth from hers with a groan, a primal satisfaction at knowing he was as affected as she grew within.

"We must slow down, lest this is over before it has begun."

His hoarse voice sparked another set of odd fluttery sensations gliding along her spine. She leaned her face against his chest. Her heart pounded, each breath rasping through her lungs like a hot wind. His fingers lifted her chin, forcing her to face the hunger in his tawny eyes.

"You're such a tiny thing. I fear if I'm too hasty I'll break you in two." His mouth curved in a sensual smile. "I must remember to take care."

She swallowed past the lump of apprehension. His hands, now resting on her waist, almost completely spanned her, reminding her once more of her nudity. The feel of his clothing against her bare skin gave her a strange feeling of helplessness. Somehow, the sensation only added to the uproar tearing through her. She shouldn't like feeling overpowered this way, yet she did.

She had little success in forcing the weak emotions aside. Her hands rested on his chest, covered by his black tunic and hard as the steel used to forge his sword. Her sex pressed against him. It didn't take long to recognize his heated bulge. A momentary panic overtook her and she pushed against his shoulders.

His grip tightened, preventing her from escaping his embrace.

"I will not let you go."

His vow sparked another tremor. His hands slid along her body, scorching her flesh wherever he touched. He cupped her bottom, pressing her more fully against his still-concealed shaft.

She met his gaze, oddly pained by the suspicion she read in his eyes. He still harbored thoughts she was unfaithful. And with Simon, no less! She almost blurted the truth then, but held back.

"What troubles you, wife?"

Something about the way he pronounced her his left her unable to think of an adequate answer. If she spoke the truth of Simon's relationship to Lyndon, her brother could be banished, or worse. Yet, if her husband believed Simon to be her lover, he faced the same fate. An answer would not be found tonight. If they thought him any threat, 'twas better Simon appeared as nothing more than a besotted guard. Someone with a claim to Lyndon ran the risk of disappearing for good.

"Tell me, what are you thinking about?"

She met his gaze, and gave a small shake before lowering her head. He tilted her chin up. "Do not keep secrets from me. 'Twill go badly for you."

She stiffened and tried to ignore the burst of panic. "I keep no secrets."

Proud of her steady voice, she boldly held his stare.

"I'm not so sure. But I don't wish to think on that now. First is the matter of your punishment."

"What? I've done nothing to warrant it!"

"Ah, but you have. Do you not recall striking me last night?"

Heat scorched her cheeks. God's blood, she had hit him. It had led to the beguiling brutal and tender kisses they'd shared. A shiver slid through her veins.

"You insulted me."

"There was no need for you to strike."

He set her away from him and a chill drifted over her. Barely a moment later, he caught her wrists in one hand. She had no time to resist as he sat on the bed and hauled her across his lap.

She kicked and twisted, trying to free herself. "You bastard, let me go! I will not be treated this way."

He said nothing while he caught her legs between his, imprisoning her further. She tugged against his hold on her wrists, but 'twas like pulling against rock.

She screamed her outrage, but his grip only tightened. With his free hand, he stroked her arse and she gave another furious screech.

"Unhand me, you beast!"

His reply was to bring his hand down hard on her bottom. She stiffened in shock, the sting of the blow not truly painful. When the second strike landed much more harshly, she began to struggle once more.

"You cruel monster!"

"I expect to be respected and obeyed. You did neither."

Another blow, and another, and another. Fire bloomed in her arse and she squirmed against his hold. Tears escaped her squeezed eyelids, but she held back her sobs, refusing to let him see any weakness. After several more strikes, however, the pain oddly seemed to fade, replaced with a heat that near matched what he'd stirred with his kisses. She stopped fighting, falling limp against his lap and waited for the next strike. When it came, she rolled her hips toward him.

The next blow seemed to take longer to come, but she anticipated it by counting the seconds between. This time, he didn't hit hard, he lightly stroked her burning skin. A moan escaped to feel the fire spark still hotter at the gentle touch.

"Your skin turns a lovely shade of pink. I find myself hoping you will disobey often so I may enjoy the sight."

His words, spoken in a gruff tone, added another dimension to the riot of thrills that took over her thoughts. And, 'twould seem, her body. What had the man done to her?

She found herself suddenly upright, her sore bottom pressed onto his leg. Burying her face into his shoulder, she whimpered at the fresh burst of pain. Oddly, her nipples remained rock hard and eager. For what? The heat and wetness coating her sex left her unable to take a steady breath.

His hand slid along her breasts and she looked up into his face. His tawny eyes caught hers for a moment, before lowering to watch while his fingers rolled her nipple between them.

Flames erupted and she made no effort to conceal the moan of delight. His touch was unlike any pleasure she'd ever known. Her heart seemed to beat in time to the throb in the heated flesh of her bottom. Her husband continued to pinch and pull at her nipple, now turning his attentions to the other.

The wanton sensations flooding her left her quivering. To her horror, she pressed her breast into his hand, wanting more caresses. A husky chuckle accompanied a sharp pinch.

"I see you enjoyed my punishment. I don't think you'll like what I have in mind next."

Before she could respond, he stood, scooping her against his chest before laying her out on the bed. The feel of the feather tick against her sore arse made her attempt to rise, but he held her down with one hand on her chest.

"Stay."

She didn't dare defy him. She had no desire to be spanked again, though truthfully, right now, she might not have minded, noting the delightful languid feeling in her arms and legs.

He peeled off his tunic and Gillian found herself unable to look away as he removed his shirt then his hose. In moments, he stood bared before her. She held his gaze and detected a hint of humor there. Did he realize how hard she tried not to look at him... there?

He reached down and took her hand. She used all of her will to hold his stare as he guided her hand to his shaft and curled her fingers around it. She froze, her eyes widening to realize how very large his cock was.

She was no fool, innocent she may be. She knew what passed between a man and woman. But now she realized just how little she knew. How on God's earth would he fit that inside her? "You are afraid?"

His voice cut into the ramble of her thoughts and she gave a nod. Finally, she dared look at the hard and warm flesh she held. Her hand, surrounded by his, barely covered half the length, and her fingers only just fit fully around. Royce began to move, sliding her along his cock. After a few moments, she shrugged him off and shifted closer, still stroking.

He gave a low groan and she lightened her grip, worried she had hurt him. When she ran her fingers over the shiny tip, a sharp hiss escaped him. She looked up and found the most intense concentration lined into his face. His eyes had closed and his lips were tight, yet parted, allowing him to suck in air. The sight set her body burning anew.

He liked her touch. Pride and anticipation dimmed her apprehension. She took her time exploring him, leaning up and using her other hand to find his balls. Another groan and he pulled her hand away.

"Enough! Lay down."

The sudden change in his tone alarmed her. At her hesitation, he leaned over and pushed her back against the pillows.

"I see you'll need instruction on how to properly obey."

She had no time to respond for he stretched out above her, taking her hands and drawing her arms above her head. He parted her legs with his and the panic returned at the helpless position. Her squirming did nothing to loosen his hold. He switched both her hands to one and used the other to land a light slap to her thigh.

"Be still. I wish to... inspect you."

Stunned by his callous words, she froze, then began to struggle against him once more. "You insult me again. Why should I obey, you insufferable oaf?"

He slapped her leg again. "You are my wife now, and under the law, mine to do with as I please. And now, I wish to see what my wife offers."

"As if I'm no more than livestock to be bought or

sold?"

"'Twould be very unlucky for you if you tempt me to sell you."

She let out a snarl of anger and fought to free herself. He caught her face with his free hand and devoured her mouth, swallowing her protests with his lips and tongue. He gave her no respite, drawing the very breath from her lungs and replacing it with a fire that threatened to reduce her to cinders. Forgotten were the angry words of moments ago. Now desire took their place, and Gillian's struggles ceased as passion surged.

\*\*\*

Royce thought he could never get enough of Gillian. He glutted himself on her mouth, finally releasing his hold on her jaw to slide his hand to her breasts. Her struggles changed and now she undulated against him, driving her hot wet pussy against his cock. Did she not realize how she tormented him? He would have to tie her down so he could take his enjoyment without fear of going mad. Just the recollection of her seeking touch on his cock made him nearly come.

He drew away, panting, staring down into her heavy-lidded eyes. The smile ghosting her mouth cooled his desire. He'd seen that look before, usually prior to being begged for some boon or favor, a pretty dress or jewels. He'd long ago vowed not to be taken in by a woman's wiles and he would hold to that oath. His wife would learn that lesson right now.

The thought of binding her to the bed arose again. 'Twould certainly help drive his point home. She would be helpless to his whims and as he imagined the ways he might torment her, his desire flared once more.

Yes, this was how he'd tame his wife. He released his hold and stood. His squire had unpacked everything, but Royce hadn't had time to ask the boy where his belongings were. He opened the wardrobe and spied what he needed. Grabbing the belt, he turned back to the bed.

Gillian raised herself up on her elbows. His mouth

watered at the sight. Her long dark hair fell over her shoulders, curling around the pale skin of her tempting breasts. Hard pink nipples poked through the ebony cloud. He ground his teeth against the uproar that left him near breathless. His gaze moved down her body, settling on the dark curls covering her secrets. Ere the sun rose, he'd uncover many, if not all, of her secrets.

"What are you doing with that?"

The waver in her voice revealed her apprehension. The sight of worry in her violet eyes set his lust to raging once more.

"Since you seem to be unable to obey, I will make sure you do. You were to be waiting here for me naked, and yet, you were not. I told you to remain still and yet you refuse. Now you will have no choice."

She leapt from the bed and took up a position on the other side. "I will not be beaten again!" He doubled the leather belt and slapped it across his palm. "I wasn't planning on beating you again, but if you don't get back into the bed, I will."

She shook her head, her dark hair floating in a wild cloud about her face. "Why must you mistreat me? I've done nothing to warrant it!"

"You haven't? I can list several reasons. You struck me last night. I found you in the company of another man, not once, but twice. You refuse to obey even the simplest orders."

She opened her mouth as if to respond, then closed it again. Pressing her lips together, she lifted her chin and folded her arms. The position pushed her breasts up further and the sight sent another powerful surge of desire to his cock.

He pointed to the bed. "Lay down as I ordered, or I will put you there myself."

"If you can."

He found he rather enjoyed her resistance. Her defiance enticed him nearly as much as her delectable body. His fingers itched to touch her again and his rational side quickly ceded to the ever-growing hunger.

"Don't try my patience further." He took a few steps toward the end of the bed, anticipating what move she might make to evade him again. He didn't plan to give her the chance.

"You are trying my patience, my lord."

The heavy sarcasm in her last words drove him past any semblance of control. He made one more step toward the end of the bed, and as he anticipated, she moved to climb over. He turned and lunged at the same time, catching her about the waist.

Her flesh against his added a whole new riot of sensation. She fought him, hitting and kicking, until he shoved her to the mattress, covering her with his body. Still, she fought on. "Bastard! I won't be treated this way!"

"Damned wildcat! Be still!"

He shifted just in time to avoid her knee as she aimed for his cock. He managed to stay her dangerous legs and caught her wrist a moment before her fist caught the side of his head. He squeezed hard. Her cries changed in tone, pain taking the place of fury. Her other fist came at him and he caught it easily. Holding them together, he wrapped the leather around them, then secured it to the bedrail above her.

\*\*\*

Stunned by the way he'd bound her; Gillian fell still, staring up at her husband. What in all that was holy had she done to deserve such treatment? Ere the wedding, if she'd had any idea he would treat her this way, she would have given in to her urges to flee.

He leaned back, panting hard from their tussle. Even as disbelief consumed a portion of her thoughts, the sight of his heaving chest left her mouth dry with a sensual thirst she'd never known. Or was that fear? She turned away, unable to look on him further.

"Now, you have no choice but to endure whatever I choose to do with you."

Her eyes snapped to his. A hint of a smile curled his

lips, heat darkening his eyes to a burnished amber. Something in his words hinted at dark pleasures. How could she possibly be anticipating this? He was a brute who mistreated her and she was trapped. Wed to him on orders of the king. Was this what her life would be like from now on? She closed her eyes to ease the sting of tears.

For several seconds, she remained thus, waiting for his next move. Would he spank her again? At the thought, the warmth in her still tender bottom seemed to blossom anew. She resisted the urge to squirm.

At the feel of fingers sliding along her breast, she sucked in a deep breath. Still, she refused to open her eyes, afraid to see his mocking face. The fingers stroked her lightly, seeking out every bit of her flesh. Her breathing came hard now, her eyes squeezed tight.

"Gillian, look at me."

She found no desire or will to resist the order. Her eyes fluttered open, her vision blurred for several seconds. His hand, still moving along her breast, curled around and gently squeezed.

Her back arched and a strangled cry escaped her parched throat. He spiraled his fingers around her nipple. She met his stare, eagerly anticipating. Too eager. She shouldn't like this fire licking at her, making her sex swell and grow slick. She should be fighting him.

When his grip tightened again, another cry escaped her and he grinned.

"I like knowing you've passion in you. 'Twill make this marriage much more tolerable." Once again, her anger sparked, but not nearly as intense this time. The riot in her body surpassed any annoyance at his arrogant mocking.

"Well, hurry up and do what you will then."

His hand tightened on her breast. The discomfort of the harsh grip somehow enhanced the ever-growing arousal.

"Don't rush me. I plan to spend the next hours learning about you. And you will have to submit."

"I've no choice, since you bound me as though I am nothing more than captive."

Another squeeze and she bit hard on her lip to prevent the moan from escaping. Was she mad to like the way he touched her? No one had ever spoken to her of the pleasure to be found with more than the simplest explanations. Most of her knowledge had been learned in secret. Nothing had prepared her for how utterly delightful this could be.

He cupped her other breast and the tumult nearly stole her wits. She panted as he caressed and stroked, every so often pinching her nipples.

"I think you enjoy being my captive."

His husked words floated through the haze. Not a single word formed to deny his. His gaze remained locked on hers. He lowered his hands along her sides. She panted as he tickled his fingers along her ribs, drawing a hoarse giggle. His pleased smile unleashed still more yearning.

When he slipped over her hips to her thighs. Gillian found herself straining toward him. He chuckled and pushed her legs apart. The heat from his hands nearly scorched. He inhaled sharply and grinned.

"You cannot hide the proof of your desire now."

He carefully positioned her legs, spreading her wider and wider. He knelt between her knees, using his own to keep her open. Heat flamed in her face.

His hands still rested on her thighs, not moving while he studied her. Through the embarrassment, his scrutiny sent waves of passion hurtling in her veins. God's teeth, she wished he would do something already, instead of keeping her in the half-maddening purgatory.

Finally, and excruciatingly slowly, he moved his hands toward her sex. She'd never imagined wanting so badly for him to touch her and near held her breath as he brushed the curls there. Just that hint of contact made her entire pussy clench, aching for something, though she didn't know what, exactly.

He tugged on her hair and she gasped.

"That hurt!"

"I know."

He liked her pain? Though, truthfully, the pull hadn't

hurt nearly as much as the spanking. Judging from the hardness of his cock, which she'd avoided looking at since he'd made her touch him, he did enjoy inflicting agony, as much as he appeared to enjoy inflicting pleasure.

He tugged again. This time, the discomfort added to the heat and she once again lifted her hips, offering herself. She shouldn't, but she did. She tugged on the leather keeping her secured to the bed. It didn't give and the added sensation of helplessness mixed into the varied tangle of reaction. React was all she could do.

"You seem impatient."

Was that displeasure in his tone? No, she clearly detected humor, and mayhap affection as well. Or did she just want his tenderness so badly, she convinced herself? Before she had the chance to think of a suitable answer, his fingers stroked right into the flesh of her sex. All thought fled as sensation took over.

She quivered, each gentle caress stimulating her beyond what she thought she could bear. God's bones, he'd kill her with pleasure, rather than pain. He paused, his finger brushing against the hardened knob of flesh where every one of the feelings in her body seemed to reside. He stroked once, twice and again. She cried out, hurtling toward something fierce and decadent and explosive. She writhed against her bonds, seeking more.

Instead, he stopped and drew away. She panted and stared at him.

"This is not about your pleasure." He leaned back. "Don't think to dissuade me. When I am finished with my... examination, then we shall see about your pleasure."

The bastard actually stroked her again, sending the settling desire back to a fever pitch.

"You're cruel." She choked the words out, wondering how in the Lord's name she thought he possessed a single tender emotion. She tugged once more on her bonds, this time seeking freedom.

"Aye. Sooner you learn that, the better off you'll be."

He resumed the gentle caresses, seeking every dark

secret in her folds and halting any response she may have planned. Honestly, she couldn't remember, especially when he gave her clit a gentle pinch. White light blinded her momentarily. Each move he made drove her deeper and deeper into a state of ecstasy she'd never imagined. Her body swayed under his ministrations. The taste of pleasure danced on her tongue and her entire body stiffened. She tossed her head. What was this madness she craved?

"Yes," she moaned, hoping he would keep on touching her this way.

He stopped again. For a few moments, Gillian didn't register the fact, until her head spun with the cessation.

"Why?" she asked.

Her entire body ached, hovering on the edge of something she'd begun to crave. He'd done this to her, reduced her to this mindless need.

"I like to watch you. If I let you come now, 'twill be over. I am not ready for it to be over. Your pleasure comes when I deem it time."

She sucked in a breath as the implications sank into her dazed thoughts. How long would he toy with her this way? The devilish grin adorning his face sent her heart into an unsteady rhythm.

However long would be longer than she could endure. Already her mind hovered on the brink of madness, so desperate to reach the bliss his touch promised.

"M-my lord, 'tis not fair that I cannot touch you."

The grin broadened. "You are my captive remember? You will remain thus."

She tugged, frustration and annoyance building again, yet not once did this soul-encompassing hunger abate. When her husband once again resumed exploring her pussy, she nearly wept.

"Please."

The plea escaped before she could stop it. He lifted his studious gaze from where he toyed with her sex. Once more, he gave a shake of his head, then shifted position.

What did he intend? Her mind raced with possibilities

as he crouched between her legs. Nay, he couldn't mean to... he did! He lowered his head, his mouth now replacing his fingers, which held her open for his exploration.

The hot rasp of his tongue, slow and deliberate, sent her eyes rolling back in her head as she desperately sucked in gulps of air. He'd positioned himself in such a way she could no longer move her hips and had to lay motionless under his sensual assault.

He plunged his tongue into her, then withdrew, moving again to her clit. He sucked it between his lips, lashing it with his tongue. Gillian cried out, her body trembling violently, hunger and pleasure mingling to overtake everything except this hot and furious carnality.

He paused then, giving her time to steady her breath, though her heart still raced madly. Her sex clenched, aching for more. When he resumed his former position, she tried again to raise her hips to his seeking mouth, but to no avail. The inability to move seemed to deepen the waves of lust rolling through her body.

On and on it went, her husband holding her still as he tormented and teased her, making her mad with this inexplicable need. Her head tossed, and the guttural cries echoing in the room surely belonged to her, but she wouldn't have recognized them had she not been so entranced by the sensations he sparked.

Finally, after what seemed an interminable amount of time when he didn't touch her, Royce sucked her clit once more into his mouth, giving one sharp pull while rubbing his tongue over the flesh. A blinding bliss exploded within, over and around her. Her body rocked with glorious delight. All else faded into the background. Her husband continued to employ the most subtle changes with his lips and tongue, altering the pleasure between fire and throbbing warmth, and her body rolled and quaked under the continuous onslaught.

When he finally drew away, breathing seemed impossible. She lay limp and sated, her body quivering in the aftermath. She didn't even realize when he reached up and released her bonds from the bedrail. Yet, he kept her wrists bound and hauled her against him.

"Rest, Wildcat. You will need your strength for what comes next."

He stroked her hair and hugged her. Somehow, the tender gesture made her want to weep. A little while ago, he'd been seemingly cold, cruel and indifferent. Then he'd given her the most incredible pleasure. Now, he was tender and caring. He kept her senses upended. Or was she slipping into madness?

# chapter four

Royce's cock throbbed with painful need. His wife's reactions had been far more than he'd anticipated. He glanced down at her bound hands. He smiled. He'd played games such as these with his various mistresses, but never had he truly wanted to keep someone as his slave. Who better to tend that need than his wife? She couldn't refuse, and even if she did, 'twould give him more reason to spank her pretty arse again.

She snuggled against him and a strange warmth crept into his bones. He frowned and pushed her to her back. Her eyes, darkened to plum with her satisfaction, flashed with confusion.

"What are you –?"

He kissed her hard, silencing her. He covered her with his body, his cock seeking and finding with minimal effort, her wet and swollen pussy. A moment's hesitation as he lifted her bound wrists and placed them over his neck. She arched toward him at the same moment he drove into her.

Her pained cry halted his motion. He knew he'd hurt her. He brushed the hair from her face. "'Tis better to have it over quickly." He winced at the thickness of his voice.

"It hurt."

She squeezed her eyes shut, one tear escaping. Her chest heaved with heavy gasps.

"I know. It won't for long."

Her watery gaze tugged at a place in him he never even realized he possessed. He looked away and remained still inside her, much as it pained his pulsating and hard cock. Her body needed to adjust. He needed to come. His teeth ground together painfully as he delighted in her wet heat and fought his instinctual needs.

Her breathing steadied a moment later. He smiled. 'Twas time to slake his own desires.

He drew back, savoring the way she clenched around him. He paused with only his tip remaining inside her. Her slick walls surrounding him spurred an exhilaration he hadn't felt in years. He slid back into her, delighting in the way her body quivered and she cried out. He did it again, maintaining a leisurely rhythm, much as his cock wanted him to hurry. But Royce didn't want this to end; he wanted to drag it out and relish each decadent moment. His wife's body pleased him well, and he wanted to enjoy her.

*You've a lifetime to enjoy her.* The thought spurred his need and his balls tightened. He grabbed her hips, holding her still as he drove in and out, her cries echoing in a strange erotic music that matched his tempo. When he slid his fingers to her clit and gently squeezed, she gave a shriek and her body rocked under his with another climax, her pussy clutching at his cock with a ferocity he could no longer resist. 'Twas more than enough to send him over the edge and he drove deep one more time, his seed exploding. He could barely see, barely hear, could only feel the fiery release as it tore through him, over and over, encouraged by his wife's slick hot pussy squeezing him so delightfully, leaving him sated and weak. He collapsed atop her. She hugged him tighter.

A shiver passed over him. He didn't want to face the realization that laying here like this with his new bride seemed somehow a missing piece of his life now put into place. Much as he hated to do it, he slid free of her body, lifting her arms off his neck. He ignored her disappointed sigh. He left her bound, but somehow she still managed to wrap herself around him.

"I liked that, my lord."

"Did you now?"

He knew she did, her uninhibited responses had told him more than any words.

"Aye. When can we do it again?"

He held back a chuckle. Instead, he let loose a loud yawn.

"Not now. 'Twill take some time before I can... besides, it has been a long day and I've much to do on the morrow."

"Very well."

He ignored the hurt in her voice. 'Twas harder to ignore the remorse poking him.

*\*\**

Gillian stirred from her brief slumber and snuggled closer to Royce. His warmth surrounded her, and his hand sliding along her back and hips roused more of the delight he'd given before. She ached to wrap her arms around him, needing to somehow ground herself against the sensation that left her spinning. But her still-bound wrists hindered her efforts.

He didn't seem to care, finding her mouth and devouring her with a ferocity that left her gasping. He gripped her breast now, caressing and squeezing and she cried out into his mouth, pressing as close as she could, seeking more of the wanton delight.

He pulled away, the moonlight filtering through the bed curtains to illuminate his tawny eyes. She held her breath at what she found.

Fire. Ravenous hunger. Possession.

With just a look, he'd claimed her. Body and soul.

Panic rose to choke her. She squeezed her eyes shut. In a matter of hours, this man had reduced her to nothing more than chattel and she had flung herself willingly into his net. Angry tears stung but she held them back. She would prove herself to him. Somehow she knew the key to making him respect her arose from the passion they shared. As brutal as it was, 'twas honest and real. She couldn't deny it.

She only had to use it to her advantage.

"What are you thinking, wife?"

His emphasis on her new title seemed a taunt. She opened her eyes and met his gaze steadily.

"I am thinking I wish you'd hurry already so I can go back to sleep."

The insult drew a flinch. Just as quickly, he threw his

head back and laughed, a hearty sound that vibrated through her and left her sex once more wet with heat.

"I think I shall have you begging ere long."

He ran a finger down her cheek and along her jaw. She fought not to shiver against the heat curling in her veins.

"You may try. My lord."

The banter left her exhilarated. He arched an eyebrow, but clearly knew she taunted him deliberately. He gave her a sly grin that gave her a second's panic. He confirmed her concerns by seizing her wrists and securing her hands above her once again.

"Damn you!"

Despite her frustration at being rendered helpless yet again, Gillian found her situation enhanced the desire pulsing along her spine.

"Aye, I've long been damned to hell, but as long as I walk this earth, I will enjoy myself. Now, I believe I said I would have you begging."

He leaned back, studying her in such a way, her heart rammed furiously against her chest. He seemed to be pondering what to do. Her breath came in short gasps as she waited.

The strike of his palm against her breast drew a sharp cry before she could stifle it.

"You bastard!"

He said nothing, just did it again. The sting left her thoughts reeling, but at the same time, she noted how her pussy swelled and ached. He paused and caught her stiff nipple in his fingers, rolling it and squeezing. She arched against him, needing somehow to press closer. He obliged, cupping her tender flesh. The echo of his slap swelled, yet now the heat licked deliciously through her. He released her and landed another light blow. Her entire body bowed toward him, the discomfort a fiery delight that tempted her to let herself burn.

His fingers suddenly stroked her sex and another cry erupted. He twirled his fingers into her and withdrew.

"You seem to have a liking for pain."

Her gaze snapped to his as he held up his fingers, glistening with her juices. Heat flooded her face and she thought she might burst into flame when he put them into his mouth and sucked.

God's bones, she was ready to beg him to take her now. Only the recollection of his mocking challenge kept her silent. Even so, she doubted she would win this battle. He held all the advantages. Worse, he knew it.

But she wouldn't make it easy on him.

He resumed his exploration of her sex while giving her breast another slap. The pleasure of his gentle stroking in unison with the sting of his palm against her flesh left her vision blurred. Her hips lifted, seeking more of his decadent touch. If she had known the marriage bed would bring such delight, she might have asked her father to marry her off years ago.

"You are enjoying yourself, aren't you, Wildcat?"

Her gaze cleared and locked on his. She couldn't find her voice to ask what he meant, why he called her that. He grinned and the turmoil in her body intensified.

"Your body seeks my touch; your cries tell me of your need. Wild and untamed." His stare pierced, pinning her more surely than his body. "I will tame you."

He plunged two fingers into her and for a moment, tenderness left her squirming for another reason. But a few moments later, the heated pleasure returned as he pumped within her, a finger circling her clit. The heat rose, until she felt as though she breathed fire, but she didn't care. Her body sang with delight, craved the inevitable explosion she knew awaited her.

He paused then, pulling his hand from her sex. He leaned in close.

"You will beg me for your pleasure."

She gave her head a shake, but when he resumed stroking her pussy, she understood. Damn him! He may be her husband, but she wouldn't beg. Let him have his way, she would give no satisfaction to his desires, even if the flames licking her body charred her to a crisp.

He continued to toy with her, each stroke maddening and delightful. He alternated his gentle stroking with sharp pinches to her nipples and light slaps to her breast. Each time, her body quivered, her hips rising to try to force his hand deeper within.

He drew back. Her breath came in harsh pants. For several seconds, he merely stared at her. With a suddenness she didn't anticipate, he lowered his head and took her mouth in a bruising kiss. She responded eagerly, desperate for any touch he gave. His tongue found every deep corner in her mouth and the onslaught left her feeling as though the bed spun.

He paused. "What do you want, wife?"

"I want you to... please, I need..." She couldn't find the words to explain, and choked on a sob.

He brushed the hair from her face. "You want to come?"

"Yes, yes, please."

He chuckled, but she didn't care that she'd given in. She had to come, ached for it so badly, she licked her lips.

"Are you begging me?"

Another sob and she closed her eyes for an instant, trying somehow to steady herself. When she met his gaze, she nodded.

"Aye. I am begging you. Take pity on me. Make me come."

He gave her a wolfish grin and rose above her. She spread her legs in invitation. She wanted that hard shaft filling her, claiming her completely.

He obliged her with one thrust, and she wrapped her legs around his waist to keep him there. He chuckled and began to move inside of her. The pain of their first coupling had faded, lost in the riot of desire clouding her thoughts.

She wanted to hold onto him, but since she couldn't, she arched her hips, allowing him to drive even deeper. Her eyes rolled, her head thrashed, as he propelled her higher and higher, closer and closer.

The feel his fingers finding and stroking her clit made her vision go red, then white, and fire erupted inside her. She felt as if she jumped from the highest cliff, her body twirling and spinning in the wind while inside, she exploded into a fiery shower of stars. From what seemed a distance, she heard Royce's guttural shout a moment before his hot seed bathed her sex. He continued to thrust, spurring the most pleasurable tremors.

When he rolled away, she almost asked him to stay, but remained silent when he freed her wrists. He pulled her close, settling her against him. He picked up her hand and studied the red marks on her wrist.

"Have that seen to in the morn."

His brusque manner left her confused and shredded the vestiges of sated drowsiness. His mood changes happened so fast, she wondered if she'd ever have warning.

Then he squeezed her a little tighter, and somehow, the gesture soothed her. So many questions danced on her tongue, but she found she possessed no strength to ask them yet. She closed her eyes. Just for a moment.

# chapter five

Gillian awoke alone, cold and shivering in the large bed. At first she'd thought to find her husband in the chamber, but it appeared he'd already left. Chimes from the chapel marked the end of the morning meal. *Jesu*, she'd been abed way past anyone else! She threw back the bedcovers and went to the door, calling for her maid.

"Edith, you should have awakened me long ere now!" She scolded the girl as she tended her ablutions.

"Yes, my lady, but your husband said you were not to be disturbed."

Gillian paused while splashing water over her face. "He said that?"

The maid twisted her hands before her and nodded. "Aye. He said you were very tired and needed to rest."

What message did he send with the gesture? She would ask, her mind clear and keen now. The light of day would help keep her sharp-witted when she spoke with Royce.

Pulling a simple burgundy bliaut over her kirtle, she urged Edith to hurry with braiding her hair. Placing the veil on top, she slipped into soft leather shoes. Ready at last, she opened the door.

The mad rush of her toilet now over, Gillian noted the aches lingering in her body. Oddly, the soreness felt good as it reminded her of the dark and wicked pleasure he'd given her last eve. She'd never have imagined some of the things he'd done. Even now, heat flooded her cheeks to think of it. To want it again.

God's blood, she needed to put this aside or she'd lose her strength again. Her eagerness to see her husband confounded her. They had business to discuss, such as Lyndon's affairs and the usual household matters. He would take over the garrison and incorporate the men into his own army. She should focus on those things only and all would be well.

Except the image of his fingers stroking her breasts, the recollection of his mouth sliding along her sex, the tantalizing torment of his cock's strokes into her body kept her thoughts somewhat scattered. No matter, she forced those thoughts aside. Time enough to think on them later.

She stopped short at the bottom of the stairs in the great hall. 'Twas mostly bare, save for a few servants clearing the tables of the morning meal.

Her husband had already left. Surely that wasn't disappointment welling in her throat. She broke her fast with a hunk of bread and some cheese from the last remaining platter.

After washing the meager meal down with some ale, she made her way to the steward's chamber. Thomas informed her the ledgers were ready for the earl's inspection. In the meantime, word had come that Edward may arrive at any time. The announcement roused another sense of panic.

While she had no doubt Lyndon was prepared to welcome her sovereign, she worried what might come about during his visit. Edward knew well she carried Welsh blood in her veins, but she hadn't yet informed her husband of the fact. She'd assumed the king hadn't kept the information secret, but her husband had yet to make mention of it, which led her to believe he didn't know. She must tell him ere the king arrived, lest he think she hid the fact for a different reason. He didn't trust her already. Certainly he mistrusted anyone with even the most tenuous of ties to the Welsh. Knowing she possessed Welsh blood would surely displease him. His reaction left her torn.

A recollection of her spanking rose up fast. Might he do worse if he learned of her Welsh heritage before she told him? A shiver passed over her. She clenched her fingers, trying not to let the memory overpower her. 'Twas no use. Her bottom burned now, as if feeling again the stinging heat that had sparked so many other sensations. Most of them were pleasant.

Was she mad? He'd beaten her. How could she have enjoyed it? Damn the man for upending so much of what she knew about herself. She'd long imagined a respectful husband, one who would cherish and value her and all she did to keep Lyndon at its best. Instead, she'd gotten a man who possessed dark tastes and wicked intentions. He was stubborn and angry and arrogant. Yet, the thought of his hands on her, even now in the harsh light of the morn, sent tendrils of heat uncurling within.

Bah! She was a fool. She had to find a way to use the heat between them to her own advantage. Her husband *would* learn to appreciate her. First, she had much to tell him, well, as much as she herself knew. Gillian had never met any of her mother's family. Gwyneth had been disowned by her kin when she'd wed William Marlowe. Surely that fact should ease any worries her husband might have.

Since she now had some time, she went in search of Simon. She needed to sort this all out and he would surely help. She headed for the doors, pulling them open and shielding her eyes against the sun.

Three steps down, the gates opened and soldiers rode in, led by her husband. He wore his mail armor, but no helm. Even from here, there was no mistaking his scowl. Gillian descended the stair and strode across the bailey to greet him.

"Good morn, my lord."

"Get inside. There is a band of warriors headed here."

He dismounted and tossed the reins to his squire while he barked orders. Soldiers from every corner of the keep came forward and assembled before him. Gillian watched while he explained the situation and ordered the gates closed. Before the keeper could do so, an arrow lodged in his throat and he collapsed to the ground.

Royce turned, unsheathing his sword. His gaze landed on Gillian.

"I told you to get inside!" he bellowed. He grabbed her

arm and near dragged her to the steps. "Remain in our chamber until I come for you."

He shoved her toward the door and, too stunned to resist, Gillian obeyed. She paused at the top of the stairs, at the same moment several men rode in to the bailey. Not Lyndon's men, not the earl's men. Welsh rebels. Just as the earl had warned. Gillian hurried inside and barred the doors. She shouted orders for the staff to find a safe place and ran for the stairs.

Here was her chance.

She hurried to her former chamber, pausing long enough to grab her bow and quiver. Adjusting the straps, she reached for the tapestry concealing a hidden door. Pulling it open, she looked up at the sky, the narrow stairs leading to the ramparts. She crept up slowly, listening to the shouts and screech of metal that signified a battle. Nearing the top, heart pounding, she paused. She removed an arrow and notched it, ready to fire the moment she took her place. With a deep breath, she ran up the last few steps.

The chaos of the battle grew louder. Screams, shouts, pain and outrage. She had never experienced a battle. The smell of mud and blood and sweat assailed her from all sides, even up here. She nodded in approval at Lyndon's archers, lined up and picking off rebels when they came through the gates. How in the world could there be so many? It seemed as if the incoming stream of riders and foot soldiers never ceased.

"My lady, you shouldn't be here!" Edgar's shout seemed to come from far away. He loosed another arrow. A scream near the gates reached them.

She lifted her bow, peering down at the open gates. Pulling the string tight, she assessed the tension and distance, then released the arrow. Her target crumpled to the ground. A combination of exhilaration and disgust for her success left her momentarily frozen before she shook her head and pulled out another arrow.

Two rebels attacked one of Lyndon's men. She let her shaft fly, satisfied at the scream of pain when one of the rebels fell. *Jesu*, when had she become so bloodthirsty? She forced the thought aside, finding a routine in the urgency of her task. Another arrow nocked, a moment to draw back the string, aiming. Another rebel down. Words of encouragement from the bowmen lining the ramparts exhilarated her.

Two arrows flew past in close succession. The rebels own long-bowmen now attacked the ramparts' defense. Gillian ducked behind the wall, carefully raising her head to peer below. The amount of Welshmen attacking Lyndon left her stomach rolling with anger. Damn them, they would not have her home!

She rose and once more fired into the melee. Her aim was true for her next three shots, until another volley of missiles sent her ducking for cover once more.

She waited a few beats then rose again, firing toward the archers gathered at the gates. She and her men took out three more before shielding themselves.

She smiled. "We will win, already their forces are failing. Come; let's get the rest of their archers."

The two men beside her grinned.

"As you command, my lady," Edgar said.

In unison, they rose, nocking arrows and preparing to fire. Mere seconds passed before they let loose the quills. All three made contact. Before Gillian could take satisfaction in their success, she spotted her husband.

With sure-footedness, he toyed with his opponent, finally striking with deadly accuracy. The outlaw fell, his howl of agony reaching Gillian's ears over the din. In seconds, the man had been replaced by one of his comrades. Royce easily dispatched him, then turned to face yet another rebel.

With horror, Gillian spotted a second man approaching her husband from behind. She pulled out another arrow, readied it and aimed.

\*\*\*

With one fluid movement, Royce dispatched his opponent. Some warning sounded in his head. He tried to ignore it, ready to face the next rebel. Despite his efforts, his gaze lifted to the ramparts.

A wild cacophony of thoughts exploded. Anger took precedence. Anger that he'd been such a fool. Her longbow aimed right at him. *Jesu*, she meant to kill him! With a muttered curse, he wished he hadn't foregone his helm.

Before he could blink, she dispatched the arrow. A ripple of air caressed his neck, the arrow flying past on a mere breath. A strangled scream from behind made him turn. He stared in amazement at the Welshman, inches away, sword still raised to strike. The arrow in his throat seemed to hold him upright for a few moments before he collapsed to the ground.

Royce spun back around, gaping at his wife, peering down from the ramparts. For a few moments, he almost forgot the raging battle. She hadn't killed him, she'd saved his life! Unable to fully comprehend her actions, he merely stared, a strange combination of shock and awe coursing through him.

As quickly as surprise and gratitude stole his breath, anger returned, renewing his strength. What the devil was she doing up there? She had disobeyed him yet again. She would get herself killed!

"Get away from there!"

His shout barely carried over the din. He lifted his sword to parry a thrust from an oncoming rebel and dispatched the man before turning his attention briefly back to his wife.

"Had I not been here, my lord, you would now be dead," she called.

He barely heard amid the chaos of the battle. God's bones, she would be the death of him yet. Catching sight of a path to the keep, he ran toward it, pushing himself through the melee. He barely had time to slash out at a few who dared try to stop him. They never attacked a second time.

He paused to see if she still stood up there. She did. An arrow skimmed past her and she ducked behind the wall.

His heart seemed to stop beating until she reappeared, another arrow ready and aimed. From the corner of his eye, Royce saw one of the rebels pointing his bow at Gillian. Once more, she disappeared behind the wall as the archer fired, only to get back up and return the volley. Her arrow struck the rebel, and she nocked yet another quill before he hit the ground.

Heart pounding, Royce saw Burke near the castle steps, engaged in combat. He pushed past them at the very moment Burke sent the rebel hurtling down the steps.

"Gillian is atop the ramparts. Keep them from gaining the keep."

Burke nodded. Royce pounded on the doors. At least his wife had the sense to bar them. He barely heard the steward's response, but his shouts had been sufficient. He pushed past the man the moment the door opened wide enough for him to pass through. He wasted no time heading up the stairs, Thomas on his heels. How in the devil had she gotten up there?

"There is a door in her chamber, my lord." Thomas urged him to follow.

When he entered his wife's former chamber, he saw the tapestry pulled away and the door open.

"It leads both to the ramparts and to escape tunnels below," the steward explained.

Royce's head spun. How had he not known this? Why did his wife insist on keeping secrets? What other secrets did she have?

"Thank you. I will be bringing my wife down, and I want her secured in our chamber. Are there any hidden doors or passages I should know of?"

Thomas shook his head. "Nay, my lord. I possess all the keys."

"Lady Gillian?"

"She has most as well, but not all."

"I want her locked in so she cannot get out. Do you understand?"

The gangly man paled and nodded.

"Aye, my lord."

"See to it while I retrieve her."

He climbed the narrow stairs two at a time and reached the ramparts quickly. He spotted his wife firing another arrow into the skirmish. A bellow of pain from below confirmed her aim was true. He forced aside a brief moment of pride, for fear 'twould soften his anger. When she moved to load another arrow, he caught her arm. She turned, eyes wide.

"Unhand me! There's no time!"

She gave a mighty tug and almost broke free, but he tightened his grip. Around them, the other archers continued, but watched their new lord warily. From the corner of his eye, Royce sensed an incoming arrow and hauled her to the stone, covering her with his body.

"What are you doing?" he shouted.

"Defending my home! Let me go!"

He stood, still holding her arm, and hauled her up with him. He shoved her to the stairs. "Get yourself below at once."

She tried to dart around him but he caught her about the waist. She swung her free arm at him and he ducked to avoid the blow. He lifted her off her feet and carried her to the stair. She clung to her bow while trying to land blows with her free hand. He dodged each one.

"You fool! You need me up here!"

"I need you to obey me for once!"

He descended the stair, tightening his grip on her squirming body. Despite the critical situation, his body responded in a way that drew a curse before he could stop it. Damn her!

He reached her chamber and set her down and released her. She made a dash for the stairs again, but he stopped her. He grabbed her bow and she stilled.

"Release me!"

He shook his head, closing his hand about her wrist and dragging her from the room. Thomas stood at the end of the hall, outside their chamber. Gillian dug her heels in to resist, but Royce refused to relent and she stumbled. He turned and caught her around the waist again, hurrying her along. He shoved her into the room.

"Stay here until I come for you." He turned to Thomas. "If the door is locked, she cannot get out?"

"Nay, my lord."

"Nay! You can't do this!" His wife ran toward him, but he quickly pulled the door shut, securing the lock into the latch. Thomas turned the key.

Gillian's pounding echoed in the corridor. Her furious screams might have roused humor in any other situation. He held his hand out.

"Give me the key."

The steward obeyed, pulling the key from the ring with shaking fingers. He placed it in Royce's palm.

"She is to remain here until I say otherwise."

"Yes, my lord."

Royce turned and strode to the stairs, anxious to return to the battle and put an end to it, now that his wife could no longer cause trouble. His anticipation to return to her and dole out the punishment she deserved hastened his step.

The chaos of the battle seemed to diminish. He hurried down the steps and resumed attacking the Welsh invaders. Which one was Godwin? He dispatched a rebel, then another, ears ringing from the echo of screeching steel. He searched the melee but couldn't find Burke. He needed his captain.

He made his way through the last of the skirmishes between his men and the rebels. Bodies littered the bailey, most those of the outlaws, though he noted a couple of Lyndon's men lying lifeless on the ground. Finally, the sounds of the battle faded and died, the last Welshman cut down. Blood and sweat tainted the air and the moans of the wounded mingled with shouts of celebration. Feeling a powerful gaze burning into his back, he turned.

Simon stood across the bailey, glowering as he stood over one of Lyndon's fallen. Gillian's guard's gaze held clear contempt. The man had to go, Royce decided. The sooner, the better.

Mayhap he could convince the king to take him as one of his soldiers. 'Twould free Royce from two problems Simon presented.

He looked away, again seeking Burke. There, coming from the stables. He headed toward his captain as the doors to the keep opened.

"The baroness has escaped!"

Royce didn't know who made the claim, but he swore, his shout echoing in the now eerily silent bailey. Burke reached him, appearing just as concerned.

"How did this happen?"

Burke shrugged. "I didn't see any of the rebels gain access to the keep."

The suspicions that rose nearly choked Royce. A red haze clouded his vision. Someone inside had to have given Anne aid. But who?

"Set the men to clearing this." He waved a hand around the bailey. "We must question everyone in the household. I am assigning the task to you."

"And your wife?"

Royce glared at his captain. "I will see to my wife."

"Aye. Did you see any sign of Godwin?"

Royce shook his head. "It's as if he is nothing more than a specter. I will see that man's head on a pike ere this is over."

Burke gave him a knowing smile. "No doubt you will."

"See to your tasks."

"Aye, my lord." Burke strode away, shouting at the soldiers in the bailey awaiting further orders.

Royce gave another sidelong glance toward Simon before turning back to the keep. He needed to punish his wife. Again.

# chapter six

Gillian's fists ached from pounding on the door. Damn her husband for locking her up like this! Kept prisoner in her own home. Not even Thomas would unlock the door. Had she no voice at Lyndon anymore?

She went to the arrow slit and peered out. From here, she couldn't see much, but the battle seemed to be ending. Where was her husband? And Simon? Had he survived unscathed? She prayed so.

She sat on the bed, but jumped up as she recalled what had occurred there last eve. She never wanted to share that bed again. She picked up her bow and lowered herself into a chair by the hearth. Taking a cloth from the quiver, she wiped the weapon down, cleaning it of the sweat from her hands and any dirt acquired during her brief time on the ramparts.

Again, she silently cursed her husband. She'd done nothing but help and he acted as though she'd committed a crime. Did he not understand that with her assistance, he stood a better chance of defeating the rebels?

The sound of the key grating in the lock drew her from her thoughts. She put down the bow and stood. The door swung open, Royce filling the frame. Her heart raced.

He stepped into the room and shut the door, barring it against intruders. She swallowed the lump in her throat. Fury still lined his face and all of it was directed at her.

"Why didn't you tell me of the hidden door?"

"You didn't ask."

He clenched his fists and took one step closer. She lifted her chin, refusing to cower.

"I will have no secrets kept from me." His voice was steady, and calm.

"'Tis no secret the door is there. It was built for escape." Yet, even as she spoke the words, she suspected he meant other secrets. She had others.

"Do not toy with me."

He stepped closer still, laying his hand on the back of her neck. He drew her near.

"Do you know how close you came to being killed today?"

His warm breath fanned her cheek. The sensation stirred things she shouldn't be thinking of. Not now.

"I was never in any danger, my lord."

"No danger? What about the arrows that narrowly missed striking you?"

"I avoided them, did I not?"

"Your sass will not help you. 'Tis bad enough you disobey at every turn, but your behavior is unseemly."

"I defended my home and will do so again, if I must!"

"The baroness has escaped."

Gillian sucked in a deep breath. "Nay! How... I don't understand."

"Someone from inside must have helped her."

She gaped at him. Surely, he didn't think...

"'Twas not I, my lord. You are mad if you think I'd do anything to help that witch."

"Nay, but the attack was also curiously timed. 'Twould seem Lyndon may have a traitor in its midst."

Gillian straightened her spine. "And you think 'tis me."

"I don't know what to think. But I know one thing. You will not disobey me again."

He reached for her bow. Curiosity piqued, Gillian studied him warily.

"My lord, what are you doing?" She stepped close to him and grabbed for the weapon, but he held it out of her reach.

"What I should have done when I first learned you possessed it. You must now face the consequences of your foolishness."

He strode to the door and yanked it open, calling for Thomas. When the steward arrived, Royce held the bow out to him.

"Lock this away where she cannot get to it. I'll decide later if I will destroy it."

"Nay!"

Her scream echoed through the room. She ran to him, but he turned, blocking her attempts to grab the bow before he handed it to Thomas. The steward stepped back when she whirled, ready to lunge. Royce grasped her arm, halting her.

"Go! Now!" His order thundered over Gillian's protests.

The tall man hurried away. Gillian called for him to stop and tried to break free of her husband's grip, but he held her firmly while he shut the door and slid the bar into place. He finally faced her, his hand tightening on her arm.

"You will not place yourself in such danger again, do you understand?"

"How could you? That was made especially for me as a gift from my father!" She again tried to pull free, but he did not loosen his grip.

"It almost got you killed today. Perhaps now you will learn when I give an order, I expect it to be heeded."

"I didn't do anything other than what would be expected if I'd been born a son." Angry tears blurred her vision as she shouted at him.

"You were born a daughter and you are my wife. I won't allow you to endanger yourself or make me look like a fool."

His bellow made her wince. She jerked her arm free and ran across the room, the bed between them somehow a protective barrier.

"Better you had beaten me instead."

"Have no doubt, I will."

"You bastard!"

He said nothing, simply strode toward her. When he rounded the side of the bed, she made a dive across. Scrambling as fast as she could, she jumped off the other side and ran for the door. Before she could lift the bar, his arm snaked around her waist, hauling her back against him. She howled her frustration, kicked, pulled at his arm, but couldn't break away. He dragged her back toward the bed. Amidst her attempts to squirm free, she found her wrists caught. As if he barely noticed her resistance, he sat on the bed and stretched her across his lap. She continued to kick and scream, but he merely lifted her skirts before pinning her legs between his.

The first blow landed, hard and sharp. She shrieked in outrage. Another blow, and another, and still another, until fire raged in her arse. She tugged against his hold, then inhaled sharply.

He paused to reach between her legs. Heat scorched her cheeks to know he'd discovered her shameful secret. She twisted her head to look at him. A shiver passed over her at the odd smile curling his lips. He returned his fingers to her pussy, teasing and stroking until her cries softened to moans and pleading whimpers. His fingers could make her forget her anger.

"Do you like that, Wildcat?"

A low moan escaped her when he thrust his fingers deep inside her. The heat in her arse added to the tumult and lust fogged her thoughts. She should be fighting him, but what he did felt too good. If he kept up, she would come, and she strained against him, aching for the release.

The sudden withdrawal of his fingers left her breathless. Gillian turned to look at him, a pang of alarm screeching along her spine to see his stern expression, his tawny eyes cold.

"No pleasure for you. You're being punished."

She barely had a moment to ponder his meaning when he struck her arse again. Hard. This time, the pain seemed more intense. He struck again and again and she squeezed her eyes shut to contain her tears. The pain blended with the desire he'd stirred, until both sensations became one raging blur. Tears burned her eyes but she didn't know if the spanking or the denial caused them.

Either way, she would not weep.

When he stopped, the fire seemed to burn hotter than ever. Her head spun when he lifted her and settled her onto his lap. Her tender bottom throbbed and she gave a screech and tried to rise.

He didn't release her.

"I will be obeyed."

She sniffed, squirming in an attempt to ease the pain in her arse. His arms around her seemed to offer comfort, but she held herself stiff.

"You're a monster." She sniffed again, wiping at the stray tear that escaped.

He chuckled. The sound rumbled through her, and she silently cursed the shiver of longing passing along her spine.

"And you're a hellion. But you will learn."

He stood, shoving her from his lap.

She stumbled and righted herself, maintaining a straight spine. He folded his arms and studied her. How she longed to know what thoughts turned in his head.

"Today's attack raised many questions."

"Such as?" She had no idea what he spoke of.

"The rebels knew my men would be patrolling the surrounding area. Someone from within told them."

She rolled her eyes. She should have expected this. "You think 'twas me."

"I didn't say that. But there are many in Lyndon who possess Welsh bloodlines."

He knew. She didn't care, really, but had no doubt the fact she didn't tell him herself made her a target of his suspicion. No reason to deny it. 'Twas not completely unexpected he'd be aware of the fact.

"Aye. Such as I."

"I wondered when you would tell me."

"'Tis common knowledge, my lord." She folded her hands together, desperate to hide their shaking. Truth be told, it came more from the unsettled arousal still spearing her. God's bones, he'd turned her into a wanton overnight!

"I would have preferred learning it from my wife

herself."

"I didn't think you didn't know." She sensed he recognized her lie, but she didn't care. Let him think what he wanted.

"Only someone loyal to the Welsh cause would aid the rebels."

"Of course."

He remained silent for a long time. Too long. Finally, he gave a curt nod.

"Rest assured, my men and I will find the traitor."

"And Anne? Will you seek her as well?"

"Mayhap."

"She killed my father. Poisoned him! She must face justice!"

Gillian's anger took over. She walked close to her husband and pounded her fist on his chest. "You must find her! Or I will!"

He caught her wrist, squeezing hard until she cried out. He shoved her away from him.

"You strike me again?"

His low menacing voice drew a shiver of apprehension. She held herself erect.

"If 'twill make you listen to reason, I will do so as often as I must!" She folded her arms and lifted her chin.

He stalked over to her, standing right before her so she had to tilt her head back to hold his gaze. She didn't retreat and steadily held his stare.

"'Twill only gain you more severe punishments."

"I don't fear you. My lord."

The hastily added respect only seemed to anger him. She didn't care, daring him to do worse than he already had. Except her poor, sore arse would suffer. She tried to ignore the lingering discomfort in her bottom. He could beat her until her skin turned purple. She would endure.

"Mayhap you should."

"I seek justice for my father. Surely, you'd do the same."

He hesitated for a moment. Gillian swore she saw a

hint of sadness in his eyes before it fled as quickly as it had arisen.

"'Tis not the same."

"And why not?"

"I decide what takes priority in protecting Edward and England. I can't be so closed-minded to focus on a rumored murder of one baron."

She didn't think herself capable of such angry pain. "My father was very important to Edward. And England. He kept the peace in this region for years and you know it."

"Aye. Edward was well-pleased with William's service. But your father would be the first to tell you England would come before him."

Damn the man to hell and back if he wasn't right. Gillian bit her cheek to keep from responding foolishly. She'd never gain her husband's trust and kindness if she continued to give in to the frustration and annoyance he always seemed to provoke.

"She killed him. I will find proof. When I do, will you find her?"

He gave a nod. "Aye. If you can prove it, I will find her and she will face justice."

"Thank you."

"I have to question some of the rebels we have taken as prisoner. You will remain here until I return."

"But I have many tasks –"

He held up the key. "Thomas will handle whatever the household needs. I want to make sure you don't get into any more trouble."

He turned and headed out the door. Gillian followed. He pulled the door shut behind him.

The thud of the bar falling into place caused her to jump. She pulled on the handle, but it held securely. She pounded on the wood.

"Bastard! You won't keep me locked away forever!"

The grate of the key rasped like jagged swords. She pressed her ear against the door, listening to his steps grow fainter as he walked away.

"Damn you!"

Her only response was his laughter, fading as he strode away.

She folded her arms and moved to sit on the bed. Just as quickly, she jumped back up when recollections of her wedding night pummeled her once more.

She eased herself into one of the hearthside chairs, wincing at the tenderness in her bottom. How long would she have to wait?

\*\*\*

Royce strode through the great hall and headed for the chambers below. Too many questions remained and he didn't want to wait for answers. His wife held many of them, of that he had no doubt, but just how deeply was she involved? He would see to her later tonight. He ignored his hardening cock as he thought of the way he would do so.

Burke met him at the bottom of the narrow stair and led him to the room where Anne had been held. It now housed three Welsh rebels. One looked to be severely wounded. Royce pointed to him.

"Question him before he dies."

Burke summoned two soldiers who dragged the man from the floor and into another room. Royce and Burke stood over the remaining two men. Their shaggy and unkempt appearance hid cunning and barbaric warriors. Their hands were bound behind them and would remain so.

"Where is your leader?"

One of the men grinned through his beard.

"You'll never find Godwin."

"Why did you attack?"

Another grin but no response. Royce kicked the foot of the other man.

"What do you know?"

"The king is coming."

Alarm rose swift. Royce reached down and hauled the man to his feet.

"How do you know? What was your plan? Tell me or you die."

"I'll die anyway."

Frustrated, Royce shoved the man back to the floor. He paced and looked at Burke, just as a piercing scream rose from the hallway. Liam came back into the room.

"He is dead, my lord. But he told us the plan was to lay in wait for Edward."

Royce spun about to face the remaining two rebels. "Your plan failed. You'll be hanged."

"Look within, Panther, to find your traitor."

The words echoed around him with each step back to the hall. He shook his head. All he needed was some ale and to discuss fortifications with Burke.

# Chapter Seven

Gillian paced before the hearth. Her stomach rumbled and she wondered if her husband would leave her to starve. He was a cruel bastard, but locked in here all afternoon had left her in an odd mood.

The bed was a constant reminder of all the wicked things he'd done to her last night. And how her body wanted him to do it all again. Every time she sat, the tenderness in her arse prompted another flurry of recollections. Now, her sex was swollen and slick, hot and achy. She couldn't be sure her hunger for food wasn't nearly as strong as her hunger for pleasure.

What had the man done to her? She was no fool and knew well what happened in the marriage bed, but last night was unlike anything she could have imagined. Recalling how he'd bound her and left her bared and helpless before him stirred another barrage of yearning.

The sound of the key drew her from her thoughts. She smoothed her damp palms against her dress and straightened her back. The door swung open. The sight of her husband filling the frame never failed to provoke that breathless sensation of excitement. She only hoped he didn't notice.

He stepped into the room, followed by Thomas, who carried a large tray laden with food. The aroma of meat and vegetables teased her and her stomach rumbled again. She gave an embarrassed glance at her husband. He merely smiled.

Yet, somehow, Gillian had the sense he possessed some nefarious plan. She didn't know if she felt more fear or anticipation.

"We will sup here this eve. Then we have much to discuss."

She gave a nod. How much would be actual discussion? An ominous warning echoed in her thoughts.

Thomas laid the tray down and departed. Royce closed and barred the door. He waved a hand toward the chair.

"Sit. Eat your meal."

She remained silent as she obeyed, knowing that even if she had no hunger, she would need to eat for the coming night.

The stew was warm and filling, the ale crisp and satisfying. They ate in silence, but he never took his gaze from her. Worried she might choke, she refrained from asking why he studied her so intently. When at last she had taken her last bite, she wiped her lips with the cloth and turned to him.

"Is there something you wish to say, my lord?"

He gave another one of those curious smiles, the ones she couldn't quite tell if they were genuine or masked some other dastardly thought.

"There is a lot I want to ask you. I learned something interesting from the captured rebels. Incidentally, they'll be hanged once the king arrives."

"Here?"

"Aye. Is there some problem with that?"

"Nay, they should be hanged for what they did, but why here? 'Tis not something that's ever happened at Lyndon."

"As a lesson to the traitor in our midst."

She held his stare steadily, his tawny eyes dark with suspicion. Did he think she was the traitor? Convincing him of her loyalty might prove to be a bigger task than she'd first thought.

"You truly believe someone here is a traitor?"

"There are many Welsh here who would protect Godwin. He is distantly related to Llewellyn. As are you."

"I wondered when you would accuse me."

"I did not accuse you."

She shook her head. "Aye, you just did. By claiming I share a bloodline with Godwin, I don't."

"Are you sure?"

She narrowed her eyes. "Aye. My father told me the tales of my mother's heritage were false. They made them up so the marriage contract would not be broken. 'Twas the only way Edward would accept the marriage."

She'd been told the story many times by her father, which proved how far he would go to keep the woman he loved. Gillian had longed for a man to love her in such a way. She had ended up with a debauched, brutal and emotionless man. A momentary despair threatened to suffocate her before she forced it aside.

"I see. Why does no one else know?"

"If they did, word could reach the king. Not that it mattered. She died when I was a child."

"When did your father marry Anne?"

"Last fall. Before the harvest. I tried to talk him out of it, but he was besotted."

Gillian's stomach churned to recall the argument she and her father had over his announcement. The Lady Anne was a good match, politically. Or so they'd thought.

"Tell me more of Anne."

"Her lover lived in the village. Aye, his name was rumored to be Godwin. I have never seen him. I suspect she used the name to provoke fear in the villeins."

"Why do you say that?"

She didn't like his tone. She felt like a prisoner being interrogated. But these questions needed honest answers. 'Twould help convince him she meant her vow she did not betray Lyndon or England.

"As you know, Godwin is named as the rebel leader, though he'd not attacked us ere now. But if she was aligned with him, 'twould frighten the serfs into acceding to her wishes. Except that it didn't always work."

The corners of his mouth curled. "Like with you?"

She gave him a conspiratorial smile. "Aye, like me. I didn't care who her lover was. I didn't fear her. When word came of Edward's order for me to marry you, that's when my father fell ill. And she claimed to be pregnant."

"And you think she's not?"

"She could very well be. But 'tis not my father's child. He said he had not lain with her since shortly after they wed." Heat scorched her cheeks to think of her father and Anne....

"Spawn of the devil!"

Royce stood and began to pace. Gillian wondered what had so angered him.

"My lord, is Godwin... will he attack again?"

"I cannot say. 'Twould seem they know the king will soon arrive. Only someone within Lyndon would know."

Anger sent Gillian to her feet. "Again, you think 'tis me!"

"I didn't say that. But I will ask you about all of those on Lyndon who may be."

"No one is! Except mayhap Anne, no one here would betray us!"

"You are naïve to think that." He held up a hand when she would have protested further. "You trust and love your people. I understand."

"'Tis the first sensible thing you've said all eve. My lord."

He gave a half-scowl. "But you should be more wary. Someone here is passing messages to the rebels. They attacked to take over Lyndon and lay in wait for Edward. Only someone within the walls would know of the king's imminent arrival."

"Anne knew."

"Aye, she did. 'Twas another reason for the attack. And yet another reason I believe 'tis someone within these walls. She was locked inside and the rebels didn't have access to the keep. Unless there are more hidden entrances than I know about?"

Gillian scratched her head. "Of course! Aye, there are two more. But they are not known to many, as they are obscure."

He stalked over to her. "Where are they?"

"By the kitchens, there is one door that leads to a

tunnel that takes one outside the walls to the forest beyond. The other led from the solar to the same tunnel. But that one collapsed years ago and was impassible. My father had it sealed off."

"So only the one near the kitchens is of concern."

He strode to the door and called for Burke. The captain appeared. He looked over at Gillian.

An unexplained uneasiness crept into her veins, chilling her. Something about her husband's captain seemed threatening. Why? He greeted her with proper respect and even gave a slight bow. Gillian looked away, unable to define what caused the wariness.

Royce ordered Burke to set men to guarding the entrance. The captain agreed, and the two men discussed other options before Burke departed. Royce closed the door and faced her once more.

"I don't yet know if we'll seal it off. But thank you, wife, for that information."

"I will do what I must to defend my home. Mayhap now you will believe me."

"Mayhap. But you possess other secrets."

Gillian folded her trembling fingers together. "I'm not sure I understand. My lord."

"I will learn them all. And I have ways of extracting secrets from even the strongest criminals. I suspect you'll be fairly easy to break."

She gasped. "You oaf! You would torture me like a criminal for no reason?"

He shrugged. "What if I think there is reason?"

"I've given you none to think so."

"I disagree. So we begin."

She shook her head, backing away when he moved toward her.

"Your insistence on fleeing suggests possible guilt."

She halted her retreat but folded her arms. "You are searching for something that is not there!"

"Mayhap. But 'tis no reason not to enjoy the search."

"What?"

"Remove your clothes."

"Wait! I have no maid, I am not –"

"Very well. Tonight, wife, I will play your maid. Turn around."

A surge of excitement jumbled into her anger. She shook her head. She would not give in.

He would not break her.

"Why must you be difficult? 'Twill go badly for you."

"'Tis a risk I'm willing to take."

He sighed. "Very well."

He grabbed her shoulders, turning her. With quick movements, he cut the laces holding her bliaut closed. Gillian gave a shriek of outrage and tried to turn, but he held her in place with one hand tightly squeezing her shoulder. He made quick work of ripping her clothes from her body, leaving her clad only in her thin chemise.

He turned her to face him. She tried to break free of his grip, but he didn't release her.

"You will answer my questions truthfully or suffer the consequences."

She lifted her chin. "Do your worst."

She refused to cower before this man who seemed always intent on breaking her. She recalled the way he'd reduced her to begging last night. Would he do the same again? Why in all that was holy did she anticipate it?

She didn't understand what he intended when he turned her once more. But when he caught her wrists behind her back, she began to struggle. 'Twas no use, he had tied her hands behind her. She tugged, but the rope binding her held fast.

"So I am to be treated as a criminal then?"

He walked around to stand before her. He gave a sly smile and folded his arms.

"You refuse to obey again. You could have simply answered my questions. Instead, I will show no mercy."

A shiver passed along her spine. She held his gaze, silently daring him to continue. His menacing grin drew another tremor. Of fear, or something else? She preferred to think the former, lest she again label herself as wanton. 'Twas not her, 'twas his own wickedness that left her nipples hard and aching, her sex slick and swollen. She could not be blamed for what he did to her. And she would never admit to desiring his debauched games.

He slowly removed his overtunic, then his shirt, and finally pushed his hose down. His cock sprang free, hard and erect.

"Before we get started, you will pleasure me."

She blinked, not sure she understood. "And how will I do that bound as I am?"

"There are ways."

His hands rested on her shoulders and he pushed her to her knees. She now stared straight at his hard shaft, understanding sprouting, even as she denied he could possibly...

"Open your mouth."

Her eyes widened as she met his gaze. "Are you daft?"

"Nay. Now do it, or suffer."

"I'll suffer anyway, you cruel bastard."

"Insult me again and 'tis another infraction for which you will be punished. Open your mouth."

She shook her head, sealing her lips. He glowered at her and reached for her head. She tried to back away, but on her knees and bound as she was, had no leverage. He curled his fingers into her hair, holding her still as his fingers pinched her nose shut.

Damn the man for doing this to her! She could hold on only so long before she needed air.

When she parted her lips to breathe, he slipped his finger in and spread her jaw wide. Before she could pull away, the tip of his cock rested between her open lips.

"Don't bite or I will beat you."

He meant it, she knew, and tried to resist the urge to do exactly what he warned against. He guided his cock further into her mouth.

The sensation was not unpleasant, as she'd feared. His hard and hot flesh held an enticing musky taste and she swirled her tongue along his length. He gave a groan and her gaze darted up. Pleasure lined his face and a responding desire burst within her. She had pleased him. Mayhap this was a way to win him over.

"Suck," he ordered.

Enthralled by the way he held her still while sliding deeper into her mouth, she obeyed and gave a long pull on his shaft. He groaned again, his hips moving in a gentle rhythm. His grip in her hair loosened, becoming a tender caress. Between her legs, her juices slid down, wetting her thighs. How could she enjoy this? 'Twas madness! Yet, she did enjoy it and knowing she pleased him gave her a strong measure of satisfaction.

She continued to suck, her tongue stroking his flesh and noting the way he throbbed within her mouth. She dared another look up at him. His eyes had closed and the lines in his face melted into delight. She recalled how he had used his mouth on her. It had been decadent and wicked, but oh so delightful. She imagined he felt the same way now.

His flesh seemed to thicken and a momentary panic set in. But he held her in place, his body stiffening. A moment later, he erupted into her mouth. Fearful of choking, she swallowed his seed, surprised to feel no disgust, only an enhanced enjoyment that she'd brought him to this point. When his softening cock pulled from her mouth, she sucked in a deep breath. She wondered how long his taste would linger. For a time, she hoped, not that she'd ever tell him that. Her sex clenched, anxious to be filled. Performing this act on her husband had stirred her desires more than she thought possible.

"You have a natural gift for that. I look forward to it again."

His voice, husked with desire and release, set her quivering anew. Before she gathered her wits, he grabbed her arm and pulled her to her feet. Her knees ached from kneeling on the stone, but she was too worried about his intentions to care. He gripped the top of her chemise and pulled, tearing the thin fabric from her body. She shivered in the coolness of the chamber, but defiantly held his stare.

His gaze roamed her body. Her nipples hardened into tight points when that tawny stare landed on her breasts. He reached between her legs, grinning triumphantly to find her wet. Heat scorched her cheeks.

"You enjoyed that as well, wife. Knowing you are so easily pleased will make my task that much easier."

"What task?"

"Getting you to reveal the secrets you keep. I'll not let my wife's mysteries jeopardize the king's safety or my holdings."

"I keep no secrets!"

But she did, and she feared what he might do to loosen her tongue. She thought briefly of Simon. His life might be endangered if Royce decided to force the truth from her. She had to keep him from learning of her brother for a little longer. Until she could be sure Simon's life would be safe from harm.

Royce pushed her to the bed and she fell upon it, wincing as she landed on her bound arms. He knelt above her, studying her. The intensity in his stare left a trail of fire boiling her blood. She found herself anticipating what he might do next.

He spread her legs, holding her wide open as he studied her.

"I shall enjoy this."

"Enjoy what?"

He said nothing, merely slid one finger along her sex. The touch jolted and she squirmed, seeking greater contact. He merely tightened his hold on her hip to still her and continued the teasing strokes. Slowly, he slid his finger deeper, pulling out and gliding up to circle her clit. The sensation ran from her core to her head, leaving her breathless, her breasts heavy and aching.

Over and over, he caressed, just the one finger lightly touching her and making her ache with lust. She wanted more and sensed he knew it. She bit her lip to keep from blurting a plea. 'Twas what he wanted and she would not give in.

But as he kept up the provocative caresses, she found her resolve weakening. He circled her clit again. She tried to lift her hips to guide him back when he moved away, but he gave her no chance. Finally, he drew away and she panted heavily.

"You are soaked, wife. I suspect you are growing hungry for release."

"Nay, merely waiting for you to finish your game."

Her husky voice betrayed the lie and he grinned.

"Your sass will win you no favors."

"I don't seek any."

"Is that so?"

He stroked her again and the moan escaped before she could cut it off. His hearty chuckle fired annoyance, which quickly vanished in the wake of desire his probing finger stirred. Suddenly, she had plenty of favors to ask, but she wouldn't do it. She bit her lip on another moan, squeezing her eyes shut.

That only intensified the arousal he ignited. She opened her eyes, breathing heavily and wondering if she would withstand him. He pulled his hand away and she sighed, relieved for the respite so she could steady her wits.

"Tell me who else here at Lyndon or in the village might have reason to rebel."

"What?" Her lust-clouded mind didn't quite understand.

"Someone on this manor or in the village is aiding the rebels. I think you can give me answers."

She shook her head. "Nay, I do not know anyone who would betray England. You must believe me."

"I don't."

His words, harsh and clipped, sparked a momentary panic. When he reached for her once more, this time cupping one breast and squeezing gently, the panic increased. Fire licked at her veins and she longed to fling herself into the inferno. He lowered his head, his tongue circling her nipple, which seemed to throb and reach for contact.

He never touched the tip, continued his tormenting licks, leaving her gasping and desperate to stop the plea that danced on the edge of her tongue.

He drew back for a moment and blew gently. The heat of his breath against her wet flesh sent another flare of fire hurtling through her. She arched her back, seeking his mouth. Instead, he leaned back.

"Too much pleasure without release can become quite painful."

She knew full well what his taunt meant. Her body ached for climax, but she knew he wouldn't give it. Not yet anyway. Not until he had something from her. What could she do? She would never betray her people. But if she remained silent, she had no doubt he could keep her on this precipice, near desperate to come, for hours. Did she fear or look forward to that?

He resumed his exploration of her breasts, using his mouth and hands to send her into a frenzy. She squirmed against him, desperate to hold onto him. But her bound wrists kept her helpless to his whims. Her fingers clenched, the raspy feel of his tongue rubbing lightly over her nipple was near enough to drive her over the edge. He pulled away.

She groaned, squirming, but his position between her legs kept her motionless.

"Ere the sun rises, you will give me the names of those who may be possible traitors."

She shook her head, caught in the throes of lust. How could he ask that of her?

"I know no one who would betray England." She gave a silent prayer of thanks her voice held strong and clear. "And I will not give a name just for my immediate pleasure."

"Very well, then. But know this; I will not stop until I have what I need."

He squeezed her nipple, hard. She cried out, but the

flare of discomfort only enhanced the delight coursing within. He repeated the action. The riot of sensation left her breathless.

"I know many ways to make someone talk."

His words held a hint of threat. Why wasn't she afraid? He eased his grip on her breast, now stroking lightly. Somehow the touch seemed more exhilarating than before.

She whimpered, thinking of the hours of nighttime stretching before her. How would she survive?

She took a steadying breath, tugging against the bonds around her wrists. She would endure, force him to respect her. If she only knew how.

*** 

Royce leaned back, captivated by the sight of his wife beneath him this way. Bound, naked and helpless to whatever he chose. He knew he needed to gain names from her, but found his concentration on that task getting lost in what he did to her.

Her body responded so delightfully to his touch, whether it be harsh or gentle, and he sensed the conflict in her thoughts. Clearly, she liked his attentions. But she didn't want to.

He smiled. He would use this pleasure between them to bring her to heel. She would learn her place over the next days and he would use her sensual nature to teach her.

He resumed stroking her breasts, her damp flesh quivering under his palm. He wanted to devour her, drive his cock deep into her warmth and taste every bit of her skin. He would, soon enough. First, he needed to focus.

"Tell me wife, surely there is someone you don't completely trust."

She tossed her head, her eyes squeezing shut. He stroked her breast, once more avoiding her nipple. He held his hand a hair's breadth from her skin. She arched up, seeking his touch.

"I will please you well if you tell me what I want to know. I know you have some idea who could be responsible for cooperating with the rebels."

"I swear, there is no one!"

He drew back and slapped her breast, savoring the way she cried out. Yet she didn't shrink away. Instead, she opened her eyes and met his gaze.

He sucked in a breath at the intense heat he saw in the violet depths. Such passion his wife possessed. Mayhap he'd been luckier in this contract than he'd first thought. The recollection of her warm mouth around his cock had him ready to drive into her now.

'Twas not time. He should be forcing answers from her pretty lips, but he found himself simply anxious to continue exploring her body. He gave her flesh another slap, admiring the way the skin pinkened.

"You can beat me endlessly, but I will tell you nothing."

"Stubborn wildcat."

"There is nothing to tell."

She cried out at the way he squeezed her nipples, both at the same time. When he released her, she panted heavily, but never took her eyes from his. He stroked her gently this time, his cock achingly hard.

"You are quite responsive. As I've mentioned, pleasure can be painful, just as pain can be pleasurable. Both together can be quite persuasive."

"You will not break me."

"We shall see."

He lowered his head, soothing her tender skin with his tongue. She gave a strangled shriek and the sound reverberated throughout him. Beneath his hands and mouth, she trembled. She tasted sweeter than the custard tarts he enjoyed at court. Her musky arousal scented the air and he could no longer think clearly.

He drew away, panting heavily. He studied her, reaching up to brush away the dark hair obscuring her face. He crashed his mouth onto hers, startled by the voracious way she responded. Their tongues dueled, and he reached between her legs to find her pussy more soaked than ever. Her cries echoed into him as he circled her clit, pinching lightly before drawing away. He rose above her, relishing her frustrated moan.

"Gillian. Look at me."

Hazed with need, her eyes fluttered open. He slid his fingers along her folds again and she arched toward him. He gripped his cock and eased into her.

He filled her slowly, delighting in the way her pussy clenched around him, welcoming him. Her legs came up around his waist, urging him on. Finally, he lay completely within her, her body trembling around him. He could no longer remain motionless and drew back, driving into her again, this time with force. Her body bowed against his. He needed to feel her touch. He reached under her, lifted her up and pulled the ties binding her loose.

Like a wild woman, she surrounded him, her mouth seeking and landing on his with ferocity, her arms wrapping around him like velvet ropes. Lust fogged his sight and he moved only on instinct.

Sharp discomfort ran along his spine. His wife's nails tore him to shreds, but he didn't care. They drove each other, frantic and needy. He tangled his hands in her hair, holding her still for his kiss.

One hard thrust and she pulled her mouth from his, letting loose a primal cry. Her body shuddered and rocked around his. The sensations drove him over the edge and he exploded with passion. He buried his face in her neck, inhaling sharply as his release went on and on, his balls squeezing over and over with each wave.

Finally, he went limp. Beneath him, Gillian had also quieted. He stared at her, thinking he had never been so consumed by lust before. And yet, this woman he was forced to take as wife had somehow ensorcelled him.

Her eyes fluttered open, and she gave him a sleepy smile. His heart lurched. Nay, he could never let her touch his heart, lest she shatter it. As he regained his wits, he recalled his original intentions for tonight. Even so, he still didn't possess the urge to question her further. He pulled free of her, her disappointed moan sending a shiver along his spine.

He stretched out beside her. She curled around him. He suspected she wanted some romantic declaration. He wasn't capable of giving her that.

"That was..." Her voice, soft with satisfaction set off another set of sparks along his spine. He wrapped his arm around her shoulders, noting the way she relaxed even further. He rather liked the way her body melded against his.

"Aye. It was."

He couldn't deny the fiery passion between them was unlike anything he'd ever experienced. The idea he could have it again filled him with an excitement he hadn't known in years. Knowing his wife ultimately took pleasure in such games as well, heightened that thrill.

And he had every reason to use such methods. Though he had yet to uncover them, his wife still kept secrets.

# chapter eight

Shouts from the bailey sent the servants running from the hall. Excited words passed among them. Royce looked around the hall for his wife, his gaze settling on her where she stood at the foot of the stair. As always, the sight of her made his heart beat a little faster. If he believed in magic, he might think she'd cast a spell on him.

She caught his gaze, the uncertainty in her violet eyes clear even from this distance. Did she not know what caused the excitement? He strode over to her.

"Edward arrives."

She nodded. "Aye. I think all is in readiness."

"He will be pleased."

Where had this need to reassure her come from? He was well pleased with the efficient way Gillian had prepared the castle for Edward's arrival. While he still harbored doubts about her loyalty and knew 'twould take some time before she became the subservient wife he wanted, her abilities as chatelaine would ultimately serve him, and Montchester, well.

"Come, shall we meet him in the bailey?"

He held out a hand and she hesitated before taking it. At the feel of her cold and clammy palm, he studied her more closely.

"Are you ill?" he asked.

"Nay. But a little nervous, mayhap."

The high pitch of her voice gave credence to her words. The woman who openly challenged him at every turn had been replaced by an uncertain girl who needed reassurance. A strong, lingering urge to calm her fears filtered through him. He shook his head, disgusted with himself. This weakness in him was maddening, and he silently cursed her. She had caused this turmoil.

Yet, much as he loathed these feelings, at this moment,

he couldn't bring himself to scold her. He led her outside but she held back, earning his fiercest scowl. She would disrespect the king?

But was he really annoyed with her or with himself for finding her becoming in a violet gown that almost matched the shade of her eyes? She lowered her head, some of her dark hair coming loose from the wimple to obscure her face. He imagined twining that hair around his fingers. He sighed.

"We must greet him when his train reaches the bailey."

Her shoulders lifted with a deep shuddering breath. He silently cursed the need to pull her close. 'Twas no time now, and he didn't dare risk letting her distract him with her charms.

"Now, Gillian."

Another rise of her chest and she nodded, this time allowing him to pull her toward the door. Royce knew he shouldn't be angry with her, but if he didn't hold onto that, lust would take over and addle his wits.

\*\*\*

Gillian's stomach quivered with apprehension. She'd never been to court, had never been presented to the king and queen. She feared embarrassing Lyndon. Or worse, her husband.

For a few moments, she'd thought him compassionate to her worries, but his harsh tone in ordering her to follow revealed the truth. All she wanted was for him to care for her, even just a little. After the last nights together, she hoped their shared passion would create a bond where she might earn his respect and affection. 'Twas clear now she had a long path ahead of her to win even that from him.

The sun shone brightly, near blinding her. She followed her husband down the steps, the king's train just coming through the gates. At the head, just before the rider carrying the royal pennant, rode King Edward.

Tall and blonde, every bit the debonair king he was rumored to be, Edward waved to the crowd and grinned, before reining in his steed to dismount. Immediately, he strode to the rider just behind. His queen.

Gillian had heard tales of Eleanor's beauty, with long blond hair and bright blue eyes. Yet, many said she was cold and greedy. Gillian saw nothing but affection and warmth in the stare the king and queen exchanged. They shared a few quiet words, Eleanor briefly touching her husband's cheek.

Gillian sucked in a breath to realize she longed to experience the tenderness that passed between the pair. 'Twas obvious they genuinely loved one another. She darted a glance in her husband's direction. He stared straight ahead.

She didn't insist her husband love her. But she did want his affection and concern. His respect. Somehow, she would gain that. Without it, she feared Lyndon faced a dire future.

Edward and his queen now approached. Gillian tried to steady her unevenly beating heart by studying the queen's sapphire blue bliaut which perfectly matched her eyes. A girdle of gold chain surrounded the blonde woman's tiny waist and the elongated cuffs of her dress were trimmed in the finest gold ribbon. Throughout her hair, matching gold bands twined through the thin braids that pulled away from her lovely face.

Gillian glanced down at her own amethyst-colored gown, one of her finest, and suddenly thought her clothing seemed inferior. She glanced toward the closest litter, where several ladies-in-waiting stepped down. All were dressed similarly to the queen, in gowns made of the finest silks and linens and tied with girdles in silver or gold.

Gillian straightened her kirtle, wishing she had more time to arrange her hair, perhaps weave ribbons through it as many of the ladies did in imitation of their queen. Her own chain girdle was not of gold, but ordinary metal, and looked, to her critical eyes, shabby in comparison.

"You look lovely."

Royce's whisper beside her ear startled her from her thoughts. She stared at him curiously, surprised by the warm smile curling his lips. How had he known what she was thinking?

She gave a nod of thanks. A warm tingle hummed in her belly. She'd never thought he could show such kindness. Had she somehow managed to break through to him? How different he looked with his face softened and without the scowl he always seemed to wear. He held her gaze for several moments. Was that actually warmth in his eyes? For her? Her head spun with the realization.

"Panther! 'Tis good to finally set our eyes upon you."

Edward's booming voice cut across the courtyard. Once again, Gillian's heart raced nervously. Royce squeezed her hand. The simple gesture calmed her even as it raised more questions about her husband.

"Your Highness, it is my pleasure, as always." Royce bowed before his overlord. "May I present my wife, the Lady Gillian of Lyndon."

Gillian sank into a curtsy, awaiting the king's reply.

"'Tis a delight to meet the woman who will tame the Panther." Edward touched her shoulder, indicating she should rise. "Allow me to present your queen, Eleanor."

"Your Highness."

Gillian once more dropped into a deep curtsy. A hand on her shoulder drew her gaze up.

Eleanor greeted her with a friendly smile.

"Lovely girl, Royce. You've done well."

Certain her cheeks had turned scarlet, judging from the heat scorching her face, Gillian gave a nervous laugh and stood.

"Aye. I should get many sons from her."

Indignation straightened her spine. So many things to say in response sparked on the tip of her tongue. She held them back, afraid to insult either Eleanor or the king.

"Treat her well, Panther." Eleanor's voice held a clear note of warning before she turned to Gillian once again. "I am fatigued from this journey."

"Of course, Your Majesty. I have several rooms ready for you and your ladies."

Gillian gave a half glance to Royce before pulling her hand from his. She headed for the stairs, aware of the queen and her ladies following. Once more she found it difficult to breathe, anxious about the queen's reaction to her modest home. 'Twas no castle like Ludlow or Shrewsbury, and the town must have appeared quite small to the royal party. Confidence wavering, Gillian clenched her fingers to steady her hands. At the top of the steps, Thomas stood in the open doors, and dropped into a deep bow.

"Welcome, Your Majesty."

"Thomas and I will see to whatever you need." Gillian's need to assure the queen she had control of the household grew stronger than ever.

"Thank you. We are most grateful, Lady Gillian."

A modicum of relief left Gillian's knees weak. Forcing herself to put her nervousness aside, she led the way up through the hall and up the stairs. The large solar had been prepared for Eleanor, with the adjoining chambers for her ladies. Gillian assumed the queen's personal maid would sleep at the foot of the bed.

Oh no! She'd forgotten to tell Royce which chamber would be for Edward. She bade the queen to enter and stepped out into the corridor, calling for Thomas. The steward appeared quickly, making Gillian thankful the loyal servant would manage the situation well for her. She explained her dilemma. Thomas gave her a reassuring smile.

"Don't worry, m'lady, I will see to it. You tend the queen and I will assist the earl."

"Thank you. I don't know what I'd do without you, Thomas." She gave him a brief hug and giggled at the flush staining his cheeks before he hurried off.

Turning back to the queen's chamber, she took a deep breath and knocked, opening the door when Eleanor bade her.

"Join us, Lady Gillian."

The queen waved toward the chair beside hers. Her other ladies gathered around the room, several watching

Gillian intently. Feeling as though she had been placed on display, she obeyed Eleanor's order and eased into the chair beside her sovereign.

The queen regarded her thoughtfully for several seconds. Unsure if she should say something, Gillian remained silent, folding her hands in her lap and thanking the Lord above no one could see how tightly her gut had knotted.

"Many of my ladies are quite jealous of you."

Eleanor's words broke the awkward silence. Gillian met the queen's piercing stare.

"Your Highness?"

"You've captured one of the most sought after nobles of the court. Several of my ladies had hoped to win his heart."

Gillian glanced at the faces of the other women, and while most watched her with cool stares, she detected no outright malice. That gave her a small measure of comfort. She pressed her damp palms against her dress.

"I had nothing to do... I mean, the contracts were made regardless of..."

No matter how she chose to explain, the queen likely thought she resented the marriage. 'Twould never do.

"Your Majesty, what I mean is that I didn't intend to interfere with any other... relationships the earl may have had."

Eleanor laughed. "Don't worry, my dear. The Panther has always been aloof, never giving anyone hope he might ask for their hand. We gave you to him because if we didn't, he might never wed. Besides, we need his strong army here near the border."

Why did she feel worse than ever? Was she not worthy, merely a tool to be bargained away? Until these last few days, she had never felt so unwanted and worthless. She twisted her hands in her lap, not sure how to respond. Determined not to allow anger and sadness to show, she focused on the household.

"The meal will be ready soon. I've ordered the cooks to

make all of their specialties. And a few of your favorites, according to my husband."

The queen smiled. "No doubt all will be delicious. You seem nervous, child. What troubles you?"

"Nothing, Your Highness. I do have a lot to prepare for the meal; however, if you need me, I will stay."

Eleanor reached over and patted her hand. The reassuring gesture, along with the understanding in the queen's eyes, eased the snarl in Gillian's stomach.

"I have my ladies to tend me. Do what you must. We will join you below when 'tis time."

Gillian nodded and rose. She hesitated, then sank into another low curtsy before hurrying from the room. Once outside, she heaved a deep breath. God's blood, how did someone survive at court? She could barely make it through a few minutes and felt ready to retch.

A few more steadying breaths and she headed below to seek out Thomas and confer with the cooks.

\*\*\*

Royce walked beside Edward toward the keep. He had much to share with the king, and worried the news might set off Edward's temper. Royce knew he was one of the few who could keep his sovereign calm when sharing grave tidings.

"Your journey went well, I trust?" he asked. He ignored the strange glance the king shot at him.

"Aye. The roads were muddy from the storms, but we fared well enough." Edward stopped, halting Royce with a hand on his arm. "What's wrong?"

"We will discuss it inside. There's trouble."

The open, friendly expression on the king's face changed to one of concern and displeasure. "The rebels?"

"Aye. Come rest, and have some ale to refresh yourself first."

"Don't toy with me, Panther. What have you learned?"

Royce resumed walking and Edward followed. He tossed over the words he would use to tell the king of what had happened in the last days without setting off Edward's rage. Thankfully, the king didn't continue to press for answers as they climbed the steps.

Once inside the hall, Royce bade Edward to sit by the hearth and summoned the steward. After requesting refreshments and confirming the king's chambers, he joined Edward, seating himself beside the king before the hearth. He hesitated. Choosing the right words would be difficult, and he knew he'd then have to justify his own actions. Or lack thereof, depending on how the king might view them.

"The baron's wife is rumored to be with child."

Edward's eyes narrowed. "Are you sure?"

"To be honest, nay, I am not. 'Tis only her claim. However, if 'tis true, Gillian says the child cannot be her father's. Apparently, William swore this to her before he passed."

"Then there is naught to worry about. Where is the baroness now?"

Royce paused again, his gut knotted. He gave silent thanks for the timing of the maidservant who brought ale and some cheese with bread. When she had departed, Royce handed a tankard to the king.

"We secured her in the chambers below. She attempted to murder my wife."

"And she still lives?"

Royce stared into his ale and nodded. "Without proof of her condition, which I intended to learn as soon as possible, I didn't dare."

The law did not allow for women with child to be tortured for information, no matter their crimes. Royce had no doubt Edward could, and would, discount the law to get what they sought, but he would not. Not until he knew for sure.

"Summon a physic and confirm it then."

Yet again, Royce took a few extra moments before answering. "She's escaped."

Edward slammed his tankard on the table, spilling the ale and almost upending the food. "Damn it to all that's holy, Langley, how the hell did that happen?"

Royce sighed. "I fear there may be a traitor within Lyndon's walls. 'Tis the only explanation."

He relayed the events of yesterday, the attack and Anne's subsequent escape. He paused to gulp a few mouthfuls of ale and continued. When he finished, if Edward's eyes had been swords, they would have felled Royce in an instant.

"Who've you questioned?"

Royce's thoughts immediately focused on his attempts to get his wife to talk last night. His mouth went dry and he tried to force the images of her naked bound body from his head.

"There are several on the manor who may hold information. I've set my men to gathering them for interrogation."

Edward nodded. "Very well. And the rebels you captured?"

"To be hanged. I'd thought on the morrow."

Edward scratched his chin, eyes narrowed in thought. "Nay. The day after, mayhap the next. I want to question them. We'll uncover the traitor ere long."

Royce hoped so, but if everyone proved as stubborn as his wife, he worried about what methods Edward would employ to gain the information they sought. When necessary, the king could be brutally ruthless. Royce didn't want those on Lyndon to turn against him, especially not when he still wasn't knowledgeable enough about the manor and its village. With the Welsh known for their heathen ways, he feared an uprising to be a real possibility. He didn't share this concern with the king, knowing Edward wouldn't care. After years of friendship, Royce knew exactly how his king achieved his goals and when to keep silent about anything he might disagree with.

Mayhap this was another way he could use his wife. The idea certainly merited consideration, in case he needed to employ such trickery. Royce knew well Edward had a tender spot for women, especially those as comely as Gillian. 'Twould seem his bride could be even more beneficial than he'd thought.

As if he'd conjured her with his thoughts, she appeared at the foot of the stairs, her face ashen. Even from his position across the large room, he saw her tremble. What had spooked her?

Edward apparently noticed Royce's focus and turned as well. He smiled.

"Your bride is quite lovely, Langley. I've chosen well for you."

Royce nodded. "Aye. But you didn't tell me she carries Welsh blood."

Edward laughed. "I didn't want to prejudice you against her before... But judging from the way you're looking at her now, though, I see it doesn't matter. You're smitten."

"I am not. She's a disobedient hellion. 'Twill take some time to train the rebelliousness from her. Must be the Welsh bloodline."

Edward's grin turned sly and knowing. "I trust you've already begun her instruction."

Royce returned the grin. "Aye. She'll learn."

Gillian's gaze landed on him and he stood. Why did he feel this sudden urge to soothe her agitation? He strode over to her.

"What troubles you?"

She shook her head. "Nothing. I just... I must see to the meal and ensure all is in readiness. The queen and her ladies are in their chambers until we summon them."

"Did something happen while you were with Eleanor?"

"Nay." She paused, her fingers twisting before her. "I... I've never been presented at court, and I... I hope all is well."

He understood. She had doubts about her worth in the eyes of her king and queen. Any would. He resisted the urge to pull her near.

"It is. You've done well."

"Thank you."

Her hoarse whisper once again betrayed her anxiety.

He took her hand, aware Edward watched them from across the room. He kept his voice low.

"The king is pleased with Lyndon. You have nothing to fear."

Her eyes searched his and he wondered if she detected his pride in her. For she had done well with her preparations. As he would have expected from his wife. Somehow, though, this slip of a girl stirred so many more reasons for his satisfaction.

"And you, my lord? Are you pleased as well?"

A hopeful glint brightened her eyes. He didn't even try to hold back his smile.

"Aye. I am well-pleased."

A hint of pink returned to her cheeks and the corners of her mouth curled.

"Thank you."

He squeezed her hand and released her. "Go tend your tasks and tell us when you are ready."

She nodded and strode across the hall, to the kitchens behind the keep. He watched her as she made her way, admiring the soft sway of her hips and the way her ebony hair fell in a fat braid down her back. He imagined wrapping that braid around his wrist as he drew her mouth to his cock. The flesh stirred and hardened. He closed his eyes and took a deep breath. Later. For now, he must finish with Edward before taking the king to his chambers to rest before the meal.

# chapter Nine

Satisfied with how well the feast preparation progressed, Gillian made her way to the barracks. Several of her husband's men lingered. She prayed for their silence about her presence. The last thing she needed was to give Royce further reason to distrust her. But she had to see Simon. The only acceptable resolution to the problem was to reveal the truth of his parentage.

She knocked on the door, relieved when her brother opened it. His brow furrowed.

"Gilly, what's wrong?"

"We must talk. Come, where none can see us."

He followed her to a spot near the bailey walls, hidden behind one of the unused outer buildings. She turned to give him a great hug.

"I've missed you." She sighed, tears burning her eyes.

"And I you. Gilly, what's wrong?"

"You must permit me to tell my husband the truth about you."

Simon shook his head. "Nay, we've discussed this. I won't risk being banished."

Gillian wrung her hands. "You don't understand. Royce is determined to uncover every secret I hold. He fears my Welsh blood means I am a spy, but I know he also has suspicions about you."

"I don't care. If they see me as a great threat, banishment will be the least of my worries. I would follow him as my overlord. At least this way, even if I am sent to Montchester, or London, or wherever, I can return. If I am banished, or worse, that will be impossible."

Gillian's desperation grew a little more, her gut knotting as tightly as her fingers clenched. She knew what methods her husband could employ to loosen her tongue. In only a few short days, he had turned her into a wanton, anxious for the pleasure he would bestow. But he could as easily use that pleasure against her, a fact she already knew well. She didn't think she could bear another night of such torture without admitting all. Even other things she didn't know; she'd likely swear to anything he suggested she held responsibility for. Heat flamed upon her cheeks to realize she would have to tell her brother some of what she'd experienced. How to do so without angering him? She twisted her hands and began to pace.

"Simon, he has ways of... he can... he knows how to make me... beg for mercy."

Simon's eyes widened, his dark brows slashing deep in his forehead. "He beats you? I will kill him!"

He turned and headed toward the keep. Gillian ran in front of him, pushing at his shoulders until he stopped.

"Nay, he... well, yes, he spanked me. But it's not that."

Simon studied her intently, his lips pressed together in a grim line. "Then what is it he does?"

"He withholds pleasure."

The confusion in her brother's dark eyes would have been laughable if the situation were not so serious.

"Explain."

Gillian turned her back, unable to face him while she relayed, as vaguely as she could, the way Royce had bound her and teased her mercilessly with sexual pleasure. Recounting the tale warmed her body, her nipples tightening and pressing against linen. The sensation only intensified the building desire, and already, her sex slickened. The thought of her husband's hard shaft filling her sparked a wave of desire so intense, it weakened her knees. She kept her explanation brief, not wanting Simon to know what a wanton she'd turned into. How hungry for that pleasure she'd become. If he looked, he would see the flush climbing her face, the trembling of her hands, her unsteady breathing. All because of her husband. His wicked ways had made her into a wild woman. A wildcat, as he'd already called her.

Simon's hands on her shoulder brought a soothing measure of relief. He would understand. He would permit her to share his truth.

"You sound as if you enjoy it."

She spun about. "He makes me! His wicked hands and... I never thought such things were possible, and yet, now, 'tis all I can think about!"

She covered her face with her hands, choking back a frustrated sob. Simon caught her wrists.

"Look at me."

She obeyed, hoping he couldn't see the need pulsing at fever pitch within. What had her husband made of her?

Simon smiled. "You should be pleased your husband knows such tactics."

"I...you... what?" 'Twas not what she'd expected.

"Most women suffer a miserable marriage bed. You are lucky."

"Simon!" She stamped her foot. "Do you not see I'm being tortured? He does not trust me and unless I tell him something, he will continue to do so. He is trying to drive me mad!"

Simon chuckled. Gillian resisted the urge to pummel him, with great difficulty.

"Enjoy it, Gilly, while you can." His humorous countenance sobered. "But do not tell him of me. Not yet. 'Tis way too soon. He won't believe you anyway, and think it a lie to cover our adulterous affair."

She shook her head. "I cannot believe you would turn away from me now. I need you to let me tell him. I cannot promise I can withhold the truth."

"You will. You are as stubborn as he. We will tell him. Eventually. But not now. Just a little longer. I have a plan anyway."

She nodded, giving him her fiercest scowl. "I will try. But I make no promises, should my husband decide to continue to mercilessly torture me."

But was it really torture if she looked forward to it?

\*\*\*

Royce watched his wife slip from behind the building with her guard. He narrowed his eyes. Gillian turned and embraced the man, and he returned the hug. They lingered far too long. Red tinged the edges of his vision. Anger near choked him as he thought of how much damage she could do with the help of her guard. If 'twas truly what the man was. Royce didn't entirely believe that anymore. Had they worked in tandem to betray his patrol to the rebels? His men were above suspicion, but this Simon appeared intent on aiding his deceitful wife with whatever she planned. What else could explain the secret meetings?

Fingers clenched, he ducked back inside, not wanting to be caught spying on her. But tonight, he would have the truth of her "guard" and what they planned. And then he would kill the man. As for his wife... a grim smile curled his lips as he planned ways to extract vengeance against his wife.

He took a stance at the end of the hall, surveying the activity of the servants preparing the tables for the evening meal. With the king in residence, Lyndon's cooks had prepared many fancy dishes, or so he'd been told. He hoped Edward would be pleased.

He sensed Gillian behind him. How, he didn't know. But he felt her presence. He turned.

She offered a warm smile, but his anger at seeing her with Simon still had hold of him. Her smile faltered at his glower.

"My lord, is aught amiss?"

He shook his head. "I am about to summon the king. Ensure the meal is ready."

She eyed him curiously and nodded before setting off to the kitchens. He could no more pull his gaze from her as she walked away than he could cut off his own arm. The lust she inspired angered him nearly as much as her deceit. Halfway across the hall, she turned and gave him another curious glance. Clearly, she sensed his anger, but didn't understand why. She would. Later, when he had her alone in their chamber, she would learn exactly what had angered him.

He sent one of his men to summon Edward and Eleanor. More men filed into the hall, many accompanied by wives or other kin, and took seats at the lower tables. So many soldiers, Edward's, his, and Lyndon's. With an army of this size, finding the rebels and putting an end to the uprising shouldn't take more than a few days.

A hand on his arm drew him from his thoughts. He looked down at his wife. Again, the rush of desire startled him, but the image of her embracing her guard reminded him she could not be trusted.

"All is ready."

Her voice wavered with hesitation. Good. He liked knowing he had her as unbalanced as he felt. He gave a curt nod and took her hand, laying it on his arm. He led her to the stairs.

The king and queen descended amid excited whispers. Gillian's fingers tightened on his arm. He fell into a bow, pleased when she sank into a proper curtsy. He could not fault her manners in any way. Edward bade them to rise.

"May I officially welcome you to Lyndon, Your Majesty?"

Royce raised his voice, silencing the murmuring.

"Thank you, Langley. We are pleased to finally be here and properly celebrate your marriage."

Edward led his queen to the head table. As they passed, the assemblage bowed. Royce let out a sigh of relief. The remote manor had done a fine job in greeting the king. At Montchester, he'd never worried, but he realized just how anxious he'd been to think Lyndon might not match those standards. With that concern laid to rest, he focused on other matters. Like protecting his new holding, and the king. And teaching his wife what happened when she dared betray him.

Her fingers still had a tight hold on his arm. He glanced at her. She held her head high, looking straight ahead. He couldn't wait to undo that stony expression. He must remember not to let himself get lost again. Her passionate response to his touch easily made him forget anything else of importance. He had questions that needed answers. Tonight, he would have them.

He eased Gillian into a chair and slid into his own, between her and the king. He'd given a brief thought to seating his wife beside the queen, but decided he would do better with her at his side. This way, he could watch her as she exchanged looks with the guard. Royce had a clear view of the man seated not far away.

"We ride out at first light." Edward drew him from watching his wife.

"Aye. With our combined armies, we should flush them out ere long."

"Then I want to question those below."

Royce knew the Welsh rebels held below would be brutally tortured for any information. He feared the reactions of those on the manor when they learned of that, for they surely would. He must tread carefully. He leaned close to the king.

"We do not have the proper... chambers for such things. If the villeins and villagers, especially those with Welsh bloodlines, turn against us, the uprising may be difficult to subdue. There's been peace here for many years. I'd thought to preserve that."

Edward nodded, scratching his chin thoughtfully. "You have a point. But I need to know what they know. I will think on how to proceed."

Thankful he'd for the moment averted potential disaster, Royce took a long drink of ale. He hadn't realized just how hard his heart had pounded. Now to reinforce the advantages they'd gained.

"The resistance is weakening. They suffered many losses during their attempt to take Lyndon. It cannot last much longer."

"And we'll be back in Shrewsbury for the trial before sennight's end. And mayhap bring others to suffer the same fate."

Edward grinned as two maids carried a tray to lay

before him. Two swans, roasted and re-feathered, their long necks crossed and adorned with small jewels, sat upon the wood.

"You've done well, Langley!"

Eleanor leaned over her husband. "I'd suggest Lady Gillian is the one who should be thanked. She advised us her cooks had something special prepared. 'Tis lovely!"

The king glanced at Royce's wife, whose cheeks flushed pink with her pleased smile.

"Thank you, Your Majesty. I hope you enjoy the rest of your meal as well."

Royce frowned. While he appreciated her comportment, he wondered what had caused her subdued manner. Was it the presence of the king and queen that had pulled the sass and fire right out of her? Or was it because of his anger, for she clearly felt it. Did she truly fear him? Oddly, the idea bothered him. He shouldn't care. He liked the way she warily watched him. His dick hardened every time apprehension clouded her eyes.

Or was her demeanor nothing more than an act? He recalled the way Anne had easily composed herself to appear demure when necessary. Did his wife share the same skill?

He discounted the idea almost immediately. She was nothing like Anne. Or was he wrong? The idea stirred his anger again. He gave her a glance. She watched him, her violet eyes wide and hopeful. He said nothing and turned back to Edward.

***

Gillian took a long drink of ale. Her husband had grown so cold suddenly. She wished she knew why. The few moments this morn, when he'd assured her all would be well; he'd seemed to show some genuine care. What had changed?

Was it possible...? Nay. He couldn't know where she'd gone earlier. Besides, he would have said something long ere now. He didn't hesitate to accuse her at any other time, why should this time be any different?

If she admitted the real truth, she worried what it might mean for this eve, when they were alone. He seemed to enjoy finding the tiniest reasons to claim she needed punishment. At least the king and queen were pleased with her efforts. That should convince her husband she deserved at least some level of respect.

God's bones, why did it hurt so much? She wanted to please him, but it seemed no matter what she did, 'twould never happen. Physically was the only way she knew he was gratified with her. If only she could find some way to carry that over to his feelings toward her.

She caught Simon's gaze and offered a small smile. Amid the raucous gaiety in the hall, she felt strangely subdued and it appeared her brother did as well. She picked a bite of the swan and chewed, but tasted nothing. The night seemed to drag on, and she wanted nothing more than to escape the din and retire to her chamber. Her former chamber, the one she'd used before...

She took another drink of ale. Royce's hand on her arm startled her and she almost spilled the goblet in her attempt to place it on the table.

"I don't want you sotted tonight."

His low voice warned of danger and delight. A shiver passed over her.

"I am not, my lord."

"Good. 'Twill soon be time to retire."

She nodded, unable to find her voice. There was both threat and promise in his words. While her mind worried, her body anticipated. She pressed her thighs together, trying to quell the need that built between them.

Fancy tarts and custards, puddings and fruits were brought out for the final course. Honey stewed fruits, normally her favorite, looked unappealing and bland. She looked around the hall, as if watching the gaiety from a distance. She certainly felt no part of it and turned again. One of Eleanor's ladies approached Simon. The interest both held for each other warmed Gillian's heart. Mayhap he could find someone who cared for him. At least one of them should be so lucky.

She glanced again at her husband. He paid her no notice, deep in conversation with the king. Surely they planned some strategy to capture the rest of the Welsh rebels. She sighed.

It seemed no more than a few minutes passed when the king stood to bid the celebrants good night. Once he and the queen had left, everyone else followed suit. She gave her brother a small wave as he headed for the barracks.

Soon, only she and Royce remained as the servants set about clearing the hall. She raised her gaze to his. A tremor slid along her spine. He stared intently, heat and menace both clear in his tawny eyes. He held out his hand.

"Come."

Why did she feel as if she were about to face her doom?

# chapter ten

Royce felt his wife's terror as he led her up the stairs. Good. She clearly knew something was amiss. She would know exactly what soon enough. He opened the door and waited for her to enter before stepping inside and closing and barring the portal.

"My lord, what troubles you?"

"Why do you think something troubles me?"

"You... you seem angry. And I suspect 'tis because of me. But I cannot fathom why."

He folded his arms. "You can't? Mayhap soon enough you'll understand. Remove your clothes."

She shivered and reached behind for the laces of her dress. After watching her struggle for a few moments, he motioned with his hand for her to turn. He made quick work of the laces, and soon his wife was bared before him. He turned her again to face him.

"Is there anything you would like to share with me before we begin?"

"Begin what? I don't understand."

"You have committed a grievous crime. One that includes severe punishment."

Her eyes widened. "I've done nothing wrong! What game are you playing?"

"'Tis no game, my unfaithful wife. And now you shall pay."

"Unfaithful? I haven't been –"

"Cease your lies. I have no patience for them. Give me your hands."

She shook her head and backed away. "Nay, you will not beat me again."

"I will not have to beat you. We both know exactly how I can make you beg."

He stalked over to her but she continued to retreat until

he trapped her against the bed.

Before she could scramble across, he caught one wrist, then the other. She struggled mightily, but he quickly wrapped his belt around both wrists, securing her. She kicked out at him, but he evaded her, lifting her and tossing her to the bed. She tried to crawl away, but with her hands bound, had little leverage. He grabbed the end of the belt and secured it to the bed rail.

"Bastard! Debauched beast! I won't tolerate this treatment any longer!"

She kicked at him again, but he caught her ankles and pinned them to the bed.

"You'll tolerate exactly what I plan to give you. And mayhap I'll loosen your tongue and get the truth!"

She stopped fighting him and her bonds for a moment. "What truth?"

"'Twould seem you withhold quite a few from me. But tonight, I will uncover them all."

"You are truly mad!"

She jerked her legs against his hold and he realized he would have to secure her better. He rose and went to the armoire, thanking his squire for insisting on bringing more clothing than Royce had originally planned. He withdrew two sashes and turned back to her.

"I've had much success getting criminals to tell me all they know. I warrant with you, 'twill be fairly easy."

She narrowed her eyes, watching intently when he moved to the foot of the bed.

Anticipating her attempts to fight him off, he knelt on the mattress, capturing one of her legs within both of his. On the other, he wrapped one of the sashes, and quickly bound it to the post. She screeched, her body heaving against him, but he quickly secured her free leg as well. He stood back to study her.

She cursed him quite heartily and tugged against the bonds holding her open and bared before him. Truly his captive. His possession.

He gave a grim smile. She was his. And he was free to

treat her as he chose. Of course, the fact that she'd so openly betrayed him, on more than one occasion, gave him solid justification. None would gainsay him for what he did with and to his wife.

The bewilderment in her eyes raised a modicum of doubt about his suspicions. Well, he would know all soon enough. He already knew well how to make her beg. Tonight he would test the very limits of her endurance.

\*\*\*

Gillian stared up at her husband, flabbergasted at how he'd so quickly rendered her helpless. Being bound and spread for him this way raised alarm, even though the excitement running through her intensified as well. Damn him for turning her into a wanton. Her body responded with eagerness. She forced herself to try to appear unaffected, but the smirk on his face told her he knew damn well the state she was already in.

"Why? You treat me as though I'm a criminal, a prisoner to be abused and mistreated. I don't understand."

He leaned back. "You have defied, disobeyed and lied to me at every turn. You've earned every punishment you've received. And you still deceive me. After tonight, you will think twice about doing so again."

She tugged against the bonds, but they held fast, leaving her helpless. Again. Yet, her pussy swelled, her nipples hard as pebbles. She couldn't hide her body's reaction to her vulnerability. Heat in his eyes revealed he saw it as well. He reached out and cupped her breast, caressing gently.

She fought against the urge to rise up, to seek more contact with his slowly moving hand. God's blood, he would kill her if he continued. Was that his intention? To kill her, slowly and exquisitely, with this maddening pleasure? Damn him to hell and back, she would survive whatever he did.

"'Twould seem you are enjoying this."

She shook her head. "You are daft to think so. My lord." She deliberately injected venom into her tone, hoping to hide some of her reckless yearning.

He chuckled then caught her other breast, now stroking and squeezing them both. Gillian gritted her teeth, desperate not to cry out. But the heat licking through her veins left her clinging to barely a thread of control. She squeezed her eyes shut in concentration.

When he stopped, the sigh of relief escaped her before she had the presence of mind to stop it. Another chuckle forced her heavy lids to open.

"I shall enjoy tormenting you tonight. By the morn, I will know all of your secrets."

A brief thought of Simon arose, but she pushed it away. Yet, somehow, she knew much of this had to do with her brother. Why didn't he just say what he meant instead of the vague insinuations? Too much confused her and with her body already aching for more of the depraved pleasure her husband wrought, she couldn't think clearly. Barely enough to deny any of his claims, even if she knew 'twas only a matter of time before he had her sharing every secret she'd ever possessed since childhood.

"I have no secrets."

"Again, you lie. But I will soon know all."

"There is nothing to know. Why won't you believe me?"

"I trust my eyes. I always will. And always before I'll ever trust a word from you."

His words hurt, and she resisted the burn of tears. He was cruel, this man she'd been given to. Would nothing change that?

"You are mistaken."

"I saw you! You and your guard passing silent messages during the meal."

Was that all? She wanted to laugh, but didn't dare. Besides, he'd shifted his hands and was now leisurely stroking her sides and belly. The fire he left in his wake seared through every logical thought.

"You are a fool to think that!"

"Then tell me why you met behind the outer buildings

today?"

She gaped at him. He did know! No wonder he thought... again the urge to laugh came over her, but she wasn't stupid. She held it back.

"Let me explain."

He shook his head. "Nay, you will say nothing. At least, not until I am ready to hear it."

"But –"

He covered her lips with his hand. "I will silence you however possible if you don't remain quiet."

He took his hand away.

"But –"

He replaced it again. "No excuses. You will suffer your punishment. Mayhap when 'tis all over, I will wish to hear your apologies and the truth."

He removed his hand and ripped a length of fabric from his tunic.

"You must listen! Simon is –"

"I don't want to hear his name." Her husband growled the words out a moment before he slid the cloth into her mouth and tied it behind her head.

She screamed, her protests garbled. The bastard had gagged her so she couldn't tell him what he wanted to know. His claim to force the truth from her was nothing more than a ploy, just so he could torture her yet again. She silently raged against the way the heat in her body rose at a rapid pace.

"You'll never want him again. I'll ensure that tonight."

God's blood, did he actually think she and Simon...? The very idea was laughable. She tried to mumble through the gag holding her tongue immovable but he ignored her unintelligible words. 'Twas a fearsome anger she saw in his eyes, but something else lingered there as well. Hurt. And somehow, her own heart ached at the sight. She looked away, indecision churning at her gut. She'd never imagined him capable of such an emotion and the knowledge drew forth a sympathy that rivaled her outrage. And her desire.

Yet, oddly, her body still anticipated the torment he

planned to make her endure. She wanted it, God save her soul. Did she dare admit it? Nay, she couldn't bear what she instinctively knew her husband would do to her. At the same time, her mouth watered at the very thought.

The need to soothe his hurt mingled with her desire. Mayhap 'twas a sign she wasn't as wicked as she'd thought. Would he believe her? Hell, she couldn't tell him anyway. God's teeth, how could she be willing to risk exactly what she'd feared most only a few days prior? The devil must have claimed her when she wed this ferocious man. No wonder they called him Panther. He would tear her determination to pieces.

His hands sliding along her skin chased her thoughts and she whimpered behind her gag. The corners of his mouth tilted up as if he found her predicament amusing. He reached up once more to cup her breasts, and she trembled with the force of the desire rioting through her. When his hot mouth closed over one tight nipple, she let out a low moan, audible yet muffled.

He licked and sucked and she thrashed her head, the lust overtaking her mind. He knew just how to call out the strongest reactions and seemed intent on doing exactly that. Already sweat beaded her brow, her skin covered in gooseflesh that only added to the turmoil.

When he scraped his teeth against her hardened flesh, a shriek escaped the gag. He repeated the motion. White fire scorched through her, her fingers clenching. Her hips lifted, her sex aching and wet and wanting to be filled. Damn him, he still wore his clothing. Which meant he had no intention of giving her release anytime soon. The notion sent her desire to a new level, and she thought she might burst into flame, leaving her nothing but cinders in its wake.

She took a deep breath, desperate to steady her spinning senses. The sight of his dark head against her pale flesh as he moved to her other breast sent another sharp pang of need through her core. He lavished her other nipple with the same exquisite attention. Gillian collapsed weak on the bed, resigning herself to the inevitable hours ahead.

As soon as the thought rose, she found an acceptance of the situation, tinged with excitement. Why not take advantage of his talents? He knew well how to draw out her pleasure; he'd thoroughly taught her that in the last few days. She could, and would, enjoy this, much as he did, without guilt. After all, he'd left her with no choice. He held all the power and control. Yet, she knew ultimately he would give her pleasure, even if she had to wait for it to happen at his whim.

At the same time, the realization also brought another thought. He couldn't win if she liked what he did. He would not outwit her.

Still, a residual dread skittered along her spine, borne of the fear he would truly drive her mad this time.

He pulled away and the glimmer in his eyes warned of his diabolical intent. To her surprise, he rose and went once again to the wardrobe. What did he seek now? Fear and excitement warred within her, neither gaining a solid foothold which left her feeling as though she floated.

When he turned back to her, she choked on a strangled cry. Nay! She shook her head, trying to shrink into the mattress.

"I gathered these from the mews."

He twirled the hawk feathers in his fingers and approached the bed.

"You are mad!" Her words were distorted, but his smile revealed he'd understood.

"Mad? Mayhap. But ere long, I think you will be as well."

He glided the tip of the feather along her cheek. Fire exploded in its wake and she turned away. But the motion only allowed him to drag the quill down her neck and to her ear. The sensation drew a chuckle, despite her effort to conceal it. When he drew the feather along her outstretched arm, she tugged mightily. *Jesu!* The torment left her exhilarated and trembling. And fearful where the feather's journey might end.

"So, wife, did you ever think your hawks could bring you pleasure of another kind?"

He dipped the feather into the hollow under her arm. She writhed and gave a little shriek at the ticklish feelings. God's bones, he would kill her, but damned if she didn't want him to continue.

He did, and she lowered her gaze to his hand as he dragged the feather toward her breast. She bit against the cloth silencing her, holding her breath as she waited, letting it out when he stroked the underside of her breast. She couldn't look away, mesmerized by the tawny feather circling her skin.

Her nipples hardened, aching for a touch, any touch, but he avoided them, content to circle around them and tease her by moving closer, then away.

He stopped and sat beside her. She wanted to scream for him to continue. Instead, she closed her eyes, breathing heavily.

"I fear you enjoy this too much."

Her eyes snapped open and she frantically shook her head. Her jumbled protests didn't hold enough conviction to convince herself, let alone him.

He gave her a wicked grin and a wink and once more drew the feather to her body. It took every bit of her determination not to urge him to hurry.

The tip landed on her nipple this time, stroking across and around it. A whine escaped, her back bowing, seeking more. He repeated the actions on her other breast and she squeezed her eyes shut to bear the exquisite torture.

The feather moved away from her breasts, down her belly. Her initial suspicions confirmed, she braced herself. Damn the man for taking his time, letting the quill meander across her skin, trailing frustration and delight. Her gasps rose in pitch revealing more than she wanted.

He moved again, settling once more between her widespread legs. The vulnerable position left her uneasy and eager at the same time. How did he stir such conflicting thoughts, so she didn't even care what he might do?

The feather skimmed her thighs, and her muscles strained. She couldn't even flail her legs, he held her so securely.

"Gillian."

Her name, uttered on a husked and shaky breath, drew her from the riot in her head. She opened her eyes and met his penetrating stare. She understood his silent question but made no attempt to give him any sort of response, lifting her chin in a dare.

"As I thought." His voice, husked with passion, seemed a caress of its own. "Stubborn wench."

He smiled, a devilish grin that left her quivering and wondering if she'd been too reckless in challenging him this time. For a few moments more, he held her gaze as his hand settled on her sex, spreading her open. She panted and tried to twist away, to no avail.

At the first stroke of the feather along her pussy, she nearly swooned. The hint of touch teased and excited. He did it again, now moving in a steady motion along her slickened flesh. He paused, to exchange the wet feather for another, and continued teasing her flesh. Again and again, until the third time he switched feathers. She sucked in a deep breath, waiting to see how he would further torment her over-sensitized sex.

The tip of the feather brushed lightly across her clit, circling and stroking, giving just a taste of what she knew he could make her feel. Each gentle stroke felt delightful, but they weren't nearly enough, and the heat roared through her.

Gillian's head tossed in a vain effort to withstand the tantalizing tease. But Royce seemed to know just where to move the feather to bring out the most intense sensations. Her entire body tensed, tight as a bowstring, her hips rising to meet the diabolical kiss of the feather.

On and on he went, until madness sank into her thoughts. Razor-sharp need consumed her, bitter, sweet and so delicious. The feather continued to dance on her flesh, until she could bear no more.

"My lord, you're killing me!" She prayed he understood her mangled plea.

\*\*\*

Though he didn't understand her words, the pleading in her voice sank into Royce's lust-dazed senses. He leaned back, studying his wife. The suspicion she enjoyed this too much rose swift and sure. He couldn't be positive if her words were a plea for him to stop or continue. He reached behind her and untied the cloth jammed between her teeth. Might he now get the confession he desperately wanted, much as he didn't want to hear it? Hearing her admit her affair with another man might push his rage past the point of any control.

But she remained stubbornly silent. So be it. His heart raced at the thought of continuing. He turned his attention to her sex. Swollen and red, the soft flesh pulsed, her hips undulating and offering herself to him. He ached to bury himself within her, but would not do that yet. Damn her, she would beg him and tell him the truth. He would have that at all costs.

He ran his fingers along her pussy and the low moan that escaped her jolted into his cock. He kept at the teasing motions and sensed when to stop. When he did, she whined, but no words came forth. Just those enticing whimpers and moans that made his cock throb.

He shook his head, giving her time for her body to come back from the edge of release. How he read her so well, he still didn't understand, but he half-hoped she would continue being stubborn. The delight in tormenting her had become a pleasure he had no intentions of surrendering.

Time to change tactics. When her squirming settled, he leaned back. A quick flick of his hand had his palm slamming into her sex. Her eyes widened, her entire body stiffening in shock with the sudden sting. Her rough cry reverberated within him, his dick now painfully hard.

He drew back and did it again. This time, her shout

sounded more like a pleased moan. She arched her back, lifting her pussy to him, as if asking for another. Knowing she took pleasure in the strike left his head spinning. Instead of repeating the blow, he resumed his soft and teasing strokes of her moist folds. Now her cries took on a desperate pitch. He was close to getting what he wanted.

He stopped touching her and leaned back, savoring the way her lids fluttered open. Her gaze remained hazy and unclear. Pain or lust? A combination of both? Mayhap.

"Why?"

The whispered word gave him pause. He found himself desperate to take her now, bury himself deep within her body. Nay! Not this time. An image of her guard reminded him of why he had taken this course of action. He would have the truth from her.

"Because I can. You will tell me what I wish, nay, what I need to know. By now, you should know I trust no one completely. You especially, have given me reason to suspect you of many things. Adultery I will not tolerate."

She shook her head. He sensed she battled her own desires, determining whether or not to give him the words he sought. The worry in her violet eyes confused him, for he somehow knew it had nothing to do with his actions now.

"I have done nothing wrong!"

He shook his head. "I cannot believe you. Not without proof."

"My word should be enough for you. I am your wife."

"'Tis not enough and you know it. Since the day I arrived, you've kept secrets from me. We both know that and we both know you still hold secrets. I will uncover them. I will not be cuckolded."

He lowered his head, swiping his tongue along her pussy, held open by his fingers. Another low wail escaped her. He drew back.

"Tell me of your lover."

"I have no lover! I was pure when we wed."

"As you know, there are other ways. Did your guard

not teach you?" He stroked his fingers along her sex and caught her clit between his thumb and forefinger, squeezing gently. The sensitive flesh swelled and quivered in his grip.

Her reaction thrummed through him, her body tightening and arching toward him. He loosened his grip, waited several heartbeats and did it again. And again. Her head thrashed against the bed, her hips bucking frantically toward him, seeking more.

"Mayhap you enjoy this too much. Mayhap I should try something else."

He squeezed a little harder this time and she cried out, a desperate wail of frustration washed over him, making his cock harder than ever.

"Nay! Stop! No more. Please, I cannot bear it."

He paused for a moment, then grinned. He caught her chin with his free hand, forcing her to look at him. Her breath came in heavy pants and a hint of madness lingered in her eyes.

*\*\**

Gillian held her husband's gaze, trying to silently tell him he'd won without giving him the satisfaction of saying the words aloud. She had no choice anymore; he would truly drive her to madness if she let him continue. The brief thought of Simon's lifeless body dumped at her feet brought a momentary surge of strength she didn't think she possessed. It passed near as quick as it arose.

"Now, I will hear your confession."

The gentle squeeze of her clit accompanying his demand almost set her over the edge, but he eased back. The frustration screeched out of her.

"Please, Royce. I can't bear any more."

"You will tell me, or you will bear a lot more than this."

She nodded, a choked sob escaping. "Very well! I will tell you!"

She took several calming breaths, her body raging. The desperation had reached its breaking point and gone beyond what she could bear. Her hesitation drew another swirl and squeeze of her clit and she arched, the release so close, she tasted it upon her tongue. As quickly as it began, it stopped when he drew away.

He bit lightly on her nipple, keeping her on the slicing edge of pleasure. 'Twas delightful, too delightful, and bordered on a delicious pain. She near forgot what she must do. Ah, yes. Simon. She prayed he would forgive her.

Another tightening of his teeth on her nipple, another stroke and press of her clit and her vision seemed to fade, the room darkening around her.

"He's my brother!"

He stilled then and she groaned in frustration. She squirmed, urging him to continue, but he stubbornly remained motionless. Her sight slowly restored itself and she met his questioning gaze.

"Your brother?"

"Aye." She barely had the strength to speak.

"But William had no sons."

She panted, forcing the words past her parched lips. "He's a bastard. Never acknowledged. Please, Royce, take pity on me. I've given you what you wanted."

He studied her for what seemed an eternity. She held her breath, her body trembling and squirming without any conscious effort. Finally, he nodded. He rose above her and she gave an excited gasp to see his erect cock pointing straight at her sex. Her hips lurched upward. He stroked himself a few times then filled her with one deep thrust. Her back arched and almost immediately, her release overtook her. When he began to pump within her, the pleasure continued, soaring higher, curling her toes. Her senses tumbled through the riot of carnal bliss.

Over and over, the waves of rapture claimed her, leaving her gasping and panting and trying to right her upended wits. Still, he moved within her, his rhythm keeping her spinning in pleasure she thought might never end.

It seemed hours before she calmed, her body quivering rhythmically around his. He pulled free of her body, and she barely had the awareness that he freed her bonds and pulled her close.

She might have dozed, she couldn't say, but slowly, she became aware of her surroundings. Royce held her firmly against him, and beneath her ear, his heart thumped. As her thoughts cleared, she recalled what she'd told him. Fear for her brother's safety gave her a sudden burst of vigor, fueled by worry.

"Royce, do you believe me?"

His tawny eyes seemed to probe right into her thoughts. He nodded.

"Aye. It all makes sense. But why didn't you tell me sooner?"

She averted her eyes and snuggled closer. "He, that is, we, feared he might be sent away.

My father never claimed him as son, though he saw to his training and well-being. No one knows. Except..."

He slid his fingers under her chin and forced her to look at him. "Except who?"

"Myself and Simon, of course, and mayhap Edward."

Royce's brow furrowed. "If Edward knew, he would have told me."

"A letter was sent. I don't know if it reached him. And I can't say for sure what it said. I didn't see it."

"I will discuss it with the king in the morn."

"Royce, what will you do to Simon?" She had to know. Fear her husband might send Simon away, or worse, took over.

"Do to him? What do you mean?"

"He is a threat to your holding." She tried to turn away again, but her husband didn't release her chin.

"He is no threat. He can make no claims on Lyndon."

She heaved a sigh. "So you will not kill him?"

He gave her the oddest look, as if he thought her daft. "Of course not!"

"Or banish him?" She still held half a breath.

He shook his head, chuckling. "Nay, I will not send him away. You ask the oddest questions, Wildcat."

"I feared, that is, we both worried you might see him as a threat."

"Nay. In fact, now that I know, I feel he can help us."

For the first time in hours, Gillian's breathing came steady. "How?"

"He is knowledgeable about Lyndon and the surrounding lands. He can aid us in our search."

"I can as well –"

"You will not! You will do nothing except tend to matters of the household."

"But I know the lands as well as any here. I can help you!"

Frustration grew again, this time with her husband's pigheadedness.

"If I must lock you in again, I will. You will not join us in our search."

"But –"

"That is an order. To disobey will get you punished. And you won't like that one."

The shiver passing along her body told her otherwise.

# chapter eleven

Gillian stopped at the foot of the stairs. She'd summoned Simon almost an hour ago. He should be here by now. She spotted Royce seated with Burke at the head of the table. Her husband looked up and caught her gaze. Her body warmed at the affection she found in his stare. Worried he might go back on his word faded. Simon would be permitted to stay, even to help.

She walked to her husband, her gaze darting to Burke. She'd not spoken much with the captain, but knew him to be efficient at keeping the men ready for Royce's orders. She caught his gaze and an uneasy tremor passed over her. Again, she detected the coldness in his eyes. The thin line of his lips gave him a menacing look. Yet, he merely nodded courteously. Nothing unseemly; as always, he remained properly polite and respectful. Still, a foreboding shiver ran along her spine.

"Good morn, my lady."

"Burke." She turned to Royce, shaking off her musings. "My lord."

Her reward was a warm smile from her husband. Her stomach gave an odd little flutter when he indicated she should sit beside him. She did, assailed by a shiver of giddy delight when he took her hand and kissed the back.

"I trust you slept well?"

"Like a babe." She had, once she'd finally drifted off. So heavily did she slumber, she hadn't felt him rise and leave her.

He placed a trencher of cheese and porridge before her. "Eat. You need to recover your strength."

Her cheeks heated and she focused her attention on breaking her fast.

She'd nearly finished when footsteps drew her attention. Simon approached the table, concern lined into his face. He gave a bow toward Royce, a nod to Burke and a glance at Gillian.

"Good morn, Simon. We must talk." Royce took a long drink of ale from the flagon before replacing it on the table.

"About what, my lord?"

Her brother sent a questioning glance her way. She tried to reassure him with a smile, unsure if she succeeded.

"Burke, leave us. The king will want to interrogate the rebels shortly."

"Aye." Burked faced her once again. "My lady."

This time, Gillian noted an unmistakable lust flickering in Burke's eyes before he concealed it. She shuddered, grateful when he turned away and strode toward the lower chambers.

"I know of your parentage. Gillian told me last night." Royce's voice, low and deep, drew her out of the troublesome thoughts. Simon turned to her. She'd never seen such anger spark in his eyes.

"We agreed." His words croaked out between clenched teeth.

"I know, but –"

Royce cut in. "I made her tell me. Fear not, you are welcome at Lyndon and always will be. In fact, we will require your assistance during the search for the rebels."

Simon shifted uneasily and looked between Royce and Gillian. She stood.

"'Tis true I had no choice. But trust him. You have nothing to worry about anymore. Trust me."

"I don't know what to make of this. I... thank you, my lord."

"You will continue your role as my wife's guard. I trust you'll keep her safe and protect her as you must."

Gillian caught the stern stare Royce fixed on her brother. The words left unspoken promised a gruesome retribution if Simon should fail.

"Of course. I would lay down my life for her."

Simon's voice rang true and strong as he made the

vow. He gave Gillian a smile. All would be well.

\*\*\*

Royce, with Burke at his side, awaited Edward's arrival in the lower chambers. The two rebels remained bound in the tiny room. Though they were injured, and weak, having not eaten since their capture, they still glared at Royce with defiance. He wondered how long they would last under Edward's interrogation.

The king entered, as always, his trusted advisor Burnell right behind him. He paused and quietly gave the other man some instructions. Burnell left the room to carry out his sire's wishes.

"These are the only ones you captured who survived?"

"Aye. The third died of his wounds but did tell of the intentions behind the raid."

Edward stalked over to the two Welshmen and kicked one of their legs. "You will die for your foolish daring. Have you anything to confess before you are hanged?"

"Godwin will win the day! We'll tell you nothing!" The scruffier of the two shouted the words.

Edward drew back and punched the man square in the face. Blood spurted and the rebel howled in pain. Edward turned to the other.

"Do you wish to add anything to your dead comrade's words? He was quite eager to speak, from what I'm told, once he realized he would soon face God's judgment."

"Lyndon is not England's. It never has been." The man focused a steady stare at Royce.

"Look to your own, Panther. The wife you gained is not who you think."

Now it was Royce's turn to clench his fists. He too took two steps toward the rebel. Edward halted him.

"Hear what he has to say first, Panther."

"He dares claim my wife is a traitor!"

"I would hear what he will say!"

The anger tightening Edward's face left Royce alarmed. Did the king believe the lies? He stepped back and Edward turned his attention to the rebel.

"You are either very stupid or very brave. No matter, you will tell what you know."

The rebel smirked. "Will it save me from the noose?"

"No." Edward spat the word out.

Royce wanted to shout with frustration. The rebel lied. Didn't he? Doubts he thought he'd dismissed rose again, much stronger than he wished.

"Then, I'll tell nothing."

Edward studied the rebel thoughtfully. "Oh, you will. Before we hang you, you will beg to tell us all you know. Both of you."

The terror in each man's eyes flared anew. Finally, the second rebel nodded.

"Very well. I'll tell you."

The first Welshman tried to protest, but choked on his words, a combination of desperation and likely blood as well, from his broken nose. The second silenced him with a nudge of his foot.

"Fear not, Igmar. I take great pleasure in telling the Panther his bride has been passing secrets to us for years. Now the king knows those he trusts most have made him a laughingstock!"

Edward gave Royce a curious glance. The suspicions in the king's eyes sparked a new round of worry. Did he believe the pronouncement? Royce didn't, not entirely, and it took all of his control to contain his rage.

"I know lies when I hear them." Edward nodded to Burke. "Fetch lard and stoke that fire. Where are the stocks?"

Royce stood back as Burke and the other the guards prepared. They dragged the Welshman toward the hearth, where the flames had been coaxed higher. With quick movements, they fastened his legs into the stocks, his feet exposed and about a cubit from the hearth. Another guard returned with the lard.

"How long do you think he'll last before he tells us all we need?" Royce asked.

"Not long at all." Edward folded his arms. "Rebels

such as he are quite brave until we use a little persuasion."

Burke removed the rebel's boots and set about smearing the lard on his feet. The Welshman tried to slide away, but held between the stocks and another guard, had no chance of escape. Together Burke and the guards pushed the rebel closer to the fire. His harsh protests and pleas for mercy echoed in the room.

Edward held up a hand. "Will you tell all now?"

The rebel looked back toward his companion. Royce scowled to see the other man shake his head.

"Nay, I will not help you any further."

Yet the fear in the man's eyes betrayed the lie. He kept silent only on the encouragement of the other. Royce found himself anxious to hear the confession but more than anything else, he wanted to know if the man spoke the truth about Gillian.

"Very well." Edward motioned to Burke, who pulled the man closer to the flames. The rebel screamed and tried to fight back, but was no match for Burke and the guards, who soon positioned both lard-smeared feet against the flames.

The screams echoing in the room hurt Royce's ears. For several minutes, Burke held the captive in place, then gave the signal to pull him back. The Welshman collapsed limply to the floor. The smell of burned flesh knotted Royce's stomach.

"We will continue until you tell me where I can find Godwin and who has been aiding them."

The outlaw remained silent, unwilling or unable to speak. Edward motioned to Burke and the screams began anew.

\*\*\*

"Could I have been wrong about William?"

Edward didn't wait for an answer, forcing Royce to follow down the narrow corridor. The rebel had lost consciousness before saying anything useful. Edward decreed they would try again. In the meantime, he wanted the other rebel hanged. Immediately.

The king continued to speak. "His wife was Welsh, distantly related to Llewellyn and his brothers. William said she'd been renounced by her family, and she's been dead for many years, but..."

"As you know, Sire, I have had doubts about Gillian myself. I will continue to work to learn the truth. She has always claimed innocence, but she's also kept many secrets."

Were there more? He couldn't be sure. He gave a moment's consideration to sharing what he'd learned from Gillian, about the truth of her mother's ancestry. Would the revelation of additional lies help, or make things worse? Edward's next words extinguished the idea.

"And if we learn she is indeed a traitor? You know what must be done."

Royce understood the king's meaning clearly. The thought of his wife executed left him cold, but if he discovered she had indeed betrayed England, he would not hesitate to hand her over. An image of her on the ramparts, bow in hand, calmed his worry. If she meant harm to England, she would have killed him. Instead, she'd saved his life. Her actions spoke more than any monk could record in his lifetime.

"She defended Lyndon, Sire, and saved my life during the raid."

Edward nodded. "'Twould seem to indicate she is innocent."

Another possible suspect arose. While Royce had wanted to share this latest with the king in private, he realized he must do so now. Why did the urgent need to defend his wife guide him now?

"Sire, did you receive a letter from William before he passed?"

"Nay, though 'tis possible Burnell has it. Why?"

"Gillian has a brother."

Edward gaped at him, anger reddening his face. "And you didn't tell me?"

"I didn't know ere last night. She admitted it. He's a

bastard. Never acknowledged."

Edward's eyes turned contemplative. "I see. Mayhap he is angered over that."

"Could be."

"Mayhap he is traitor."

Royce nodded. "Mayhap."

The idea made more sense with each second. Who was Simon's mother? If he was indeed the traitor, 'twould explain much. And Gillian would be free of suspicion. The relief he felt startled him. He told himself 'twas only because it would save him the shame of having a traitorous wife.

"I have told him I will require his aid in securing Lyndon. He will bear watching. I will set him to tasks so that Burke and I can do so easily."

Edward nodded. He stepped aside as two of the guards dragged the bloodied rebel from the chamber. Royce half-dreaded the next hour.

***

Gillian heard the commotion in the bailey and excused herself from Thomas. There would be time for the ledgers later. She lifted her skirts and strode down the steps, surprised to see so many people milling about the tall oak near the smithy. Royce stood nearby, Edward before him. To the side, Eleanor and her ladies stood, whispering. She hurried across the bailey, pushing her way through. When she reached the tree, she froze.

One of the captured rebels, his face bloodied and bruised, knelt in a wagon underneath the lowest branch. His hands were bound behind his back. The horse harnessed to the cart shifted, and the wagon lurched. The rebel swayed but held his position.

What next caught Gillian's attention was the noose hanging from the branch. She covered her gasp with a shaky hand and approached her husband.

"What's happening?" Although she had little doubt, the inane question lisped out anyway.

"We hang one of the rebels."

Her sickening suspicion confirmed, she looked from the rebel to the king and back to her husband.

"Now? Here?"

"Here. I told you of our plan. And as you have no permanent gibbet, this must do."

"We've not had a need for one ere now."

"I will remedy that soon enough."

"Must you do this?"

"Aye. And likely again tomorrow, when we finish our interrogation of the other."

The oddly suspicious look in her husband's eyes sent a shiver of anxiety along her spine. He seemed to be looking for something, but what? She turned to Edward, who also watched her with a strange expression.

"Sire, why must we do this here? Now? In full view of everyone?"

"We send a message, Lady Gillian," Edward said. "This criminal refused to speak. He attacked Lyndon, therefore England, with plans to ambush me. He stands by his treasonous actions and faces justice. Any who think to follow his path will know what they face when they are caught."

"But why now?"

Royce grabbed her arm, forcing her to face him. "It must be this way. The king wishes it. You dare much in questioning him."

"We've been at peace here for many years. In a sennight's time, we've now become a focus of the rebellion. Since you arrived!"

"He came on my orders, Lady Gillian." Edward stepped closer, his blue eyes icy and cold. "Forgive me, Sire, but so much has happened in the last weeks. First my father, and now..." The lines in the king's face softened. "Your father shielded you from much. But we have no choice. This man committed treason and must pay with his life."

Gillian gave a bleak nod. She turned to study the rebel. He stared back at her, an odd smile curving one side of his mouth. Royce's hand on her arm tightened. She looked away, and caught Eleanor's gaze. The queen bore an expression of understanding and sympathy, though she said nothing.

The executioner, likely one of Edward's men, climbed into the wagon. His face obscured by a black hood, he hauled the rebel to his feet and secured the noose around the condemned man's neck. The executioner then jumped to the ground. Gillian looked away as he gave the order.

"I die willingly for you and our cause, Lady Gillian!"

Her head snapped up at the rebel's shout; a moment later the creak of the wagon's wheels sounded eerily loud in the sudden silence.

"What? You lie! I am not one of you!" she shouted.

"Ultimately, we will win!" The outlaw stared right at her. Too stunned to speak, she gaped at his grinning face. The wagon seemed to move very slowly. Aware of stares upon her, she turned away at the moment the cart drew out from under the Welshman.

Her gaze landed on Edward, who again eyed her with suspicion. He must think her a traitor now, too. She backed closer to Royce, but his tight grip on her shoulders warned she'd find no sanctuary with him.

Edward spared a glance at the twitching body of the rebel, then slowly strode closer to Gillian. She could read nothing in his stone-like expression. Not even the chirping of birds could be heard in the ominous silence.

"Are you in consort with the rebels, Lady Gillian?"

She shook her head. "Nay, Sire. Ere the raid, I have never seen him before."

She looked around at the lingering crowd, some moving closer to the king and Gillian. Beyond Edward, the body of the rebel caught in its death throes seemed to mock her.

"Royce, will you see to this?"

"Aye, Majesty."

Gillian looked up at her husband and fear sliced sharply into her. His stony countenance warned she was about to suffer again under his hand. Excitement sprouted in the midst of her worry. She ignored it, aware that an accusation of treason could subject her to far worse than any sexual torment her husband put her through.

"Nay, you cannot think I have betrayed you, Sire!" The desperation in her voice was due to Royce's ever tightening hold on her. "'Tis Anne who is behind this!"

Edward said nothing as Royce pulled her toward the keep. She stumbled once, but he righted her. Where was Simon? He could make them see the truth.

Several times, she caught the glances of soldiers or servants. Many bore expressions of surprise and sympathy, but a few actually appeared pleased by her predicament. Had she been a fool to think everyone here was loyal to England? To her? Had she protected them for naught? She made note of who looked satisfied. If they would betray Lyndon, they betrayed her and she owed them nothing. She would tell her husband their names once they were alone in their chamber.

She shivered at the thought of what he might do to her this time. An eagerness for him to touch her, in any manner, poked through the bedlam of emotions, but fear kept it from taking over.

He said nothing as he dragged her through the great hall and up the stairs to the lord's chamber. He shoved her into the room. She stumbled and nearly fell, but he made no move to aid her. She pulled herself upright and met his gaze defiantly.

"You know I am no traitor!"

He folded his arms. "I don't know what to believe anymore. Your insistence on keeping secrets has not worked in your favor. Daring to question the king's actions only makes you more suspect."

"What will you do to me?"

"Whatever I must to ensure you are indeed loyal. For now, I have more urgent tasks to see to. You will remain here until I return and decide what is to be done with you."

He turned and left the room. She ran to the door,

hearing the now-familiar sound of the bar sliding into place, followed by the rasp of the key in the padlock. She slumped, wondering how such a promising day had turned into such hell.

\*\*\*

Royce found Edward in the hall and joined him before the hearth.

"What have you done to the girl?"

"She's locked in our chamber for now. I will see to her later. First, I must –"

"My lord, what have you done with Lady Gillian?"

Simon's angry shout preceded him by mere moments. His dark eyes flashed in anger as he stalked over to stand before Royce.

Royce stood. "She is secure. For now."

"Surely you know she's no traitor!"

"We know nothing of the sort."

Edward's words drew Simon's attention from Royce. He paled at the sight of the tall king rising from his chair.

"She would never be disloyal to you, Your Majesty." Simon bowed.

"How can you be so sure?" Edward asked. "Both rebels have said she passes secrets to their leader."

Royce leaned close to the king. "This is the brother, Sire."

"I see. And are you loyal?"

"Of course, Sire. I would never betray you, nor would Gillian. Our father was your man until the end."

"You hold no anger at not being acknowledged?"

Simon hesitated. "I won't deny I would rather William had recognized me, but I harbor no malice."

"We shall see."

"May I speak with her?" he asked.

Royce shook his head. "Nay."

"What will you do?"

"'Tis not your concern. I suggest you worry for your own neck, rather than my wife's."

Again, Simon's face turned white. He gave a nod, another brief bow to Edward and strode out of the hall.

"They could be working together."

"Aye." Royce didn't dare gainsay the king and risk his wrath. Not until he was sure his wife had not betrayed them all.

\*\*\*

He approached the tiny hut with caution. Did his lover wait for him as he'd ordered? He saw movement at the window and smiled. Already his cock ached for her. It had been too long.

He smiled again, thinking of how the rebels had turned the king's suspicion toward Lady Gillian. His plan continued to grow stronger each day. Once he had satisfied himself Anne was safe, he would see to reinforcing his army for another attack. He must strike while Edward remained at Lyndon, lest he lose his chance to win this once and for all. And once the king was slain, he would take the crown for himself. Not even his cousins had dared attempt the English throne. But he would.

He reined in his horse and dismounted securing the beast to a nearby tree. He looked around. So far deep into the forest, 'twould take days before anyone reached this hut. By then, Anne would be safely away with his heir secure in her belly.

He knocked once on the door and it swung open instantly. He found himself greeted by a warm body thrown against him, arms and legs encircling him. He grinned and stepped inside, kicking the door shut.

Her mouth upon his grew frantic and his cock hardened at the feel of her in his arms. He'd missed her. Soon, they would never be separated again.

No words passed between them as they tore at each other's clothes, until both were naked. He swept her into his arms and laid her upon the small cot in the corner. He wasted no time with preliminaries and suspected she didn't care either. He stroked his hard shaft twice then spread her legs. With one thrust, he was home.

He remained motionless for several moments, savoring her silky and wet warmth. All too soon, his urgency grew, her hips bucking to urge him on. Her nails scratched along his back and arms, spurring him on as he pounded into her. In mere moments, the rocking of her body around his had him exploding in delight, his shout matching her cries of completion.

Sated, he lay with her, his heart slowing.

"I've missed you so much," Anne said. She lifted herself on one elbow, her green eyes glowing with satisfaction.

"And I you. The plan is working well. I must see you to the village on the border, though." Her gaze reflected her concern. "Why?"

"Several reasons. Edward plans more searches and I fear they might eventually find you. Also, I would see that the babe is safe. The king will not hesitate to execute you even if you are with child."

Something in her expression alarmed him. He held her chin, forcing her to look at him. "What's wrong?"

"Nothing. I just... my baby, I fear for the child's safety."

He nodded. "'Tis why I want you away from here."

"Will you come visit?"

He shrugged. "Mayhap, though I fear 'twill be some time. The plan is working. Lady Gillian is under suspicion of aiding the rebels. Us."

A delighted glow lit Anne's eyes. "How I wish I could see her pay for all that she's cost me."

"She will hang eventually. She is now locked away and subject to her husband's interrogation."

"And no one suspects you?"

He shook his head. "This has turned out to be much easier than I expected. 'Tis true the traitor is in their midst. By the time they realize, 'twill be too late."

The feel of her warmth against him soon had his cock stirring again. He covered her breast, squeezing and caressing until she arched against him. He took her mouth in a bruising kiss and rose above her.

# Chapter Twelve

Gillian paced the chamber, chewing on a fingernail. She'd been locked in for the past three days and feared she might soon go mad.

The only respite had come when the sun disappeared, replaced in the sky by the moon, and Royce joined her. Only then could she forget she remained under suspicion. Her husband's wicked games filled the long dark nights. She had given him the names of several of Lyndon's villeins on the first night, the ones who were clearly pleased with her predicament. Still, Royce refused to declare her free of suspicion. She supposed he did it in order to continue his torture. If only she didn't enjoy his underhanded tactics to get her to speak. God's blood, if she had anything to tell, surely he knew she'd have shared it by now. Her thoughts ran wild, recalling how he kept her release at bay for hours, until her head pounded mercilessly with need and her core felt as if it would burst.

Her body warmed to recall the harsh way he'd finally taken her. Her breasts throbbed, still aching from his rough and painful handling. At the same time, she again yearned to feel his palm landing on her flesh, the bite of the strike sparking a heated delight. She moaned and fell back on the bed. With nothing to do, she could only dwell on such musings. Was that his intention? To make her think of nothing but his touch, no matter how harsh or gentle?

When he brought her meal this eve, she must ask him to bring her needlework, or the ledgers, or something to occupy the long hours. She missed the bustle of tending her home, she missed her hawks and she missed Simon. She worried for him. Royce had informed her that her brother was also under suspicion, and closely watched. He would tell her nothing more.

She feared her brother might be locked below, a

prisoner subjected to the king's whims when he wanted information. The second rebel had been hanged the day before. Royce had shared the news along with more disturbing information. The torture they'd subjected him to had not changed the outlaw's insistence she was in collusion with the rebels.

Who conspired against her? Who had been loyal to Anne and would continue her evil ways? While Royce's men questioned those she'd named, none had been proven to be traitors. And she still remained locked in here, under suspicion.

What would it take for her to win her husband's, and the king's, trust?

The rasp of the key drew her from her thoughts and she stood. As usual, the sight of her husband filling the doorway set her heart to racing. She clasped her hands before her.

He carried a tray and stepped into the room, kicking the door shut. He held out the dish. She stepped closer and took it. Now unencumbered, he immediately barred the door. She tried not to scowl, fairly sure she didn't succeed before setting the trencher on the table near the hearth. Her stomach rumbled at the smell of the stew.

"I will be letting you out on the morrow."

Hunger forgotten, she met his stare. Excitement bubbled. "You will?"

He nodded. "Aye. But you are not free."

His cold voice sent a shiver along her spine. The contrast of his husky murmurs of last night echoed in her memory.

"I don't understand."

For the first time, she noticed the sack he carried. He reached inside. Her stomach rolled when he withdrew its contents.

An iron shackle, with a chain attached, sparked a terror she'd never known.

"When you are outside this chamber, you will wear this. I will determine where you are needed and you will be secured there until I return for you."

"So I am still a prisoner. In my own home."

"Until I can be sure you are no longer a threat, I will ensure you cause no harm."

She folded her arms and sneered. "You are vile! I've done nothing wrong!"

"You've said that before. And yet, there is still reason to believe you capable of treason."

"Then hang me now! Nothing I say will convince you otherwise!"

He paled at her words. Was that a hint of panic in his tawny eyes? Before she could be sure, his expression hardened again.

"Nay, you will not hang. But I will have the truth from you one way or another."

She shook her head, disgusted with his insistence on treating her as a criminal. Even so, she knew what methods he would use to draw his presumed truth from her, and her body reacted with that damnable heat. She dared another glance at him and the knowing glint in his eyes revealed he deduced just what she felt. She turned her back.

A knock on the door sent Royce across the chamber. Thomas stood in the corridor, concern etched into his lean features. Royce gave her a warning look and spoke to the steward in low tones. Gillian stood silently, but try as she might, could not make out their words.

Her gaze landed on the stew awaiting her. The aroma wafted to her and her stomach rumbled, reminding her she'd eaten nothing since breaking her fast this morn. She moved toward the table, but before she reached it, Royce stood before her.

"There are signs of the rebels nearby."

She glared at him. "And?"

"And I will be riding out on the morrow with my men to find them. Your brother goes with us."

A tremor of alarm shuffled along her spine. "Why?"

"Because I would know if he is in consort with the Welsh. 'Twill be a good test."

She didn't answer, noting the veiled threat. Did Royce have some other nefarious plan for her brother?

"Nothing to say, wife?"

She met his stare defiantly. He smirked, as if he knew the thoughts tumbling through her head.

"Very well, then. Eat your supper; you will need your strength tonight."

Why did the shiver of delight explode in her sex, making her slick and hot and wanting his tormenting touch already? With a shaky breath, she sat and reached for the stew.

*** 

Royce watched his wife help herself to her supper. She paused and looked up at him.

"Are you not eating, my lord?"

"I've already taken my meal below. That is all for you."

Her violet eyes widened in surprise, then softened in gratitude. She must be starving by now, as he'd given orders that she was not to eat until he brought her the food. Much as he hated treating her thus, he knew Edward expected him to get whatever secrets Gillian possessed by whatever means possible. But more and more, Royce began to believe she truly was innocent of the rebels' claims.

The last three nights had been a delight for him, and near torture for her. Yet, she'd enjoyed every moment, he felt sure of it. Even now, despite her anger and defiance, he read desire in her gaze.

No doubt she'd enjoyed the way he'd coaxed the names from her, giving them easily. While he wished those names had given him the information he sought, he found himself oddly pleased her compliance had worked in his favor. Since then, she'd had nothing more to share, and by now, she surely would have, if she indeed knew anything more.

Still, he must use caution. The only alternative was allowing Edward to handle her interrogation. Royce truly feared what the king might do, knowing how impatient his overlord could be in passing judgment, sometimes before having all the facts. While his loyalty to Edward never wavered, he found himself anxious to keep his wife from suffering the same fate as the hanged rebels. After tonight, he would know what to tell Edward on the morrow.

Finally, Gillian pushed away the trencher and gave a loud sigh. Drawn from his thoughts, he met her gaze at the moment she lifted her cup and took a long drink of wine. When she lowered the cup, her tongue swiped along her lower lip. His cock stirred at the thought of his plans for her this eve. Still, he waited, staring into the flames dancing in the hearth, casting the room in a surreal glow. His wife sat silently as well, her head lowered. She appeared to contemplate her entwined fingers.

How long they remained thus, sitting quietly, listening to the crackle of the logs in the fire, he wasn't sure. The chapel bells indicated it had been over an hour. He'd not realized how comforting it felt to simply sit beside her. God's bones, he'd surely gone daft, finding contentment with a woman who could very well be a traitor. Yet, he found himself disavowing the idea more and more.

"Do you wish to eat anything more?" He pointed to the custard tarts on the tray. When she shook her head, he found himself glad of her choice.

"Very well. Remove your clothes."

Her hesitation drew him a step closer. Instead of her obedience, his reward was the defiant lifting of her chin, while her hands clenched at her sides.

"You refuse my order?"

"And if I do?"

He savored the way her face paled at his slow smile. "I think you know. If I didn't know better, I'd think you sought punishment."

"If you didn't know better, you'd be nothing more than the king's jester."

He wanted to laugh at her bold insult. How he restrained himself, he might never know. Instead, he took another step closer. He noted her swallow, but admired her refusal to cower. "You have a choice. Remove your dress or I will cut it from you."

Her hands rose quickly to the back of her gown, fumbling with the laces of her kirtle. When she had loosened all she could, she turned her back to him. He undid the rest and she slowly slid the dress from her shoulders. The chemise followed as did the hose, until she stood naked before him. His heart thudded, cock straining against his braies.

He pointed to the floor before him pleased when she obediently knelt. He said nothing, merely watched her. He yanked off his tunic and folded his arms. She looked up at him. The anger in her stare only made him harder. He chuckled, laying his hand on her cheek.

"You please me, wife."

Surprise flitted across her face. "Then you believe me?"

He shook his head. "I still don't know what to believe."

"Surely by now, you realize I've done nothing against England."

He shrugged. "No matter. Remove my hose."

"Nay, you cannot think what those rebels said is true!"

"Stop talking, and obey."

"But –"

He moved his hand to cover her mouth. "I had hoped not to have to bind and gag you tonight, but I will if you force me. Obey the order."

Instead, he felt the sharp bite of her teeth. He yanked his hand away.

"So be it."

He reached down and grabbed her arm, hauling her up and against him. With quick movements, he turned her, then bent and pulled the sash free of her gown. He wrapped it quickly around her wrists, securing her. Soon, she knelt before him once more and he tugged at his hose, freeing his aching cock.

"I only have one use for your mouth tonight."

Tears glimmered in her eyes and for a moment, he found himself tempted to release her. Until he recognized the fury also glinting in her shimmering violet gaze. He gave a grim smile, even knowing that after tonight, if she revealed nothing more, he would declare her innocent. But he couldn't share his intentions just yet. If the slightest chance remained she had indeed fed the rebels information, he had to see it through. On the morrow, he and Edward would observe the brother.

In the meantime, he would take great pleasure in her fiery emotions.

"Do as you're told."

Hesitation accompanied a narrowing of her eyes, yet, she sucked in a deep breath and leaned forward. With her arms secured behind her, her balance was precarious, so he stepped closer and placed a hand on her shoulder to steady her.

The first tentative swipe of her tongue along the head of his dick nearly had him coming already. He gritted his teeth, savoring the hesitant way she explored him. When her lips opened to enclose the tip of his cock, his knees nearly buckled. He braced himself, sliding his other hand into her dark locks, holding her in place, surging into her sweet mouth.

Her inflamed gaze moved to his and he nearly lost himself then. Somehow, he regained control, once more entranced by the movements of her lips and tongue. He held back as long as he could, but she sucked greedily on his aching flesh and he was no match for her innocent instinct.

With a roar, his fingers tightened on her head and he exploded into her mouth. Through it all, she held his stare, swallowing every drop of his seed. When she drew away, she licked her lips and it was almost enough to send Royce to his knees beside her.

Once he regained control, he pointed to the bed. "Lay yourself down at the end and present your arse for me."

The sorrow in her eyes almost undid his determination to punish her until she begged for him to stop. He folded his arms and fixed a fierce glare on her.

Slowly, and with much difficulty, she rose to her feet then made her way to the bed. As instructed, she laid her upper body on the mattress, her arse fully exposed. With his foot, he kicked her legs wider apart, the sound of her startled gasp sending fire to his cock.

He stroked her flesh, savoring the way she quivered under the touch. Slowly, he let his fingers roam over her, pushing her legs still wider as he slipped his thumb between the groove of her cheeks. He found her tiny hole and pressed lightly against it. She stiffened and tried to rise. He used his free hand in the small of her back to hold her down.

"Nay! My lord, please no!"

"Silence!" He lightly circled her hole and soon, her resistance faded. Her hips wiggled in the most delightful way, her flesh clenching at the teasing touch. He continued for a few more moments, until pleading gasps escaped her.

Without warning, he raised his hand and brought it down hard on her arse. She squealed and again fought against his hold, but she was no match for his strength. He struck again and again, relishing the way her skin reddened and grew warm. He paused to stroke her gently once more and a hitching sob echoed around him. When she quieted, he once again spanked her, hard, over and over, until a hoarse shriek erupted.

He stopped, soothing her tender skin with a gentle caress. Her arousal scented the air, hardening him further. He slipped a finger along her pussy, pleased to find it soaked. His seeking fingers gathered her moisture then once more he found her rear entrance. She stiffened again, but soon calmed as he used his fingers, wet with her juices, to lubricate her. With a couple of strokes on his hard cock, he moved into position behind her.

At the first feel of his cock near her bottom, she cried out and tried to move away, but he kept a tight grip on her bound wrists.

"Nay! Don't do this!"

"I will gag you if I must. Now be quiet. I am going to

enjoy your pretty arse tonight and you will not refuse me."

A choking sound echoed in the chamber. A sob? His cock lurched between her fleshy cheeks. He moved slowly, pushing against her resisting muscles. Her entire body tensed.

"Relax and 'twill go much easier."

"My lord, please!" Her raspy voice held a tremor of fear.

He pushed harder, hearing her whine and plead, but not making sense of her words. Her tight muscles tried to repel him, but he gave one more shove and was inside, her tight passage clenching hard. Slowly, he continued to move deeper, but knew he would not last long.

Her high-pitched cries urged him on, and he moved gingerly within her. She shrieked, trying to squirm away, but the motion only impaled him deeper in her warmth. He used his free hand to stroke her back soothingly, glancing down at her tear-streaked face.

He stilled his movements. "Gillian, be calm. You will find pleasure in this if only you would obey."

"'Tis hard to be calm with your cock up my arse, you pig-headed oaf!"

He chuckled. "Very well, then."

He resumed his leisurely pace, enjoying each clench of her muscles. He reached under her and found her clit, and tickled it. Her moans took on a different sound then, hot and full of need. He continued to torment her with the twin sensations, stroking in and out while he circled and flicked at her clit. Her entire body trembled violently beneath him.

His head seemed to float far above his body, the pleasure running through him so intense it stole not only his breath, but his wits. With every squeeze of her clit, Gillian's arse clenched nicely around him, the pleasure lunging higher. She moaned and cried, and he thought she begged, but couldn't be sure. The lust had hold of him and he didn't want to relinquish its fierce grip.

He stroked her sex, sliding two fingers up into her pussy while his thumb continued its teasing dance around her clit. To his surprise, she actually pushed back toward him, driving his cock and fingers deeper inside. Her harsh pants mingled with his. She continued to move with him, her voice and body urging him on. No longer able to resist, his balls tightened, moments before his seed erupted with force. Beneath him, his wife's body rippled and clenched, a keening wail coming from deep within her. He continued to fuck her with his fingers, even as he pulled his softening dick from her body. Another fierce trembling and sharp cry erupted and she came again on his hand, soaking him. He eased away and rolled her to her back.

Holding her gaze, he lifted his hand and licked her juices from his fingers. A shudder ran through her and she sucked in a deep breath, desire darkening her eyes to a deep purple, the color of the night sky just before the dawn. His cock stirred once more, but he ignored it as he pulled her up. He turned her and cut the sash holding her wrists together. When she moved to face him, he pushed her back to the bed.

"We are not done yet."

She rolled, scooting away from him, but he read the eagerness in her gaze. Her full lips, swollen with passion, curved into a sly smile. He crawled up along her passion-slicked body, pinning her against the headboard, relishing the way her breasts rubbed against his chest with each of her shuddering breaths.

"You'll not escape me that easily, wife."

He lowered his head and took her mouth in a bruising kiss. Her arms wrapped tight around him and she opened her legs in invitation.

# chapter thirteen

Royce rode beside Edward as they made their way through the forests. He and the king were far enough ahead to be out of earshot of the other men. Good. He wanted no one to hear, not even Burke.

"I don't believe Gillian is the traitor, Sire."

Edward nodded. "I suspect you are right."

"If she had anything to tell, she would have by now as I ... excuse me?"

"I believe you, Panther. While I harbored some suspicion after the rebels claimed her, I quickly realized she was not in league with them."

"Why did you not tell me?" A bitter annoyance, one he often felt with Edward's sometimes illogical decisions, roused anew. This time, a strange panic also lurked in his thoughts.

"I am telling you now."

A recollection of Gillian's angry tirade after he'd chained her in the kitchens rose in his thoughts. She'd called names he'd heard many times, though the ones he'd not recognized roused amusement. The way she'd hurled several cooking pots at his head when he'd left ensured a later punishment, though he suspected 'twas half the reason she'd done so to begin with. His wife had admitted liking the torment he inflicted upon her.

"Gillian will be pleased to know she is no longer under suspicion."

"You must not tell her."

"Why not?"

"I would not have her give the brother any reason to think he is beyond suspicion. You are watching him when he is not with us?"

Royce nodded. "I've set men to the task. He remains

unaware."

Edward nodded. "Good. We depart for Shrewsbury within a few days. I hope the threat from Lyndon is soon quelled. Parliament convenes and there is still the matter of the trial. I'll have no challenges to the sentence."

The last Welsh prince languished in captivity in Shrewsbury, waiting to likely be put to death. Daffyd had been unsuccessful in his attempt to overthrow the king, as Godwin would be.

If they ever found him.

"Here!"

A shout from the men behind had Royce wheeling his horse around. Several of the soldiers had dismounted, swords pointed at a tight cluster of trees and bushes. The men held off, awaiting his command. Royce withheld the order, worried the tiny hut concealed in the grove's midst might be a false lead.

He dismounted and strode over to the crude shelter. He slammed open the door, not surprised to find the hut empty. Still, anger at failing to remain ahead of the rebels burned.

No longer.

He heaved a deep breath, determined to regain an advantage over the rebels. He ordered several men into the hut before following. Standing just inside the door, he studied the gloomy interior.

The table was free of dust and the blankets on the cot looked fresh.

He turned to Edward. "A rebel hideout."

The king nodded. "Aye. I want the forest searched for more of these huts. They're nearby, I can feel it. Flush them out."

"Aye, Your Majesty."

Burke bowed. Something Royce had been considering for months arose again. He would speak to Edward about it this eve.

"If you find any of the rebels, finish them on sight."

Burke nodded and turned back to the men. With shouted orders, he mounted before leading his group of knights deeper into the forest.

Royce watched until he had disappeared among the trees. He thought about the days when they'd been boys and Burke's father had been executed by Henry. Burke and his mother had been banished and it had been many years before he'd found Royce again. By then, Royce had inherited his title and lands from his deceased father, and had happily given Burke his captain's position. Edward had concurred, even encouraged the appointment. Royce felt sure once he settled the plan with the king, Burke would be restored to his former prestige, as he deserved.

He followed Edward back to their horses. Satisfied his captain would accomplish what was necessary, he ordered Lyndon's men to accompany them back to the manor. This ensured Simon remained with him and under constant observation.

"Sire, I would ask a favor."

"What is that?"

"I wish to bestow Apshire upon Burke once all this is finished."

"That old decrepit estate? Whatever for?"

Royce explained what he'd planned. While the old, mostly abandoned lands consisted of little more than a small crumbling keep and a few other buildings, it could still be rebuilt and become prosperous once more. Burke had made several scouting missions to the lands, which lay a little more than a day's ride south, to determine the state of the manor. From his reports, Royce believed Burke could restore the keep and find villeins to work the land. He looked expectantly at the king when he finished his explanation.

Edward nodded. "The idea has merit. I will think on it."

\*\*\*

Gillian wiped her brow, the heat from the fires in the kitchen overpowering, even in the chill of the autumn air. A mug of ale was held before her.

"Drink, my lady."

Dilys, one of the many cooks who helped feed Lyndon's residents, nodded in encouragement. Gillian accepted the offering.

"Thank you." She took a long drink, her thirst quenched for the moment.

"My lady, how long do you think your husband will... that is..."

Dilys' words faded and she twisted her hands on her apron. Several of the other kitchen workers moved closer.

"Keep me chained like a criminal?" Gillian finished for the girl. "I don't know. He thinks I am a traitor to England. I suppose I'm lucky he hasn't hanged me yet."

"Oh, no, my lady, you are no traitor!" Another of the younger girls spoke up.

Gillian smiled. "My husband apparently doesn't agree. Come, we must finish the supper preparations. The men will return soon. I don't wish to keep the king waiting."

On her order, the servants dispersed to their tasks. Gillian sipped at her ale. Dylis still lingered nearby.

"Did you want something else?"

Dylis looked nervously around the room and stepped closer. She nodded, speaking in a low voice.

"I saw one of the guards go through the door. To the tunnel."

The traitor? The excitement burst upon Gillian suddenly.

"Who was it? When did you see this?"

Dylis hesitated again, a deep red staining her cheeks. "I-it was last night. After all were abed. I..."

Her hands twisted frantically in the apron and Gillian feared the girl would tear it to shreds.

At the downcast eyes and ever-darkening blush, Gillian understood.

"You needn't tell me who you were meeting with. But you must tell me who you saw."

Dylis raised her head and met Gillian's gaze. "'Twas Jervais."

Gillian frowned. Jervais was a close companion of

Simon's. No wonder her husband and the king suspected her brother. She must get word to him, warn him. And mayhap give him the chance to prove his loyalty.

"Dylis, I need to see Simon. I know the earl has assigned him to help with the searches while I am chained here, but the moment they get back, can you get word to him?"

"Aye, I will do it. I will tell..."

Gillian smiled as Dylis broke off once more.

"Might there be a wedding in the spring?" she asked.

Dylis' eyes widened, yearning evident in her dark gaze. "Oh, my lady, I hope so."

"Please keep me advised."

Dylis nodded and turned back to her work. Gillian took another sip of her ale and turned her attention back to peeling vegetables. The stores grew lower each day and she knew 'twas from feeding the king and his party.

A sudden silence fell over the room, the crackle of the flames at the open end the only sound. Aware of the servants looking beyond her, she turned. Eleanor stood at the entrance. Gillian sank into a deep curtsy.

"Your Majesty. Is there aught I can do for you?"

"Rise, Lady Gillian. I have sent for the steward to free you."

"But... Your Majesty, my husband and the king have – " Gillian stood, her questioning gaze focused on her queen.

"Two stubborn fools, to my eyes."

Eleanor offered a smile just as Thomas came up behind her. He quickly unlocked the padlock around the shackle.

She was free! She longed to dance with joy, but refrained, aware the queen watched her closely.

"Come, I have much I want to discuss."

Gillian followed Eleanor to the hall and sat beside her before the hearth.

"Do you have everything you need, Your Highness? If there is something not to your liking –"

"Nay, naught is amiss. But I think I may be able to help you. One of my ladies has become quite taken with one of the men in Lyndon's garrison."

"I see," said Gillian. But she didn't.

"She snuck out of our chamber last night. To meet with him." Lyndon appeared to be a hive of amorous activity. Gillian supposed 'twas likely with all of the extra people about. Gillian's heart raced.

"Lady Gillian, she saw someone making their way to the secret door." Eleanor chuckled at what must be a surprised look on Gillian's face. "Yes, my dear. My husband shares most everything with me."

Gillian nodded. "Yes, I would expect Royce to have informed the king of the doors."

"'Twould seem the guard at that door has been neglecting his duty. You should inform your husband."

Again, Gillian found herself confused. "Have you not mentioned this to the king?"

Eleanor shook her head, her long blonde hair falling into her face before she brushed it aside.

"Nay. I think 'twould do you and your brother well if you provided this information to the earl."

Gillian gaped. The queen offered help to prove her innocence.

"But Your Majesty, I don't understand."

Eleanor leaned over and patted Gillian's hand. "Men can be quite foolish sometimes. This would be best coming from you and your brother, rather than someone else. I've ordered Lady Madelaine to declare she has told you of this. I will act surprised when I am eventually told."

"Why?"

"You are no traitor, anyone with eyes that function can see that. But my husband is desperate to end this rebellion and will accept as fact the barest clues. And not only will he have a real target for his rage, you and your brother will be cleared."

Gillian wanted to laugh with her joy. "I don't know how to thank you, Your Highness. Please tell me how I may show my gratitude."

"No need. But you must speak with your brother first."

"Why must I tell him?"

"Because he is the one who Lady Madelaine snuck out to meet."

Gillian didn't know how to respond, so she merely nodded. Simon and Lady Madelaine? Why didn't he say something? Now she understood Eleanor's insistence. Had Dylis sent a message already?

"I will speak with him soon. As soon as I can get word for him to meet me without raising –"

The wooden doors burst open and Royce and Edward strode into the hall, followed by several of their men. At the sight of her before the hearth, Royce stopped short. Anger blazed in his golden eyes, but after glancing at Eleanor, he remained silent. The sudden silence seemed to make Gillian's heartbeat echo through the room.

"How dare you disobey! Who freed you?"

Royce's roar left Gillian on the verge of breath-stealing panic.

\*\*\*

Royce had never been so angry. His wife had used her charm to have Thomas free her from her shackle and therefore the chores she'd been tasked with tending in the kitchens. He took a step closer, fists clenched, his anger taking hold.

"I freed her, Langley."

Royce stopped at the queen's words.

"Why, Your Highness?" His confusion deflated his anger.

"Because the poor girl has suffered enough. She is your wife, and should be treated with respect. Not like one of those rebels you fools seem to think she is in league with."

""They named her as conspirator." Edward strode over to his wife. "How dare you interfere with a man's right to punish his wife!"

Eleanor waved a dismissive hand at her husband. "You know as well as I Lady Gillian is no traitor."

"You are not the one to make that judgment."

Royce remained silent as Edward and Eleanor argued. He moved to stand beside Gillian. She peered up at him with defiant eyes. He didn't dare tell her he believed her innocent; his plan with Edward required him to continue to suspect her, at least outwardly. Aware that several of the servants had paused in their work to watch the royal couple argue, he barked orders for them to leave the hall.

He leaned over to his wife's ear. "You may have won the queen's favor, but you will be punished for this."

"I have no doubt. My lord."

The acid in her voice almost drew a chuckle but he suppressed it. Yet, he noted a spark in her gaze that betrayed her excitement. He also looked forward to this eve.

"Langley, please excuse us." Edward took Eleanor's hand and pulled her to her feet, hurrying across the hall to the stairs.

"I suspect Eleanor will also face chastisement."

"For what? Recognizing the truth?"

"You would do well to curb your tongue. I should whip you for your insolence."

A brief moment of panic flitted into her eyes, her lips pressing together. As quickly, she resumed her detached expression. Still, the sight of her alarm tightened his balls. He grabbed her arm and hauled her from the chair, following Edward's path across the hall. Once inside their chamber he shoved her in. She stumbled and fell to her knees. He checked the urge to help her to her feet.

"You make me a laughingstock."

"That is your own doing! Everyone on this manor knows I am no traitor, yet you and the king stubbornly refuse to accept that. You are punishing me for nothing but the word of two cowardly rebels about to meet their death. I have given you the names of those who were possible traitors, and yet you still treat me like a criminal."

"Your behavior and refusal to obey make you suspect."

"Behavior? What have I done? Nothing!"

"The keeping of secrets is a very real reason to suspect

you."

Her fists came at him so fast, she landed two blows before he subdued her. His jaw ached where she hit him, and he grabbed her wrist before she struck again, twisting her arms behind her back. Still she fought, slamming her foot onto his boot.

"Stubborn Wildcat!" He trapped her legs between his, stilling her attempts to kick him. "Let me go!"

"You have now lost the freedom I gave you this morn. You will remain here until I have exhausted my investigation."

"You bastard! I've done nothing to deserve this!"

He said nothing, merely turned her to the bed, forcing her face down onto it. Again, she kicked out, but he avoided her legs. Grabbing a sash that lay on the floor from her past captivity, he quickly wound it around her wrists. He turned her again, lifting her so she sat on the bed, resting up on the headboard.

"I will return shortly."

He left the room, anxious to seek out Burke and find out if his captain had learned anything about Simon.

# chapter fourteen

Gillian tugged at her bonds, cursing her husband. Surely someone must hear her shouts. Royce had likely threatened anyone who dared come to her aid. Her arms had gone nearly numb. She scooted to the edge of the bed and stood, waiting a few moments to ensure she could balance. What could she use to get free?

Her gaze landed on the ewer and basin on the table beside the wardrobe. She moved cautiously across the room, halting completely when she thought she heard someone on the other side of the door. When no one entered, she resumed her trek across the chamber. She stared at the porcelain. The notion tempting her grew stronger with each heartbeat, but she knew the noise would attract attention. 'Twas the only way. She turned and with her bound hands, sent the ewer and basin shattering to the floor. She studied the broken pieces. Spotting several that might serve her needs; she carefully stepped amidst the shards and slowly lowered herself. With her hands behind her back, she couldn't see, but her fingers finally closed on a piece she deemed the right size.

Taking a deep breath, she rose once again and returned to the bed. She willed her hands to steadiness, but due to her bonds, her efforts were lackluster at best. Still, she maneuvered the broken piece of porcelain until she was able to slip it between her wrists. With slow and careful movements, she used the shard to cut through the sash holding her arms behind her.

The edges were not as sharp as she'd hoped, further slowing the process. She bit her lip, concentrating, maintaining a mostly steady movement against the cloth until finally, with a sharp tearing sound, she made a significant cut. She tugged with her arms and the ties ripped, freeing her. She dropped the glass, trying not to cry out with the pain of the sudden movement. Her stiff arms didn't want to respond to her commands, but slowly feeling returned. She let out a few deep breaths, her stomach rolling.

She'd best not be sick, not after she'd shattered the washbasin. A few more deep breaths calmed her senses, and a few tentative motions soothed the discomfort in her arms. She set about clearing the larger broken porcelain pieces. She'd need a broom for the rest. She carefully set the shards aside and turned to the door when it swung open.

Panic rose up to choke her, but dissipated just as quickly when she recognized Simon. She let out a happy cry and ran to him, hugging him tightly. She'd missed him these last days.

He set her away and closed the door. "I don't have much time. Your husband is in conference with his captain and the king, and could return at any moment. Dylis said you needed to see me."

Gillian nodded. "Yes, I have some news; someone was seen near the hidden door at the kitchens."

Simon's eyes widened. "Are you sure?"

"Aye."

"'Twould seem the door is not as secret as we thought."

"'Tis my husband's fault. He has announced it to all. But that's not important. Simon, the woman who saw this person said it was Jervais."

Simon shook his head, his dark eyes filled with disbelief. "Nay, couldn't be. He was –" "With you? In the barracks?" Gillian folded her arms.

"Of course, where else would we be?" The red staining his face drew a laugh.

"I know you were with Lady Madelaine."

"Nay, I was..." His shoulders slumped. "Aye. I met with her."

"Are you planning to ask for her hand?"

He shook his head. "I cannot. I am a bastard and have no hope for a lady such as her."

"I suspect if you went to Eleanor, she'd help."

"Gilly, stop. Tell me more. Who saw Jervais?"

"Dylis did, though she wasn't sure who it was. Madelaine confirmed 'twas Jervais. She told the queen, who came for me. You know what happened then."

She scowled, still furious that her husband insisted on treating her as little more than a slave, to be chained and worked. Even so, the thought of his physical possession of her sparked the now-familiar heat. God's bones, the man had turned her into an insatiable lunatic! She shoved the thoughts aside.

"We must tell my husband at once."

"Tell him what?"

Gillian near choked on the lump blocking her throat. She turned, stomach churning anew at the sight of the rage etched in her husband's face. She took a deep breath.

"We have word... that is, this afternoon, when Eleanor, Queen Eleanor came to me, she shared something of import."

"And you didn't tell me this before?"

"I needed to confirm something."

Royce stalked over to her, but she refused to cower, despite the violent way her knees trembled.

"What was that?"

"Where my brother was last eve."

Royce settled his stare on her brother, but Simon also stood firm.

"Tell me, traitorous wife, what did you learn?"

The ice in his voice drew a shiver of fear, but she pushed it back. Lifting her chin, she held his stare.

"That one of Lyndon's men, Sir Jervais, was seen exiting through the kitchen door."

"And who saw this?"

Royce looked between the two of them, his fierce glare more ominous with each passing second.

"I did."

Simon's voice rang out before Gillian could speak. She turned and gaped at him.

"Arc you daft? I know 'twas Dylis who saw. Shc was

meeting with... she saw him. 'Twould seem whoever was set to guarding that door was not at his post."

"I will address that matter myself."

"I think you should worry about someone in your own troops." Gillian wondered why she insisted on baiting him this way. The stubborn fool deserved it.

"I will see to it. Now tell me, who is Dylis?"

Something in his tone and expression seemed softer. Definitely less angry. Had she finally gotten through to him?

"One of the maids. She feared telling me because she was not... that is not the point. Jervais and Simon have been in the garrison together many years. I thought Simon might be able to help."

"How would you help me?"

Though he directed the question to Simon, Gillian responded.

"He knows Jervais well, and I thought mayhap he could watch him without suspicion."

"So you are plotting again, behind my back?"

"Nay, I am trying to help you!" Her throat hurt from screaming at him. Did the man have wood for a head?

"Explain."

"My lord, your wife was trying to bring you proof that neither she nor I are the traitor. Since you will not listen to anything she says, and continue to mistreat her, we must do it ourselves."

Royce stalked over to stand before Simon. "You are already on a precarious perch. I have no reason to trust you."

"Nay, you don't, but I am trying to prove myself. If you won't permit me to do that, 'tis no matter, is it? You eliminate the threat, whether 'tis real or not."

The two men continued to rail at each other. Gillian tugged on her husband's arms. He shrugged her off as though she were no more consequential than a fly. She reached for him again, the sight of his fist landing in Simon's gut drawing a scream of fury. Simon doubled over, gasping, then righted himself. He swung at Royce, who blocked the blow and struck again.

Gillian turned on her husband, her own fists flying. A brief spark of satisfaction arose when he grunted as she landed one solid blow on his chin, followed by another to his gut. Again and again she swung, kicking at the same time and avoiding his attempts to subdue her.

"You idiot! We are trying to help you. Simon is no threat!"

She continued to pummel him, raging at his foolish and stubborn pride, until he finally caught one wrist, then the other, halting her attack.

"Quiet, you hellcat."

He nodded behind her. She looked over her shoulder.

Edward, Eleanor and Thomas stood in the doorway. Gillian groaned and her head fell against Royce's chest.

A bark of laughter echoed in the chamber. The king thought this funny? She met Royce's gaze. He appeared as flabbergasted as she.

"Panther, you've quite a task before you taming that one." Edward chuckled and walked across the room.

"Sire, I can explain..." He fell silent when Edward held up a hand.

"No need. We heard the screaming and Eleanor explained all." The king's expression sobered. "We must use caution, but I would like you and Sir Simon to join me. Thomas, send for Burke and see the queen and Lady Gillian to the royal chamber."

Her husband released her. For several moments, they stood in silent contemplation, studying each other, until he finally followed the king from the room. She had no chance to say anything at all to Simon before he too followed.

Eleanor held a hand out to Gillian. "Come. Let my ladies wait on you while you have your chamber... seen to."

Gillian followed Eleanor's gaze around the messed room, the broken porcelain and overturned table and chairs. Her mind still tumbling with all that had happened, she let herself be led from the chamber.

Royce closed the door after he entered the chamber behind Edward, Simon and Burke. He waited for the king to begin. Edward turned and directed a fierce glare at Simon.

"We know you and Lady Madelaine were together last night." Edward shook his head when Simon made an attempt to protest. "She has already confessed the affair. What do you plan to do? Eleanor demands you make things right for her lady-in-waiting."

Simon looked so pale, Royce feared he might pass out. He moved closer to catch the man, just in case. He might land on Edward.

"I... will be happy to have Lady Madelaine as wife. If she will have me. Sire, I am but –"

"She'll have you. And we are well aware of who you are. Fear not, you'll be given the means to support your wife. The queen insisted upon that." Edward's mouth quirked in a half-smile, which just as quickly disappeared. "And whilst you are still not completely free of suspicion, this explains at least some of your secretive actions. Royce and I agree you are not who we seek. For now."

While the unspoken warning was clear in the king's icy tone, Simon's body lost its tension. Royce caught the king's glance and nodded. Edward lowered himself into a chair.

"Who is Jervais and how did he come to be here?"

"He's been a knight in Lyndon's garrison for many years. The baron took him on when he was still a squire."

"Does he possess any Welsh blood?" Royce asked, taking up a position beside the king, He studied Simon closely. The man didn't appear intimidated, though worry lined his brow.

"Not that I am aware. His father is a silver merchant, wealthy enough to foster Jervais out."

"Do you know his family?"

Simon shook his head. "I have never met them. He is from near York."

Edward stroked his beard, his gaze contemplative.

"What do you suppose he might have been doing sneaking around last night?"

Simon shrugged. "I don't know, but I plan to find out."

Royce nodded and turned to Burke. "Keep a close watch on Jervais, but allow Simon to attempt to uncover the man's true loyalties."

This would be another test of Simon's loyalty. Part of him hoped the bastard son would prove true to England, for he worried about his wife's reaction should her brother turn out to be a traitor.

"Aye."

Burke nodded his agreement, but the hostility in his eyes confused Royce. He watched his captain closely, wondering at the anger he seemed to direct at Simon. Had the two men argued? If so, surely Royce would know. Why did Burke appear to despise Simon?

"We depart in the morn for Shrewsbury," said Edward. "Panther, you'll need to come with us."

"Sire, with respect, I feel 'tis a bad idea to leave Lyndon with the rebels still at large."

"Leave Burke in your stead. And most of your men."

Royce didn't like it, but didn't dare refuse the king's orders. "Very well, I will advise my wife."

Edward shook his head. "Tell her she must join us."

Royce hadn't expected to bring Gillian, as he would be spending most of the time in Shrewsbury closeted with the king and other lords.

"But I thought —"

"She's been claimed a traitor by two of the rebels. She must witness the execution to lay any further rumors to rest."

Royce understood. She must show her support for the king in public. He nodded. "Very well, Sire, if you think that will work."

Edward held up a hand. "We no longer believe her to be a traitor but sometimes even my word is not enough."

Royce grinned at the king's grumbling. "She will likely not bc happy."

"Well, she's married to you now; surely you planned to move her to Montchester."

"We've never discussed it at length. She's never been to court. This I know."

"My wife will see to Lady Gillian. She's looking forward to it."

Royce wondered if Gillian would as well. While she got on well with the queen, what she would deal with at court was a very different matter. He worried about what lay ahead.

Edward turned once more to Simon. "Uncover what you can from Jervais and work with Burke to determine if he conspires against us. When the Panther returns, he will decide the best way to use what you've learned."

"Yes, Your Majesty."

Simon bowed and turned to leave, Burke on his heels. Once they were alone, Royce turned to the king.

"I worry the traitor will announce I am no longer here and they will think Lyndon is unprotected."

"If Jervais is the spy, he'll know just how protected the manor is with your men in residence."

Royce nodded, knowing to argue further would not change Edward's mind.

"You don't like my decision, Panther?"

"Nay, Sire, 'tis only that I worry for my wife. She's never been away from Lyndon."

"And still she's as fierce as any knight in either of our armies. I suspect your wife will do very well with the court." Edward chuckled. "You have a bruise already on your chin."

Royce scowled and rubbed the spot where Gillian's fist had landed. He knew well his wife's capabilities. Still, a few particular nobles came to mind and he scowled.

"Are you truly that worried for her?"

Royce said nothing. Edward laughed.

"I suspect I know what troubles you. Never fear, should any of your former... paramours pester your wife, I suspect she will reduce them to shreds."

Royce gave a curt nod, conceding the point. "Aye. I had best go tell her."

"Away with you."

Royce turned to the door, Edward's laughter echoing around him. While he wanted to see Gillian right away, he needed to speak with his captain first. He found him in the great hall, deep in conversation with Simon.

He strode over to the two men. "Simon, go about your business. Let none suspect you. Burke, I would speak with you now."

He motioned Burke to join him by the hearth. He pointed to a chair, then seated himself in the other.

"I am counting on you to keep Lyndon safe while I am gone."

"Of course, Royce. I will defend the manor with my life. But is it wise to leave the brother unattended?"

"Edward and I are reasonably sure he isn't the threat, though some doubt remains. Work with him, but if you learn anything suspicious, send me a message."

"I will. Is there anything else?"

Royce nodded. "I've already discussed this with Edward, and will do so again in Shrewsbury. But I want you to know that there is a real possibility you will be given Apshire to rebuild."

Burke said nothing for several moments, surprise widening his eyes. "Why?"

"You've served me, and the king, well these past years, despite what happened under the old king. Edward bears you no malice, and you are deserving of the title. It's merely a barony, and will need rebuilding, but you know the land better than even I do. And it will reassure me to know I have allies in this area when I am at Montchester."

"I don't know what... thank you."

"I expect Edward to make the declaration after Parliament ends."

Burke grinned. "Me, a baron?"

"As you always should have been. I am glad we can restore your position."

"My thanks, Royce. 'Tis your doing in taking me on as your captain. I owe you much."

"Never forget that."

Royce laughed, his captain joining in.

# chapter fifteen

Gillian returned to her chamber, relieved that the mess she'd made had been cleaned up. After being with the queen and her ladies for the last hours, she was exhausted. She stretched out on the bed. She would rest for just a few moments.

The feel of hands sliding up her legs drew her from slumber. Still groggy, she forced heavy lidded eyes open. Royce leaned over her, her skirts around her waist and his hands seeking her sex. Heat rushed through her at the wicked smile he gave her.

"You were sleeping so soundly, I almost couldn't wake you," he said, his fingers moving ever closer to her pussy.

She should protest, especially after the way he'd treated her the last several days. But as always, the fire he stoked consumed any rational thought. At the first touch of his warm hand on her sex, she moaned, her hips tipping up to give him better access.

"I feared you wouldn't wake before we leave in the morn."

His seeking fingers stroked and caressed, and her sex dripped with excitement. Somehow, his words filtered through the haze. Awareness came slowly, but the fog of lust finally broke away.

"You are leaving?"

He said nothing, slipping two fingers inside her, stroking her until she near forgot what he said. How she held onto the barest thread of her wits, she'd never know.

"Royce, please tell me. Why are you leaving?"

He continued his sensual assault as he responded.

"Edward has called a Parliament in Shrewsbury, where we will hold the trial. You will come with us. We should return within a fortnight."

She had no chance to question him further, for he

leaned down and took her mouth in a devouring kiss. His tongue was like hot velvet, and she moaned, wrapping her arms around his neck. He continued to torment her sex, until the lust threatened to once more consume her. She drew away, gasping for air. He ran a finger along her cheek, his other hand still teasing her sex.

"Please, my lord, I need..."

"Yes, you do, but you're not going to get it yet."

He withdrew his hand and she whined in protest. She tried to pull him back to her, but he resisted her efforts.

"I would make this night last, to hold me through the coming days. I suspect we'll have little time together."

Her heart raced with excitement, her thoughts awhirl with ideas of what wicked games he might play with her now.

"Why must I come with you?"

"Since you were publicly named as traitor, Edward believes your presence will put the last of those rumors to rest. Simon will remain here, with Burke, to defend Lyndon"

She gaped at him. "So you believe us now?"

He nodded. "I believed you several days ago."

"You... what do you...? I don't understand."

He grunted and sat up, pulling her against him. She pushed away, wanting to see his face as he spoke. There was a hint of regret in his tawny eyes.

"Please explain why you continued to keep me locked up when you knew I was innocent."

Another grunt.

"Edward and I... we believed Simon was the traitor. Keeping you under public suspicion was a way of trying to make him reveal himself."

She shook her head, anger rising to take the place of her passion. She pushed him away.

"You are a fool."

"I had to be sure."

"Because of that there are others who believe me in league with the rebels."

He nodded. "Aye, which is why your presence at the execution is required."

"Execution?"

"Edward will assuredly condemn Dafydd to death for high treason."

She thought on his words and realized she had no choice. The king demanded she be there. She met her husband's gaze.

"And what finally made you realize you were wrong?"

"The queen and her ladies have a talent for uncovering secrets. And sharing them. 'Twould seem Lady Madelaine was your brother's reason for his suspicious behavior."

"I know that!" She stood and began to pace, evading his attempts to draw her back to him.

"Gillian, I would do it again."

She whirled to face him. "I know that too. You are the most mule-headed man I have ever encountered. I'd expected you to be smarter though."

His eyebrows slashed down and he stood.

"Even though I declared you innocent, I will not tolerate your disrespect."

She folded her arms and lifted her chin. "And what of your disrespect for me?"

"What do you mean?"

She shook her head. "You treat me like a criminal! Locking me away with no good reason. If you believed me innocent of the claims of treason, you could have told me. I would have helped you and the king. I still can. And I will."

"Aye, you will. By standing at my side during the trial and execution."

"Are you sure Lyndon will be safe?"

"Burke and your brother will work together to ensure Lyndon is secure. And they will investigate the other possible traitor. Burke is more than capable."

She hesitated, unsure whether to tell Royce about her discomfort with his captain. She had no wish to anger him again, but the recollection of the way Burke had leered at her remained clear and fresh in her thoughts.

"Royce, I... I don't know how to tell you –"

"Tell me what?"

She took a deep breath. "I don't like Burke."

The confusion in his gaze would have been laughable under any other circumstance.

"Why not? He is my loyal captain and as you are my wife, he is sworn to protect you and Lyndon."

She shook her head. "I don't like the way he... looks at me."

There, she'd said it. She held his stare, her anger rising anew when he threw his head back and laughed.

"Why are you laughing?"

"Ah, Wildcat, you are innocent in so many ways."

He walked over and drew her near. His hands along her back gave comfort as well as spurring her banked desire. If only her husband would always be so gentle with her. At the thought, she almost laughed. His harsh treatment of her excited her, more than she wanted to admit.

"I am no longer a maiden, my lord."

"'Tis not what I meant. You are used to Lyndon's men, who show you nothing but respect and would never dream of besmirching your reputation."

"Again, you make no sense."

"You are quite comely, Gillian."

He tilted her chin up. His compliment suffused her with warmth and the desire in his eyes turned the warmth into flames. Her sex slickened and swelled, anxious for him to fulfill the unspoken promise.

"Do you think so?"

He nodded, a hint of a smile twitching at the corners of his mouth. "And likely Burke does as well. But he will never harm you in any way."

She thought on his words, still holding his gaze. Before any response formed, he covered her mouth in a deep kiss, one that claimed and branded her as his. Her fingers curled into his tunic, his tongue sending the heat within to searing heights.

He drew away, a finger tracing the path his mouth had just taken across her lips.

"Turn around."

She obeyed, the excitement bubbling ever more ferociously as he undid the laces of her gown and slid it from her shoulders. She remained still as he removed her chemise and stockings, until she finally stood naked. He turned her to face him once more.

The fire in his eyes seemed to burn, his gaze moving over her hungrily. She lifted her chin, the delight in knowing he found her pretty giving her pride and confidence.

"Lay down."

Again, she obediently followed his instruction, climbing up on the bed. When she turned to face him she stiffened. Held taught between his hands was another sash. Despite her confusion, her body heated at the knowledge of what was to come.

"Why must you bind me?" She winced at the tremor in her voice.

"Because, wife, I want to take my time with you, and I fear if you touch me, 'twill not happen."

Her heart raced, her sex swelling. His words sent the fire in her veins to a pitch she thought she'd never survive. When he took her wrists, she didn't resist, allowing him to bind her hands together and fasten them above her head.

Her breath came in pants, eagerness and anxiety mixing together to leave her in a state of anticipation and frustration. She already ached to feel his touch. As he removed his clothes, her gaze locked on his finely formed body, and her pussy grew ever wetter. When he turned to her, his cock hard and erect, she licked her lips.

Royce chuckled. "You've become quite the wanton."

"You've no one to blame but yourself, my lord."

"Aye. I will take full responsibility." He climbed into the bed beside her. "Just as I will when your disobedience is finally curbed."

"If you weren't such a mule-headed oaf –"

"And your lack of respect is atrocious. Whatever shall I do with you?"

"I suspect you'll punish me, whether I truly deserve it or not."

He nodded, casually reaching out to grab her breast. She arched toward him, the feel of his fingers rolling her hardened nipple a delight she never wanted to end. He leaned over and sucked the tip into his mouth, laving her flesh with his tongue. Her eyes fluttered closed as waves of pleasure swept over her. He drew away, the cool air in the chamber leaving her skin pebbled and hard with the loss of the heat of his mouth. She moaned in protest.

The sting of his hand against her breast startled her. Her eyes snapped open, meeting his curious gaze. The shock of the blow faded, replaced by a warmth seeping into her breast. She sucked in a sharp breath.

Royce repeated the motion, and again, the sudden spark of pain quickly dwindled, replaced by the ever-intensifying fire. He soothed her with soft caresses, which seemed to spread the pleasure deeper into her body. She wanted to tell him what she felt, but another slap to her other breast halted her words. The conflicting sensations of gentle caresses on one side, the sting of the strike on the other, created a tumult that left her gasping for air.

"You find pleasure in the pain."

'Twas not a question, but she nodded anyway. She did enjoy it, and she couldn't hide it. When he grinned, the delight in his eyes bloomed, warming her anew.

"Are you sure you've never been to court?"

She shook her head, her voice still elusive.

"I think this marriage will suit us both. At least when we are alone. I suspect you will attempt to undermine me everywhere else."

Though she knew he teased, annoyance still sparked at the condescension in his tone. "Mayhap if you listened to me, you'd see there are times I am knowledgeable and right." "Mayhap. But right now, there is only one thing I want to hear from you."

His meaning became clear when he once more lowered his head, sucking her flesh between his lips. Gillian bit her lip to hold back a cry, the notion of defying his wish adding to her excitement. He chuckled against her skin and she knew he understood.

She grinned herself, almost letting loose a delighted moan when he scraped his teeth against the hardened tip. She clenched her jaw, her fingers curling into fists to resist the urge to hurry him. He would work hard to achieve his desired result she determined, even as the combination of his mouth and hands soon had her writhing beneath him.

He drew away and the sight of his heaving chest attested to the desire that gripped him as well. She gave him a sly smile and spread her legs in invitation.

He laughed aloud. "Wildcat, you surprise me at every turn."

With those words, he covered her with his body, easing himself to his elbows. His cock rested against her pussy, but he made no move to enter her. She lifted her hips, still silent, holding his gaze.

He brushed the hair from her face and shook his head. "Nay, Wildcat, you will sing for me before I give you what you want. If you insist on this game, be warned, I will show no mercy."

Her breath caught in her throat. She pressed her lips into a smile. 'Twould be fun to see which of them broke first.

*** 

The seductive smile curving Gillian's lips threatened to make Royce come without even being inside her. He could enter her with one move, but he would forego his own pleasure just to torment her. His feisty wife would not win this battle of wills. He wanted to hear her beg before he allowed her release. He wanted to impress himself in her memory for the long days ahead. He forced thoughts of their departure aside, not wanting anything to dim his enjoyment of his wife's charms this eve.

He took his time stroking along her sides, her belly and

her arms, the feel of her heated skin a torment and a delight to his senses. He followed the path of his hands with his mouth, kissing and licking until she moaned in pleasure. He tempered that with sharp nips of his teeth, drawing a surprised squeal and the most charming shudder.

Finally, he cupped her breasts in his hands, gently rolling the hardened tips between his fingers. A violent quivering shook her from head to foot, her head thrashing against the pillow. He lowered his head and sucked one rosy tip into his mouth. She cried out, arching against him. Each tremble of her body echoed into his own, making his cock almost painfully hard. He bit down lightly on her breast. The wail that echoed around him shivered along his spine. He lifted his head to study his wife.

In the firelight, her face glowed, her eyes darkened to a deep violet. She licked her lips, taunting him with a wink.

"Wife, you risk much."

"Aye. But I think you like it."

"Hellion." Briefly, he dipped his fingers into her sex, surprised to find her so wet. Whatever she'd been about to say got lost on a strangled moan, her hips rising to meet his hand. He pulled away, grinning at her whine of protest.

"Not yet wife. You must beg me properly for your pleasure tonight. And even then, I may not be persuaded."

"You are evil!"

"But I think you like it."

She scowled at his echo of her earlier words. Lifting her chin, she looked away. Her dare enflamed him. She would beg ere long.

He resumed his casual exploration of the body he'd come to know so well. He knew that if he skimmed his fingers just above her hip, she'd quiver and moan, and if he stroked the underside of her breast, her cries took on a higher pitch. Up around her neck and shoulders set off a multitude of tremors, while caressing her inner thighs made her tense in anticipation. He alternated between light teasing touches and harsher strokes, landing a few more slaps to her breasts and savoring the way the pale skin pinkened.

Still, except for a few moans and gasps, she remained stubbornly silent. Smiling, he moved lower along her body, settling between her legs. He reached under to cup her arse, using his elbows to spread her thighs. He glanced into her flushed face, surprised to find her watching him steadily. Almost daring him. He gave her a smirk and lifted her pussy to his mouth.

A keening wail escaped her at the first stroke of his tongue. He continued, savoring her musky and decadent taste, finding her clit and sucking it between his lips. She writhed beneath him, trying to press closer. Her legs trembled wildly around him, warning she fast approached her climax.

He drew away, grinning at her groan of frustration.

"You will kill me, my lord, if you continue this game."

He shook his head. "Nay. But if you wish your pleasure, you know what you must do." "You are cruel to tease me this way."

"If 'tis cruel, then 'tis your own doing. You can end your desperation very easily."

She pressed her lips together.

"Stubborn wench."

He resumed his leisurely tasting of her sex, wondering if mayhap he tortured himself with this game. His cock remained achingly hard, and he grew near as desperate as his wife. He wanted to bury himself in her hot, wet depths. His head nearly spun with need. Yet his need to hear her begging overcame his desire, and he foraged on, again swiping his tongue along her clit.

He stopped again and this time, she gave a soft sob. Soon. He would hear what he longed for soon.

After giving Gillian a few moments to calm herself, he began again. He doubted he would ever tire of toying with his wife this way. Her sex had grown so hot, he feared he might actually scorch his tongue. 'Twould be worth the pain, he mused, wondering how he had become so enamored of teasing her this way. Mayhap 'twas because he knew the glow in her eyes after she came would warm him through the difficult days ahead. He devoured her pussy like a man starved for food.

When he stopped this time, she cried out in vexation. He watched her closely, relishing the rise and fall of her breasts that came with each ragged breath. Her violet eyes clouded with lust, her lips swollen from where she'd bitten them, mayhap in her attempt to remain silent. He ran a finger along her folds, and she gasped.

"Please, my lord, take pity on me. Please."

He held back his triumphant grin. He held her stare for a few more moments, watching the desperation climb.

"Since you asked so nicely, wife." He lowered his head, finding her clit and sucking it between his lips. She gave a joyous cry as he lashed her with his tongue, still sucking. As an added torment, he drove two fingers into her, pumping her as he continued to suck on her clit.

A ferocious quiver shook her, a hoarse cry ringing out through the chamber. Her body bucked beneath him, so violently, he almost lost his hold. Wave after wave passed over her body, his name torn from her lips in a rough shout. His heart raced, his cock aching, knowing relief would soon follow. He continued to suck, driving her release on for what seemed hours.

Finally, she quieted, and he drew away. He slid up, covering her with his body. He remained motionless for a few moments, studying her. Her heavy-lidded eyes betrayed her satisfaction, the small smile curving her lips telling him he'd pleased her well.

"You see? All you had to do was ask."

"I'd strike you down if I could." Her voice, still rough with ecstasy, shivered along his spine.

"I'm sure you would. But now 'tis my turn."

To his great delight, his wife spread her legs in invitation. He smiled again, reaching down to stroke his steel-hard cock.

"Hurry! Take me now!"

He obliged her, entering with one swift stroke. They

groaned in unison, and he remained motionless, savoring her hot muscles clamping around him. He could come without any effort at all, but he wanted to delight in this, make it last. It could be some time before he could enjoy her again, and he didn't want to rush a moment of this night.

But all too soon, the urge to move, to stroke himself along her slick flesh, overcame him. Intending to move slowly, he soon lost all restraint. Gillian's legs came around him, holding him near and she lifted her hips to meet his strokes.

"Yes, Royce, yes! Fuck me!"

His wanton wife surprised him again and he could no longer hold himself back. He increased his rhythm, pounding harder into her and knowing she felt the same exquisite pleasure as he when she chanted his name on each thrust.

His balls tightened, and though he tried, he lost the battle to hold out, erupting with a violent surge that rocked them both hard against the bed. He reached up and tugged the bonds free. She wrapped herself around him, holding on tight as he finally collapsed against her, weak with pleasure.

# chapter sixteen

Royce woke her before dawn despite her resistance to his attempts to draw her from slumber. Her body needed more sleep, and she longed to curl under the blankets a little longer. 'Twas not to be. He drew back the covers and landed a hard swat to her bare arse. Shocked into wakefulness, she squealed and rolled away.

"Rise, wife. We depart for Shrewsbury."

"Very well. Can you send for my maid?"

He nodded and tugged on his hose. The moment the door closed behind him, a powerful wave of nausea swept over her. Fearing the worst, she ran to the washbasin, retching violently over it. When the sickness passed, she fell into the chair, weak, her limbs shaky, and more tired than before. After a few moments to steady herself, she stood, just as Edith entered to help her prepare.

When she joined her husband in the hall, she had recovered considerably. Several trunks were piled near the door. She strode to her husband's side.

"You will travel with the queen and her ladies. The weather is fair, so we should arrive before nightfall."

"And you?"

"I ride beside the king. There is much to plan and discuss." He bent down and placed a chaste kiss on her cheek, near her ear. "But I would rather you rode with me, so I might enjoy the delights of your body to liven the journey."

Heat flooded her face and a shiver of delight skittered along her spine. Her sex ached already for him. When he drew away, he gave her a wink and a half-smile.

"Away with you, say your goodbyes and join the queen in the bailey."

Another hard swat landed on her arse and she glared at him, even as the sting, muted by her dress, shook through her, sending those familiar tendrils of heat through her veins. He would pay for teasing her this way.

She made her way out to the bailey. Hearing her name, she turned, shielding her eyes against the sun. Simon made his way through the people.

She hurried to him, pulling him close for a hug. "I will miss you."

"You'll be gone a fortnight at most. All will be well."

"Simon, do me one favor."

Her brother nodded. "Anything."

"Watch Burke as closely as you watch Jervais. I have doubts about him."

Simon looked around the people in the bailey. He stilled, apparently spotting the subject of their discussion.

"I must agree, Gilly. Something about the man concerns me as well, but your husband and the king trust him."

"Well, I don't. And Simon?"

"What is it?"

"Guard your own back. 'Tis only a matter of time before all know the truth and there are those who might perceive you as a threat."

"Why do you say this?"

"Call it instinct. And sisterly worry."

He grinned. "All will be well, you'll see. Now go on, I will see you soon enough."

She turned to see her husband waiting. She leaned up to kiss Simon's cheek and made her way to Royce, who promptly guided her to the queen's litter. Eleanor smiled warmly as Gillian gave a curtsy.

"Have you ever been to Shrewsbury, Lady Gillian?"

"No, Your Highness."

"Well, we must tell you all we can during the journey. Thankfully, 'tis not a very long one. Come."

Eleanor climbed the steps into the large and ornate carriage. Gillian gave Royce one last look and followed. She sat across from the queen, and beside Lady Madelaine. Her brother's betrothed. The other ladies must be in the other carriages behind this one. All too soon, the carriage jerked. They were off.

\*\*\*

"Panther, are you listening?"

Edward's angry voice jolted him from his thoughts. "I'm sorry, Sire."

"Is there trouble again with your wife? I thought you'd finally stopped fighting her."

"Aye. I have. But I still possess concerns."

"She will get along fine with the nobility."

Royce mostly agreed, but he knew of at least one person who might cause trouble. Not to mention the countless others who took pleasure in spreading malicious lies for whatever gain it brought them. The king chuckled at his worry.

"Your wife is near as fierce as any of your men. And more than capable than some."

Royce gave a curt nod, conceding the point. Still, he'd learned that despite her bravery and loyalty, and her stubborn insistence on defying him at every turn, she possessed a tender heart. One that could easily be shredded when subjected to the conspiracies and intrigue lurking in every corner. Many plotted against the king and his lords. Those loyal to the king plotted against each other. And the women...

"Anyone who dares so much as a whisper of an insult to your wife will find themselves the recipients of her hellfire. Or at the tip of your sword."

Royce chose not to respond, earning another laugh from Edward.

"You've been smitten with your wife since the day you arrived."

Despite himself, Royce leveled a fierce glare on the king. "I am not smitten!"

"You forget, my queen has ways of uncovering gossip. Everywhere."

Royce averted his gaze from Edward's knowing one. His mood grew darker as the king continued to find amusement in the situation.

"The villeins of Lyndon say the moment you laid eyes on your wife, you were besotted. To the point you threatened to put out the eyes of any of your men who looked at her with kindness!"

Despite his annoyance, Royce laughed at the absurd gossip. "Rumors are based on false interpretation and easily proven such."

Edward's expression sobered. "Aye. Still, 'tis obvious you care for Lady Gillian. As she does for you."

The proud and pleasing warmth at those words left Royce momentarily startled. He quickly re-gathered his thoughts. "I will concede we've reached an accord that works well for us."

Edward chuckled. "I'm sure it does. Make sure it works for all, as well."

The unspoken words reminded Royce doubts still hovered over his wife. He vowed to prove those doubts wrong. The king's next words drew him from the dire thoughts.

"Have you told Burke of your intentions for Apshire?"

He nodded. "Having him remain at Lyndon is a test of his abilities. I think you'll find he's quite capable of running a manor such as Apshire. Once it is rebuilt, of course."

"Of course. I also think he is a good choice. I could use more forces along the border as well, and he's proven his loyalty."

Royce's thoughts turned to Gillian's concerns. A brief unease sparked, but he forced it back. His wife did not know Burke as he did. She worried for naught.

"After the trial, I suspect you'll have no more trouble with traitors." Royce knew the outcome had already been decided but for the formality. Such a sentence usually led to rebels laying down their arms and surrendering their fight.

"Mayhap. Godwin still eludes us. I have a hunch he'll be in the crowds at Shrewsbury. 'Tis why I've not announced which day the trial will start. I won't until the very morning."

"A wise decision. We must position the men carefully. Once the pronouncement is made, the crowds will be in a frenzy."

The king nodded his agreement. "We'll be ready and we'll catch him this time, I have no doubt."

Royce had several, though he didn't dare voice them.

# chapteg seventeen

The king's train crossed the bridge into Shrewsbury with much fanfare. Royce, riding beside Edward, usually enjoyed the cheering crowds, but this time, he only wanted the dreaded task that lay ahead over and finished. Everyone knew Dafydd awaited trial, and most assumed the outcome. The question everyone seemed to be shouting was when would the trial occur?

Royce turned to the king. "Would be best to get the Parliament over with quickly."

Edward shook his head. "Let the bastard wait. I assure you, after this, no one will dare rise up against me again."

Royce nodded and fell silent. Edward's gruesome plan for Dafydd was one of the times he disagreed with his friend. 'Twould make matters much simpler if Edward was not king, but there it was. If he dared mention he thought the execution distasteful, he could very well incur Edward's erratic wrath himself. He thought of Gillian and her anxiousness to be back at Lyndon. Once she learned of Dafydd's sentence, he worried she'd speak out against Edward's choice.

"Come, we will rest and take a meal before retiring. I will not make any pronouncements until morning." Edward reined in his mount and slid from the saddle before the steps to the castle. He looked up to the open doors. Burnell, having ridden ahead, descended until he stood before Edward.

"How was your journey?" the chancellor asked.

"Fair enough. Who has arrived?"

Royce half-listened to the list of barons and earls who had come to attend Parliament and the trial. He perused the bustling city, knowing Edward had likely been right. Once these people witnessed the Welsh prince's execution, their thirst for blood would fade.

Royce handed over Viking's reins to the groomsman and walked toward the queen's litter. The crowd was much larger than he'd anticipated. He paused as the door to the carriage swung open and Eleanor appeared. She hesitated a few moments, ever aware of those who watched. Two guards assisted her on her descent. Royce found himself looking beyond for his wife, the king's mocking words of earlier taunting him anew.

Yet he couldn't help watching for her, needing to know she was as secure as the queen. One by one, the queen's ladies in waiting descended the litter, the three traveling with her soon taking up positions around her.

Finally, the last to depart, Gillian stepped from the carriage.

He found himself noting similarities between his wife and the queen. The regal way she carried herself, with confidence, even though he knew she must be terrified, raised his respect for her even more.

"Panther! Welcome back!"

Royce turned. A tall blonde woman wove through the mob. He had not seen Lady Joan FitzOsborne in some time. He eyed her warily. She was as lovely as he remembered, but suddenly, he could not think of why he had ever been drawn to her. Now, all he wanted was a dark-haired violet-eyed spitfire to warm his bed. Lady Joan seemed a very pale comparison. Still, the woman could be trouble.

"How I have missed you! It has been almost a full year since we have last seen each other." Royce nodded. "Aye, and much has changed since then. I understand you are soon to be betrothed."

Lady Joan's face saddened. "Aye. To the king's nephew."

"You are not happy with the match?"

Royce glanced out over the crowd. Where had Gillian disappeared to? He looked down at Lady Joan once again. She smiled prettily he supposed, but he found her to be fake as the jewels around her neck.

"Perhaps you will sit with me at supper this eve." She

offered a smile that gave her the appearance of a snake.

Royce shook his head. "Nay, my lady. I am recently wed, as I'm sure you know. And now, I must find my wife."

Royce disengaged his arm from hers and turned, once more searching the crowd. Where had Gillian gone? There, walking behind the queen while Eleanor greeted her subjects. Royce strode to her, shoving aside anyone in his path. He didn't care who he insulted, the need to get to her, and away from Lady Joan, intensified with each moment. Just as he reached her, she was pulled away. Royce seethed to see Hugo deLacey, a baron from the south, draw her to him. When Gillian tried to unsuccessfully wrench free, Royce's vision hazed red.

He had just reached the pair when Gillian's fist connected with deLacey's jaw. Clearly stunned, the man released her, staggering back.

"You stupid oaf! How dare you!"

The blow and her sharp rebuke eased Royce's fury and he grinned. His Wildcat could easily subdue a weakling like deLacey. He moved closer, concealing his humor and forcing a scowl.

"What do you with my wife, deLacey?" he demanded.

Gillian spun about, her eyes wide and oddly fearful. He gave her a reassuring smile.

"Wildcat, you are surely a match for many of the men here!"

The relief and pleasure lighting her eyes sparked a responding jolt within him. He turned back to deLacey, his fury returning as he stared at the man who dared put hands on his wife. He took two steps toward the shorter man, whose thin frame trembled like a sapling in a strong wind.

"I didn't know she was your wife!"

Fists clenching and unclenching, Royce inhaled sharply. He had no time to waste on this foolish excuse for a man.

"Tread carefully, deLacey, lest you find yourself dangling from the end of a sword."

He turned to his wife and grabbed her wrist, pushing

his way through the crowd once again.

\*\*\*

"Come, Gillian."

Once again, she was pulled along by her husband, who stopped not once when he entered the castle. Gillian barely had time to look around the richly decorated hall before she was hauled up the stairs. Servants were everywhere, coming in and out of various chambers. Several eyed them curiously as they passed, though all did bow in deference to her husband's position.

Royce finally stopped outside an open doorway. Two maids inside scurried out before he entered, pulling Gillian along with him. He released his grip on her arm once the door closed. She'd likely bear bruises on the morrow. Did the man not know his own strength?

The chamber was large, and before the hearth a large tub waited, filled with steaming water. How she longed to get in and soak away the aches from her journey, yet the urge to lay across the large and inviting bed was also strong. The choice between sleep or bath was a difficult one. She would wait to see what her husband decided first.

A knock interrupted her thoughts. She opened the door. Royce's squire, Duncan, stood outside, his eyes wide as he shifted nervously from foot to foot.

"I am here to help my lord." The boy lowered his eyes and stepped into the room. Royce motioned him over and sat upon the stool. In minutes, her husband's armor had been shed. All the while, his scrutiny of her remained intense. When Duncan reached for Royce's tunic, her husband stilled the boy's actions.

"That is enough. See to my armor."

Duncan nodded and gathered up the heavy mail. Staggering under the weight, he left the room. Once more, Gillian was alone with her husband. And his anger.

"My lord, I would..."

"Stay away from de Lacey." He did not look at her while he spoke. Instead, he began to strip his clothes away, leaving them in a pile on the floor. He stepped into the tub while she gaped at him. Did he think she had gone with de Lacey apurpose?

"Do you accuse me? I saw the woman you flirted with. And all I did was free myself of that odious man's grip."

"Are you jealous, Wildcat?"

Was that a pleased smile she glimpsed before he turned away? Damn him, she would not stand for this.

"Jealous? Nay. Yet you accuse me of seeking out another when you do exactly that!"

"I did not seek her out. She is a friend, betrothed to the king's nephew. I knew her ere I wed you. You did not know de Lacey. Did you?"

"Of course not. How could you think I would go willingly with that simpering fool?"

"Many of the court ladies speak highly of his talents. Few are imperious to them. I will not have my wife's name bandied about in castle gossip."

"Who is this man you despise so much?" she asked.

"None of your concern. He is sneaky and greedy and would take all I have were I to give him a chance. He seeks to unman me at every opportunity. Seducing my wife would ensure my humiliation."

Gillian's anger prevented her from finding humor at his laughable notion.

"Do you think so little of me, my lord?"

"Nay, Gillian. You are just a woman, and cannot understand what a man like him will do to gain his goal. He is ruthless. Keep yourself away from him. Come, wife, and wash me."

Gillian went to stand behind him. Her husband's low opinion stung. That he could so casually order her about after insulting her rankled. Her determination to make him understand he wrongly directed his anger at her was matched only by her desire to let the fool think what he wanted.

Spotting the bucket of unheated water beside the tub, she knew just how to cool her temper. Spurred on by the mischievous need to show him how she hated his insulting assumptions of her, she picked up the bucket. Royce had leaned his head back. His eyes were closed and he was oblivious to her movements. She tipped the bucket, spilling the cold water on his head.

His roar of outrage gave her immense pleasure. He jumped to his feet, sputtering. She backed away. His furious glare scorched her, yet she struggled to contain her laughter. She turned and ran for the door, intending to leave him alone with his insufferable arrogance. She had just grasped the handle when his arm snaked around her waist, hauling her off her feet and against his wet chest. God's blood, if she had only been faster!

"You try my patience endlessly."

His low, even voice made her tremble with conflicting emotions. The urge to laugh remained strong, but fiery heat tempered the humor. No matter how wonderful his mouth felt pressed against her ear, she struggled to hold onto both her anger and humor. Yet, despite his callous treatment, her traitorous body still responded to his every word or touch.

"Nothing else seems to cool your foolish anger! You still insult me at every turn! I won't stand for it anymore. Do you truly think I would cuckold you with that...that awful man?"

She shuddered at the very idea and twisted in his grasp, in an effort to face him. He squeezed her tighter and she stilled.

Huffing a harsh breath, she said, "The man was vile and assaulted me with no reason. I did nothing wrong."

"True." His grip on her waist eased. "You defended yourself well."

"So you worried for me?" She hadn't realized just how desperately she wanted that assurance. Still, Royce's heavy-handed tactics had grown tiresome. Despite his avowals of trust, he still possessed doubt about her loyalty. Yet, when he set her down, turning her, his intense scrutiny revealed his concern.

"Aye, Gillian, I worried for you."

Her heart felt lighter. These rare moments when he showed her affection gave her hope. When he wasn't acting an arrogant beast, he was a husband she was glad to have. 'Twas a shame the beast ruled his actions more than his heart. She lifted her chin.

"Yet, you still distrust me."

He shook his head. "You don't understand the importance of appearance."

"No, I don't. You are telling me you must act like you think I'm a traitor for other people's benefit? It makes no sense to me, and to be honest, I think it utterly stupid!"

To her surprise, he laughed, throwing his head back. She gaped at him, wondering how he possibly found humor in this situation. When he hugged her tight, her head spun faster than ever.

"You are a Wildcat, a fitting mate for the Panther," he said when his laughter faded. "More people should follow your way of thinking."

So many emotions raged through her, but surprise and happiness overwhelmed the rest. He actually sounded proud of her. The small flame of hope grew brighter.

He sobered, gripping her chin and forcing her to look at him. "Do not forget that as my wife, you are a target for my enemies. Never give anyone an opportunity to ..."

"Yes, I understand." She met his stare evenly.

"Do you truly?"

"More than you will ever know."

His eyes narrowed before he gave a curt nod. "Good. Now, I believe you have a task to see to?"

He arched an eyebrow and released her, returning to the tub. She shook her head, even though her blood heated at the thought of touching him again.

# chapter eighteen

The festive sounds of the musicians did little to ease Gillian's sour mood. Exhaustion, brought on by the journey, followed by her husband's intense and passionate lovemaking, served to make her long for her bed. Instead, she sat amidst the king's welcome feast, while Royce all but ignored her while discussing strategy with Edward.

She glanced around the room. Wine and ale flowed freely, with many of the guests sotted. Was this what court life was like? She'd seen many glances cast her way, as curious people wanted to see the Panther's bride. She wished she'd been seated at one of the lower tables; she might not feel like one of the roasted pigs on display in the center of the hall.

Continuing her study, her cheeks heated. In almost every corner, a couple appeared entwined together in intimacy, each pair more wicked than the last. Across the hall, a gentleman even went so far as to lift a lady's skirts, while she laughed and slapped his hands away. This wild chaos was nothing like the feasts at Lyndon.

"So this is the Panther's bride."

Gillian looked up into the disdainful blue gaze of the woman she had seen with Royce earlier. Anger stole her breath momentarily, as the woman perused her clothing, her expression mocking. Gillian's jaw tightened. She lifted her chin.

"Aye, I am Countess of Montchester. And you?" She kept her voice even. She would show no timidity in front of this woman who reminded her of a rabid dog, her eyes shining with menace.

"This is Lady Joan FitzOsborn." Royce's words drew Gillian's attention. Finally, her husband paid her some notice. Stung it had taken this woman's presence for him to speak to her, she kept her gaze firmly on Lady Joan.

"I understand this is your first time away from your home." Though Lady Joan directed the words to Gillian, her eyes remained focused on Royce. Without looking at her husband, Gillian lifted her hand and placed it upon his on the table. Her ring glittered in the light. She held back a smile as both her husband and Lady Joan turned their attention to her.

"Aye, but with my husband by my side, wherever we are feels like home."

One perfectly arched blonde eyebrow lifted over Lady Joan's eye. Underneath her hand, Royce's trembled and he coughed suddenly. She never pulled her gaze from Lady Joan.

"Aren't you lucky?"

Joan's mocking words inflamed Gillian's simmering anger. Before she could speak, Royce squeezed her fingers.

"Lady Joan, your betrothed beckons." He nodded toward the lower tables. The blonde looked over her shoulder, lips pressed together in a thin line.

"Excuse, me, my lord. Countess." Yet Lady Joan ignored Gillian, focusing only on Royce. "We will speak again, my lord. Soon."

Gillian studied her husband's icy expression and shivered. She'd felt that cold stare on her more than once. Yet, when he turned to her, a different man met her gaze.

His eyes warmed to liquid amber, his mouth curved in a slight smile. Her heart raced to recognize his affection. Forgotten was the haughty Lady Joan, the shameful courtiers. Gillian could only gaze transfixed at her husband, as he stared almost lovingly at her. Despite their tumultuous start, Gillian finally felt her marriage would not be an endless prison of misery.

Royce leaned close, his mouth hovering near her ear. "I have no desire to stay for the entire feast. But I find I am still hungry."

His low voice and insinuating words started a heat that quickly spread through her core. Her fingers trembled in his. Her body already prepared for him, her sex growing slick and hot. She pressed her thighs together in a vain effort to quell the fire.

"There are more courses to be served, and the sweets have not been brought out." Hard as she tried, she couldn't keep the tremor from her voice. His wink told her he noticed.

"I have something much sweeter for you to enjoy."

She licked her lower lip, her breath hitching in her throat. "Mayhap we can leave now."

He threw his head back and roared with laughter. When he calmed, his grin left her heart racing in an erratic rhythm.

"I have indeed created a Wildcat. I will make our excuses to the king."

She found her impatience growing when Edward lured her husband into another discussion of strategy. Another course was served, but she no longer had any appetite for food. Finally Royce turned to her, offering his hand while he stood.

"Come, I would depart now."

Happiness bubbled in her when he slid an arm around her shoulders, holding her close beside him. His fingers toyed with her hair, the gentle touch stirring all sorts of shivery sensations. He guided her toward the stairs and when they passed the lower tables, she caught Lady Joan openly staring. The man beside her angrily forced the woman to look at him. Though Gillian couldn't hear his words, she knew he scolded Lady Joan. She shouldn't be so pleased to see the woman's disappointed humiliation. Had marriage turned her into a bloodthirsty shrew?

The stroke of her husband's hand along her arm chased her thoughts. She looked up to see his warm smile as he guided her up the stairs. 'Twould seem she worried for naught.

\*\*\*

Royce led Gillian into their chamber where Edith tended the fire. He ordered her out, shaking his head at the timid woman as she nearly ran from the room. Gillian's chuckle drew his attention.

"Why does she fear me?"

"You are an intimidating man, my lord." Laughter laced her words.

"You are not intimidated."

"Nay. I see you for what you really are."

He arched an eyebrow. "What would that be?"

"A man who likes people to fear him, though in truth, you are not as terrifying as you think."

He stepped closer, loving the way the firelight illuminated her slender neck when she tilted her head back. He ran a finger along her skin, savoring her shiver.

"There are those who say I am the fiercest knight in Edward's army."

"I'm sure in battle, your nickname holds true. But the Panther I know is as fierce as a kitten."

He grabbed her arms, pulling her against him. "I've shown my ferocity many times, and will again, should it be necessary. And if you dare speak such inanity to anyone else, you will be punished for it."

"Fear not, I have no plans to ruin your reputation. For now."

The sparkle in her eyes stirred him as much as her body against his. She taunted him deliberately and he gave a moment's thanks that his wife enjoyed the darker side of pleasure near as much as he did. Already his cock had hardened to steel, and he wanted to be inside her. Now.

He took her mouth in a devouring kiss, thrusting his tongue deep. He would never tire of her taste. Or her eager response. Her hands pulled at his tunic, and he drew away.

"Calm yourself, Wildcat. I would have this last. And you have not completely agreed to keep my secret, have you?"

Her wicked grin set the blood to boiling in his veins.

"I may need to be convinced."

"Ere long, you will be begging for my mercy."

She stood straight, meeting his gaze brazenly.

"I hope so."

"Remove my clothes."

She arched an eyebrow and for a moment, he thought she meant to refuse. After a brief hesitation, she set about undoing the laces of his overtunic, instructing him to lift his arms so she could pull it off. But he was too tall, and she frowned.

"I cannot reach." She strode to the bed and climbed up, rising to stand. He grinned as she beckoned him with one finger. He moved to stand before her and she was now able to pull the tunic over his head. The shirt underneath came next, leaving his chest bared. She paused then, a wicked smile curving her lips as she stroked his shoulders and chest. Her nails scraped against his nipples and he shivered under the rough caress. He'd taught his wife well, he realized, as her soft hands moved over his skin, leaving trails of fire in their wake. He held her knowing gaze, allowing her the freedom to continue. When her fingers trailed lower, he inhaled sharply, gritting his teeth at the sensation of her untying the laces of his hose. She slowly pushed them away, her gaze lowering to land on his straining cock as it was freed from confinement.

"'Twould seem you are ready for me already, Panther."

He growled in response, grabbing her around the waist and hauling her against him. He drove his tongue deep into her mouth, even as he kicked his hose aside. He lowered her to the bed, his cock settling against her wet and hot pussy, her legs opening to welcome him. Despite the need raging through him, he held back, content to devour her mouth and savor the feel of her damp fire.

She pulled away breathing heavily. "Now, my lord. Please."

He gave her a lazy smile and shook his head, drawing a finger down her neck. "Not yet. I would make this last."

Once more she began her teasing torment with her hands, stroking every part of him she could reach. His head spun with the desire to plunge into her. Somehow he managed to refrain. Instead, he caught her wrists, raising her arms above her head and holding her in place.

"You tempt me beyond my endurance. But I will have control."

She giggled, the lilting sound wafting over him like a soothing melody. He studied her, her skin burnished in the firelight, eyes glowing with lust. The sight almost made him come right there, without even being inside her.

"You will not move." He curled her fingers around the bed rail. "If you let go, you will be punished."

Her chest heaved with a heavy breath, her pink-tipped breasts trembling. He lowered his head to take one hard peak into his mouth. She gave a throaty moan, arching toward him. Using his lips and tongue, he teased her flesh, savoring each quiver as it passed over her. When he moved to the other breast, she sighed his name. He lifted his head, relishing the way her heavy-lidded eyes opened and she gazed on him with desire.

"Remember, don't let go."

\*\*\*

Gillian tightened her grip on the rail, wondering how she possessed the strength to remain as he ordered. She ached to hold him near, to run her hands along his heated flesh. His head lowered again, tormenting her breasts briefly with raspy strokes of his tongue. Delight coursed in her veins, her body singing with delight. His hands and mouth moved along her flesh and she wanted more than the gentle and unhurried caresses. She wanted him to take her hard, to unleash the flaming passion lurking beneath the tender arousal he stirred.

She undulated toward him, trying to convey without words what she wanted, but he seemed not to notice, leisurely exploring her. He knew well which spots spiked her hunger, returning often to tease the curve of her hip, the top of her thigh, the underside of her breast. Her head thrashed, frustration mixed with the need.

"P-please, my lord."

"Patience, Wildcat."

He trailed his fingers along the juncture of her thigh

and she cried out, willing him to her sex. But he determinedly avoided her pussy, content to stroke everywhere but where she wanted him. Need pounded in her head.

"Royce, you will kill me this way!"

The shake of his head against her belly added another layer of torment, his hair brushing across her sensitive skin. One finger slowly slid along her moist folds and she gave a loud sigh of pleasure. Finally!

After several moments of that single finger moving ever so slowly across her aching flesh, she once more ground her teeth in frustration. The sensations he stirred pleased her, but it wasn't enough.

"Please!"

Her rough voice echoed like a roar in the room. He chuckled, but before she could rail at him for teasing her this way, he lowered his head and slid his tongue along her sex. She nearly swooned from the intensity of the lust taking her over. He used his hands to hold her open, exploring deeper with his tongue. Not as satisfying as his cock, but she didn't care. Pleasure thrummed through her and when he caught her hard bud between his lips and sucked hard, she was lost, her body bucking wildly against the tumult exploding her senses. Her vision went red, then white, and then she couldn't see at all, could only let the tempest roar around her. Royce continued to plague her with his mouth, drawing out the waves until she thought she would be reduced to cinders before he finished.

As the waves of delight ebbed, she gasped for air. Sensing his gaze on her, she forced her eyes open. The smug satisfaction in his smile drew a weary laugh. He moved up her body, reaching for her hands.

"You obeyed very well, wife."

Her fingers were stiff and aching from gripping the rail so tightly. She ignored the numbness in her shoulders and wrapped her arms around his neck, finding his mouth with hers. The taste of herself on his lips sent her desire soaring once more, and she opened her legs. The feel of his cock sliding against her flesh, slick with her juices, nearly had her on the edge of release once more.

"Now, Royce. Now!"

He obliged her with one hard stroke, seating himself deeply within her. For several moments, he remained motionless, studying her. He brushed the hair from her face and finally began a slow thrusting that refired the inferno of moments ago.

She met each of his strokes, until he grabbed her hips, holding her still so he could drive harder into her. This was what she wanted, the full measure of his desire, knowing it was for her alone and that she returned it, likely tenfold. She clung to him as if he were the lifeline in a raging sea, until she was exploding once more, tumbled in the wild waves. She cried his name, reveling in the way he answered with a shout of his own, his cock pulsing wildly within her. It was several minutes before they quieted, their harsh breathing making a strange music that rang in the chamber.

The motion of him rolling to his back drew a surprised squeal. He said nothing as he settled her atop him, his softening cock still inside her. She basked in the way he gently stroked her back and snuggled closer. If only they could stay thus forever. Thoughts of the morrow weighed heavily upon her.

"What troubles you?" Royce's question broke the suddenly uneasy silence.

"Nothing."

"You've gone as hard as a plank. Something is bothering you."

She hesitated. "The trial and the ... I... "

He gave a nod. "I understand, but you must be there. I will be beside you, and as we'll be beside the king, it will tell everyone Edward trusts you."

"I know, but... 'Tis brutal to watch another put to death."

He said nothing, leaving her to wonder just what was going to happen in the coming days.

GiaNNa SimoNe

# chapter nineteen

The sun had not yet completely risen when Royce escorted Gillian to the meadow behind the abbey. Throngs of people had already gathered, all eager to watch the execution of the Welsh prince. The scaffold faced the covered dais where most of the court waited.

Parliament had not taken long to convict Dafydd for his crimes. The sentence of death was to be carried out immediately. Gillian prayed this would be quick.

She was glad she'd not broken her fast this morn. When she'd awoken, with a terrible rolling in her stomach, she had refused any food, sipping only some ale to try to settle herself. It had helped for a while, but now, sitting here near the king's seat waiting to watch a man be put to death had started the rolling anew.

The excited murmurs in the crowd grew louder. Edward and Eleanor rode up to the dais amidst the cheers of their subjects. Edward took a stance before his chair and held up his hands to silence the cheers of the people. It took several minutes for the crowd to quiet enough for the king to speak.

"Today is a glorious day for England, for she stands victorious against those who seek to destroy her. The tongue of man can scarcely recount the evil deeds committed by the Welsh against our progenitors, but God has, after the prince had been slain, destined Dafydd as the last survivor of the family of traitors, to be the king's prisoner after he had been captured by men of his own race."

With those words, the crowd once more burst into wild cheers and hollers.

Almost instantly, the crowd parted and several horses rode into view. At the center of the corps, a riderless horse was led. To her horror, Gillian saw the horse pulled a small load, a man, tied by his hands to the horse's harness. Prince Dafydd of Wales.

The horse was held still for several moments. A knight stepped forward and mounted the beast, spurring it to a trot toward the scaffold, dragging Dafydd behind him. Jeers and curses filled the square, and a member of the crowd below threw something at the prince, yelling obscenities so all could hear. Soon, the throng pelted him with rotten food and refuse until the horse stopped at the scaffold steps. The animal, clearly spooked by the chaos, pranced nervously under the hands of the knight.

The executioner stepped forward and raised his hand for silence. The crowd quieted. The horse calmed somewhat as the executioner began to speak.

"Prince Dafydd, in a trial by Parliament, you have been judged guilty for the crimes of murder, for profaning the week of our Lord's passion, and for plotting against the life of our sovereign, His Majesty, King Edward. You will be held as an example to all those who would stand in your place."

The crowd erupted into cheers and shouts of encouragement. Shuddering, Gillian wondered how the crowd would react if they knew of her mixed blood. She wrapped her arms around herself and pushed the thought aside. She glanced at her husband. His face bore no expression as he watched the scene below.

Dafydd was cut loose, hauled to his feet and dragged up the steps to the platform. Despite the dirt and streaks of blood and refuse covering him, he held himself defiantly, watching the crowd. Gillian saw no fear in him as he stood tall, facing his punishment with regal bearing and grace. She could not help admiring his bravery in the face of death. When the time came, she feared she would not meet her own demise so well.

The prisoner turned his gaze toward the dais, his lips curved ever so slightly in a mocking smile and nodded to Edward. Royce's sharp intake of breath at the blatant disrespect in Dafydd's gesture vibrated through her.

Against her side, his hand curled into a fist. Keeping her eyes focused on the prisoner, she reached out and took her husband's hand in hers, loosening his fingers and twining them with her own. He closed his eyes briefly then bestowed a small but concerned smile.

"Are you unwell?"

Startled, she shook her head. "Why?"

His brow furrowed. "You look pale."

"I am tired, my lord."

"When we are finished, you are to return to our chamber to rest. Parliament will meet again and I must attend."

She gave a nod, once more focusing her attention below. The crowd jeered the prisoner, yet the taunts seemed not to dim his spirit. One of the guards yanked on his arm, leading him to the waiting noose. A hanging then. It would be over soon and she could rest, as her husband wished. Then the executioner began to speak, forcing her to focus on what was happening before her.

"For such despicable crimes, you are to be drawn and quartered!"

Gasps and murmurings, shouts and applause, came from the crowd. Such a brutal sentence hadn't been passed in many years. She met Royce's gaze. Had he known of this? Why hadn't he warned her?

She looked past her husband to the king. Edward wore a pleased smile. A shiver passed over her. If he hadn't been convinced of her innocence in the uprising, she feared what could have happened.

She squeezed Royce's hand for support.

*** 

The force of Gillian's grip nearly crushed Royce's fingers. He watched her closely, still displeased at the lack of color in her cheeks. She looked ready to swoon. He motioned to Burnell. The chancellor approached, his face etched with concern. "Panther, is your wife ill?"

"She is unused to such things as this." He absently waved his hand at the crowd. "Perhaps some ale will help settle her."

Burnell nodded and motioned to a nearby attendant. Within moments, he handed Royce a cup. As he held it to his wife's lips, Royce's gaze met hers. Her eyes were bright with unshed tears and her lips trembled slightly as she sipped the ale. *Jesu*, she could wound him so deeply with just a look! How he wished he could take her away from here.

He looked away, sensing Edward's gaze on him. Gillian's hand had resumed its death grip on his. He pulled his fingers free and covered her hand, trying to soothe her with soft caresses.

"Is anything amiss, Panther?" Edward asked.

"Nay, Sire. Gillian is merely tired."

At the king's nod, he turned back to his wife. She sipped the ale slowly. He noted how her gaze moved everywhere within the meadow, except to the scaffold below.

With a deep breath, he focused his attention on the execution. Though he was glad the traitor was getting the justice due him, he disliked Edward's punishment. The death was slow and painful, and difficult to watch.

"My lord, I..."

He covered her mouth with his fingers. "Give none cause to think you bear sympathy for this outlaw. Rumor has already harmed you before."

Her eyes sparked at the reminder. "Thank you for believing they lied. If you hadn't..."

"It's behind us, and now is the perfect time to ensure none ever doubt you again. Difficult as it may be, you must appear to be pleased with the... this."

"It won't be easy."

He shook his head. "Nay. Not for any of us."

The warmth of the autumn sun grew as Dafydd was publicly tortured. Not once did he utter a sound, accepting his punishment in stony silence, not responding to the executioner's or the crowd's taunts and verbal jibes. Throughout it all, Gillian inched slowly closer to Royce until she leaned into him. Her wide eyes and trembling gave away her distress. He wondered if he'd ever be able to pry her fingers from his.

The crowd's yells and murmurings grew quieter as Dafydd was lifted to a cross-shaped table on the gallows, his ankles and wrists bound firmly. He heaved against the ropes binding him, but could not free himself. The final part of the execution was moments away.

As the executioner approached the prisoner, hot poker in hand, Gillian turned her face into his chest. He did not force her to watch, but she turned back once, just as Dafydd gave a scream that curled the hairs on the nape of his neck. Royce heard her moan and looked down at her. Her eyes widened before she sagged limply against him in a faint.

She almost slipped from her chair before he caught her. Someone pressed a cloth doused in vinegar into his hand and he held it under her nose. She stirred and pushed his hand away. Her eyes slowly opened, their violet depths filled with horror.

"Is it over?"

"Almost." He helped her back into the chair. She shook wildly, and he slid his arm around her, holding her near. She buried her face against his shoulder. He held her, stroking her hair softly. Every time Dafydd screamed his agony, she jerked as though she could feel the traitor's pain. Edward glanced over at her from time to time but thankfully said nothing.

"'Tis almost over, Wildcat." Royce murmured the words against her ear. "Soon we'll return to our chamber."

"I don't know if I can wait much longer. I feel ill."

"Don't look anymore."

He cupped her head, shielding her view of Dafydd's final moments. The executioner lifted his axe, the crowd now eerily silent. The only sounds echoing in the meadow were Dafydd's cries of pain. The axe fell. The cries ceased.

The still crowd erupted into wild cheers. But there was still more, as the executioner quartered the prince's body to the mob's excited screams. Madness overtook the throng and many rushed the scaffold, fighting to get at the pieces of the body. Edward apparently had also noticed, for he dispatched several troops into the chaos, hoping to calm things.

Royce set Gillian away from him, his gaze traveling her face. A tear rolled down her cheek. He reached up and brushed it away. He needed to get her away from here.

"'Tis over."

She nodded in reply to his words. Slowly, she stood, extricating herself from his embrace. He reached for her, determined to keep her from seeing the gruesome display on the platform below, but he wasn't quick enough. She gasped and swayed uneasily on her feet. He reached for her as she fell back against him.

"Gillian, come, let's..."

"I'm going to be sick."

She bent and retched at his feet. He supported her head and shoulders until the spasms passed, then lifted her into his arms.

"Panther, why did not you tell us your wife was ill?" Edward questioned him as he got to his feet.

"She was not ere now, Sire. I am afraid the execution was... difficult to watch."

"Our apologies for insisting on her presence," said Eleanor. "Mayhap a rest will help her feel better."

"I will take her to our chamber immediately."

He carried her off the dais, ignoring the questioning glances directed their way. The crowd finally began to disperse, blocking his path. Muttering a curse under his breath, he ducked into the castle through a side doorway, pausing to set Gillian on her feet. She swayed slightly, then leaned against him, her cheek pressed against his chest.

"'Twas more horrible than anything I have seen before." Her shaky voice cut through him like an icy wind.

"Come, let us retire."

He guided her through the maze of corridors and rooms until they climbed the stairs that led to their chamber. Once inside, he closed and barred the door.

Gillian walked over to the bed and lay across it.

"Are you ill?"

She shook her head. "Just... I was very tired this morning, and the execution..."

"It's over. Parliament will resume on the morrow instead, and after that, we travel to London with Edward."

Gillian sat up, dismay curling her mouth down. "London? I had hoped to return to Lyndon. There is much to prepare for the winter ahead."

He inhaled sharply. He supposed she needn't accompany them to London, but the thought of being away from her left him oddly unhappy. Had he grown so fond of his bride that he now would cater to her whims? Nay! The very idea was laughable. Still, if he convinced Edward to travel ahead of the queen, Royce could escort Gillian to her home and return to her much more quickly than traveling with a royal train.

"Mayhap you won't need to go. I'll speak with the king. We will be very busy and I won't be able to watch over you as you will likely need."

He couldn't resist the jest, pleased when she smiled in recognition. While he enjoyed the rebellious antics of his wife, he found he also rather liked this easy rapport between them.

"You accuse me of being trouble?"

She rose and stood before him, her violet eyes piercing.

"Since the day I arrived at Lyndon. You try my patience endlessly."

"As you do mine. My lord."

Her eyes sparkled with laughter. He grinned.

"Cheeky wench."

Before she responded, he took her mouth, wrapping his arms tight around her and lowering her to the bed once again.

# chapter twenty

When the litter finally came to a stop in the bailey, Gillian gave thanks. Her stomach rolled from the constant uneven motion, and her head pounded. She longed for nothing more than her soft bed.

The door opened and her husband held out a hand to aid her down. He frowned.

"Are you ill?"

"'Tis the third time today you've asked. Nay, I am not ill. I am merely tired from the last days."

"You are home now, and you can rest again."

He still eyed her curiously as they walked toward the steps. Residents of the manor all clamored forward to welcome them back. Joy at being home, among her people again, pushed back the queasiness.

Simon pushed through the crowd, bowing with respect. Gillian smiled, her delight at seeing her brother dampened by the sight of Burke coming up immediately behind. Despite Royce's dismissal of her suspicions, his captain's presence still left her uneasy, as if waiting for a sword to swing at her head. She thought of her husband's words the first night he arrived. Her gaze settled on him as he greeted Burke. *Jesu*, she hated admitting he was right. A bow would do her no good in close quarter.

Simon pulled her close for a hug. "I've missed you. How did you fare through...?"

Gillian shuddered at the recollection. "'Twas awful. But it's over, and my loyalty has been proven for the entire realm to see."

Simon chuckled. "You sound displeased."

She let out a heavy sigh. "'Tis frustrating that some would take the word of an outlaw over my own."

"You've been publicly accepted by the king."

"Until someone else decides my loyalty is

questionable." Her gaze slid toward Burke, deep in conversation with her husband. "Simon, did you notice anything amiss?"

"There are some things we must discuss. In private."

While she understood Simon's reasoning, she did not wish to do anything that might raise Royce's suspicions again. Secrecy always roused problems. Still, there wasn't much choice. She needed to be sure before she brought any of her misgivings about Burke to Royce's attention. She must have some sort of proof and hoped Simon had obtained it.

"I will send for you once I have unpacked. Apprise my husband of the normal activities, but say nothing of anything else. I want us both to speak to him together."

"Very well. I am glad you are home."

She smiled. "As am I."

The heat of her husband's hand on her shoulder chased the chill of her worries. She turned and allowed him to escort her up the stairs and into the hall.

Seeing the festive mood in her home, Gillian's heart swelled. How long had it been since Lyndon had been filled with laughter? She felt the joy was a good omen.

The next hours passed quickly. Edith quickly settled Gillian's belongings, and while Simon and Burke updated Royce on the issues of security and the rebels, Thomas assured Gillian the autumn crops had been gathered and tallied. The season had been successful, so much that there was more than enough to last the winter.

Alone, she took a seat before the hearth. How odd that after weeks of turmoil and despair, all now seemed calm. But she couldn't shake the sense more doom lay ahead. Tomorrow, the king arrived and Royce would join him on the journey to London. For a moment, she wanted to ask her husband to take her along. Nay, she must remain and oversee the manor. Besides, the illness on just a short trip to Shrewsbury had been bad enough. The thought of a fortnight's worth of travel left her queasy once more.

A tap on the door drew her attention. She stood and hurried to open it. Simon pushed in and quickly closed the door behind him.

"How goes it with my husband?"

"He and Burke are inspecting the barracks. He wants to expand them and permanently place some of his men in Lyndon's garrison."

She nodded. "I expected that. What of Burke?"

"He has some secrets. Several times when I approached his conversations with Henry, one of your husband's men, he would stop speaking."

"That is not enough, Simon. What about Jervais? Anything that ties them together?"

"I've not seen Burke give him any attention. And Jervais has done nothing untoward in the last week."

"There must be something. Has he done anything that appears to harm Lyndon?"

She needed some sort of proof that Burke plotted against her, or Royce, before she dared tell her husband.

Simon shifted. "Not exactly, though there is one thing I found odd. Three times, he disappeared for several hours."

"Neglecting his duties?" This could be something useful.

Simon shook his head. "I cannot say, but twice I saw him ride in from the southern edge of the forest. But he'd headed north when he departed. When he returned, he appeared agitated. Kept looking around to see if anyone noticed him. His horse was in a lather, he'd been ridden hard and fast."

"Something to do with the rebels?"

"I don't know. I want to follow him next time."

Gillian paced, considering Simon's words. Leaving in one direction, returning from another wasn't enough to raise alarms, but she sensed this was crucial.

"Very well. But be careful. If he's consorting with traitors, he'll do anything to keep from being discovered."

"I will use every caution. We'll uncover something soon."

"Yes, well until we have some proof of Burke's wrongdoings, we cannot tell Royce. Mayhap by the time he returns from London." She hugged her brother. "Thank you. Now, go prepare for supper. I'm famished and wish to find Royce so we may eat."

\*\*\*

Sunlight filtering through the shutters woke Gillian. She stretched, finding herself alone. Just at the moment she realized the day marked her husband's departure from Lyndon, a large wave of nausea rolled over her. She flung back the bedcovers and hurried to the washbasin. The sickness had come upon her so fast; she had barely enough time to reach the basin before emptying her stomach.

Weak and shaky, she slumped on the floor, willing strength back into her limbs. She'd thought once she'd returned from Shrewsbury, the memory of the execution growing more distant, the sickness would go away. When she finally regained enough strength to stand, she strode to the door and called for her maid. If only Royce hadn't insisted Edith bed down in the great hall with the others. Then again, she had no wish for the woman to witness the carnal games her husband liked to play. At the recollection of last night, heat slithered along her spine. She would miss him in their bed most of all. A month. He would be gone only a month. The time would surely pass quickly.

Once dressed, she hurried to the hall, dismayed to see the tables had already been cleared. She had no desire for food, but feared Royce had already left. At the sound of her name, she turned, relieved to see her husband, fully dressed in his mail, helm in the crook of his arm, standing by the doors.

Her smile would not be contained as she made her way toward him. He drew her close and slid his lips across hers in a gentle yet, soul-searing kiss. Again, the realization of how much she'd long for him dampened her mood. 'Twas not fair he must leave when they finally had reached an accord in their marriage, one that gave her hope for a happy future.

"I will miss you," she said when he drew away.

"And I, you." He gave her a smile and ran a finger along her cheek. "I will return anon."

She nodded and hugged him, wishing she could stay in his arms like this forever. A cough beside them drew her from her reverie. Burke stood at attention. When Gillian met his dark eyes, she suppressed an apprehensive shudder. Despite her husband's assurances, misgivings rose again.

"Ah, Burke. You will follow the countess' orders, and rely on her as well. I am depending on you and Simon to keep my home and my lady safe."

The delight bubbling through her at his words made her smile. She turned, Simon approaching.

"The king is ready, my lord."

Her brother looked happy and Gillian supposed Lady Madelaine had something to do with that. She recalled the queen's assurances that arrangements for a wedding would commence upon her and Edward's return to London. Gillian looked forward to attending court.

"I must go," Royce said. He pressed another kiss to her lips and released her.

She nodded, the burn of tears growing stronger. She followed him out of the hall and down the stairs, across the bailey to where the king and his train waited. Edward sat tall in the saddle, clearly impatient judging from his scowl. Royce mounted.

"My lord, wait!" Gillian grabbed his leg. She pulled a ribbon from her hair and handed it to him. She urged him to lean down. He did, eyeing her curiously.

"You give me a favor?"

She gave him a sly smile and lowered her voice. "You may use it on me when you return." Understanding sparked in his eyes and he chuckled. "I cannot wait, Wildcat."

She stepped back. Royce wheeled his destrier around and fell into place beside the king. She waved, forcing the smile to remain until he had vanished through the gates. Only when he disappeared from view did she let her tears fall.

Simon's arm around her shoulders opened the floodgates. She turned into his embrace. When had she lost her heart to her husband, to be so upset to see him go? Why did he have to leave when they'd only just reached a place where they could be happy? She silently railed at the unjustness of the situation, then forced the tears to stop. She had a manor to run and protect, and wanted to prove herself capable to Royce upon his return.

\*\*\*

The recollection of the tears welling in his wife's eyes soured Royce's mood. He watched over the uneven landscape ahead, hoping the trip would take less time than he anticipated.

"Panther, are you listening?"

Edward's angry voice jolted him from his thoughts. "I'm sorry, Sire."

"You'll be back to your wife soon enough. I'm glad you've finally stopped fighting her."

"I suspect she'll still defy me. She's willful and stubborn."

"Aye, as are you."

Royce ignored the comment. "We have finally reached a solidarity that works well for us."

Edward chuckled. "I'm sure it does. Once matters are settled in London, I expect you to finish the problem here with the rebels."

Royce nodded. "Burke has stepped up patrols. He's uncovered and destroyed several camps.

Soon, there won't be any place for them to hide."

"And the brother?"

Royce hesitated. His instincts told him Simon was indeed loyal and honorable, but Burke clearly remained displeased at having to include Gillian's brother in all matters requiring Lyndon's safety.

"I don't think he's a threat, Sire." He ignored the way Edward peered at him.

"But?"

"Burke is concerned, but I think 'tis only because he'd

hoped for a clear command in my absence."

"He'll have Apshire to worry about soon enough. Is Simon worthy of running Lyndon when you return to Montchester?"

"From his reports, I think he can, though he is still green. But he knows Lyndon as well as Gillian."

"And the soldier in Lyndon's garrison?"

"So far, he's done nothing more to warrant suspicion. He's still being watched."

The king nodded. "Crush them, Panther."

"I will, Sire." Royce heaved a deep breath. "We should reach London in less than a sennight."

"And thankfully Eleanor and her ladies are travelling separately," Edward remarked.

At that, Edward spurred his mount. Royce followed, anxious to have this journey over so he could return home.

*** 

With the gates lowered and the train no longer in sight, Gillian turned back to the keep. The weeks seemed to stretch ahead to the day when they'd open again and Royce would ride into the bailey. She said nothing as, flanked by Simon and Burke, she climbed the steps.

Inside, the hall remained a hive of activity, as though the king still remained a guest. As if the lord also lingered in residence. Was she the only one to miss his presence? He'd been here for a short time, and already Gillian couldn't imagine Lyndon without Royce. At the same time, she knew when he returned and the rebellion subdued, they would leave Lyndon for Montchester.

She shivered. She'd never been north. The idea of leaving her home made her stomach roll anew. She made her way to one of the chairs before the hearth.

"What troubles you?" Simon asked.

She shrugged. "I fear I am not well."

"What ails you, my lady?"

She looked up at Burke. Ice in his stare left her chilled, her heart racing with a momentary panic.

"'Tis nothing. I am merely sad to see my husband

depart."

"He'll be back ere you have time to miss him," Simon assured her.

"You're right. For now we must determine how many men will continue to patrol the forests."

She met Burke's wide eyes. Clearly, he hadn't expected her to participate in such plans.

"I will handle that," Burke insisted. He took the seat beside her and leaned on the arm. "Royce has given me instructions on what should be done. I've been overseeing the patrols since you left for Shrewsbury."

"Aye. And he has given me direction as well. Now that I've returned, my word stands as law in his absence. Simon, please determine which men you will take with you when you patrol."

With the exception of one, Lyndon's men would remain loyal to Simon, or so she hoped. They'd served beside him for years. Her orders would help seal their allegiance.

"Simon is not captain, my lady," Burke insisted.

"True, but he possesses knowledge of this manor you do not. Simon will now oversee the patrols."

Burke looked away, the muscle at the base of his jaw tight with anger. His fist clenched a little tighter. Finally, he returned his gaze to her.

"Very well, my lady."

She caught Simon's gaze. The moment of accord soothed her agitation. Making it clear she held control over Lyndon had never felt so frightening. Then again, her husband's captain displeasure at being usurped shouldn't surprise her. Most men would react the same when placed in similar circumstance. Agitating him would likely only set him further against her.

"Burke, I shall need you to provide whatever guidance Simon should need, but especially, I will need your assistance in ensuring Lyndon's men are trained properly as my husband would wish it. I suspect your expertise will be exactly what is needed. It's been over a month since

Montchester's men arrived, 'tis time for the men to form one united garrison."

The odd expression he fixed on her left her wary. Forcing her composure grew more difficult, especially when the queasiness threatened. She clenched her fingers and jaw to contain the urge to retch. Finally, Burke nodded.

"Very well, my lady, if that is what you wish."

Why did she sense he mocked her? "It is. Now, if you will excuse me, I must speak with Thomas."

She stood, relieved when both men left the hall to tend to her orders. Suddenly exhausted, she sent a maid to delay her meeting with Thomas and climbed the stair to her chamber.

\*\*\*

He stared at his lover, anxious to finally be out in the open. To show the king and the world that Llewellyn's line continued. He ran a hand over her burgeoning belly. He hated hiding Anne like this, but her safety, the safety of the child, mattered more than his wishes. 'Twas still early, she'd been free of Lyndon barely a month, and the only way to ensure his unborn son lived would be to keep the babe's mother tucked away where none might find her.

"The Panther has left for London. With the king."

Anne laughed with excitement, grabbing his hand and holding it to her chest. "By the time they return, it will be too late. Lyndon will be ours."

"His wife remains."

Immediately, Anne's eyes turned cold. She turned away, scowling.

"That little harlot has been the bane of my existence since I met William. From the very start, she tried to talk him out of marrying me. Thankfully, I convinced the old fool she was being selfish."

"She has her husband under some sort of spell."

A sly smile curled her lip. "Then he is very stupid, or she is indeed a witch."

"And now all know Simon is her brother. None feel him a threat."

"We'll think of something to bring suspicion back to him. Have your men all been informed?"

With a nod, he took a seat near the fire. Anne handed him his ale. "The money raised went toward convincing all of them that Royce is no longer fit. The way he stares after his wife has them worried."

He caught her hand and drew it to his mouth, placing a kiss in the palm. "Some of them think the king is also in favor of removing Royce from Lyndon. I'd thought convincing Lyndon's troops would be easier, but they are loyal to Lady Gillian."

"I will think of something. When can I return?"

"I'm not sure. Anon, I hope. Give me time to form a plan that will turn the people of Lyndon against Gillian, and 'twill be sooner."

"I already have an idea."

He grinned and pulled her into his lap. "Good. Now, let me show you how much I've missed you."

# CHAPTER TWENTY-ONE

Crossing the snow-covered bailey, excitement left Gillian's knees trembling. All too quickly, though, her hopes were dashed by the pronouncement 'twas just a messenger. Yet another with likely the same message.

There had been several messages from Royce so far, each one delaying his return for varying lengths of time. He'd been gone nigh on three months now. Winter had settled in, and the nights seemed to drag on forever. The way her body ached for his touch left her unable to sleep as she needed. Saddening her even more was the realization she'd been away from her husband for most of their marriage.

When Royce returned, he'd find a big surprise. Each week, Gillian's belly grew larger as the babe within grew. All at Lyndon now knew. She'd refrained from mentioning her condition in her return letters, fearing if she told him, he would return posthaste. While she wanted that more than anything else, she feared what it might do to his reputation and relationship with the king. He'd advised that Edward demanded his aid in resolving a bitter dispute between two rival barons. There had been much blood shed on both sides, and no resolution appeared near. Gillian wondered if her husband would arrive before the babe.

The gates opened and the rider came to a halt in the inner bailey. He dismounted and handed the sealed parchment to Gillian. She quickly opened the message, scanning it for good news. As usual, her mood soured upon reading her husband's words.

"He is delayed again. He says another fortnight at most. 'Tis less time than the last messages."

She slapped the parchment against Simon's chest, her gaze focused on the disheveled rider before her. Something about him seemed vaguely familiar, but she didn't know why.

"Come inside and warm yourself by the fire. I will have more questions."

She didn't wait for them to follow her into the keep. The hall was mostly quiet now. Where had Burke disappeared to? She wanted an update on the reinforcements near the old kitchens she tasked him to oversee. Lately, he'd been difficult to locate, always seeming to be out on some errand or another. Though Simon had followed him several times, as yet, Burke had done nothing to indicate he possessed nefarious plans.

"I've had a maid bring the messenger a meal."

She looked at Simon. "Good. Join me while I question him."

She strode over to the table by the wall and took her seat at the head. Leaning forward, she studied the man. Where did she know him from?

"Did I meet you at Shrewsbury?" she asked.

The man shook his head and took a long drink of ale from the tankard before him. "Nay, I have been in London since the summer."

"I have the strangest feeling I know you, but I can't think of how. For now, tell me how my husband fares."

"He is well. He is quite busy with the king."

"Yes, his message told me the politics are taking longer to resolve than he'd hoped. But what else can you tell me?"

"He can tell you nothing."

Gillian looked over to where Burke entered the hall, surrounded by several soldiers. She didn't recognize them from Lyndon's garrison, or her husband's army. And beside him...

Rage turned her vision red and she stood. "You've found her!"

She glared at the woman her father had married. Anne looked well, her belly large with the child she carried. Where had she found such a fine gown?

Burke gave a strange smile. "Yes, I have. But then, I've

known where she was the entire time."

Gillian's eyes narrowed as confusion took hold. Aware of Simon rising behind her, she straightened her spine. "What are you talking about? All this time, you've known where this murderer has been hiding and you never told us? Or Royce?"

Her voice rose on each word until she shouted. She pulled her dagger from her belt and strode toward Anne, noticing for the first time the way Burke held the woman's hand. Realization and shock halted her mid-stride.

"Explain yourself."

Burke chuckled, but the loathing in his eyes belied the sentiment. "You are a fool, as is your husband, and most of all the king. All these years, I've been biding my time, with help from my lovely baroness."

He lifted Anne's hand and placed a kiss on the back. Gillian fought the urge to vomit.

"You vile bastard! How could you betray him? He gave you everything you have; Edward is granting you a manor of your own."

Burke sauntered toward her and she tightened the grip on her dagger. Behind her, the sound of Simon's sword unsheathing grated on her ears. Her heart raced. She'd been right, but how she wished she was wrong.

"Yes, surveying those lands made it very easy for me to plan. Perhaps you are unaware I was banished as a child, when the old king stripped my father of his lands and had him executed. Banished me and my mother. So I returned to her family. In Wales."

Even as the thought formed, Gillian tried to deny it. "You're Godwin."

"And you are very smart. My lady." He sneered with the last words.

She lunged with the dagger, but Burke easily evaded the move. He reached for her, but Simon's sword at his throat stopped him.

"My men will kill you and the countess if you so much as nick me."

Simon looked around as the men gathered close, swords and knives at the ready. He caught Gillian's eye. She could barely breathe, but gave Simon a nod. He lowered his sword.

"Take him below," Burke ordered.

Two of the men grabbed for Simon. Gillian jumped in front of him.

"Nay! Leave him be!"

"I want him locked away. My loyal clansmen have already taken control of the garrison. He is the last."

Burke grabbed her arm, pulling her from her brother and yanking her dagger away. She screamed and fought against the traitor's hold, but Simon was dragged away to the chambers below. Finally with a mighty pull, she yanked free of Burke. She turned to face Anne. Wasting no time, she strode over and slapped the woman.

Anne screeched in rage, moving to return the blow, but Gillian stepped free of her reach. "You bitch! I've longed for this day. And while I can't kill you now, rest assured, your day soon approaches."

"Murderer! You will pay." She spun about. "All of you will pay! When my husband learns of this."

"Your husband won't be returning."

She froze, leveling a terrified stare on Burke. "What have you done? If you've harmed him in any way, I will see you hanged!"

"For now, he lives. But when he attempts to return here..."

The unspoken threat lingered in the air. She looked around at the men surrounding her. Welsh rebels, every one of them. As was the messenger. But if Royce hadn't sent the letters who had?

"You sent these false messages!"

"Aye, as I've sent false messages to your husband. He is involved with political strife, but your responses are keeping him away longer. He has no idea how very much you miss him, especially during the cold lonely nights."

Flames scorched her face to hear her words tossed

back at her. Royce had never received those missives, didn't know how she longed for him.

"He thinks you are content without him. He is in no rush."

She shook her head. "Nay, he won't believe that."

Burke shrugged. "Doesn't matter. He won't be returning to Lyndon, ever."

He reached for Anne, and Gillian forced her shaking legs to hold her up while the two watched her in contempt. She refused to cower before them, and swore she would have her revenge.

"Lock her in her chamber."

Before Burke finished issuing the order, two men had hold of Gillian's arms and dragged her up the stairs. She fought against them, but soon found herself in her chamber, the door closed and barred from the outside.

She pounded on the wood until her fists ached, her voice hoarse from screaming. There was no secret door in this chamber, she was truly trapped. She paced, her anger giving her strength. A strong kick drew her attention to the babe. She covered her belly.

"We'll find a way out of here, little one, I promise." If only she had some way to get a message to Royce. Where was Edith? Burke likely had her locked away as well.

Much as she wanted Royce to return to Lyndon, she wanted him to stay away until she had figured a way to warn him of the threat.

She finally collapsed on the bed. At the moment, she could do nothing.

\*\*\*

Royce stood in the bailey of the White Tower with Edward, waiting for Viking to be brought from the stables. He didn't like the feeling that had accompanied his wife's latest letter. Something had seemed different than the last messages.

"Have you given more thought to what might be amiss?" Edward asked.

"The Welsh are involved somehow, I'm sure of that.

But both Burke's and Gillian's missives indicate all is well."

He didn't want to admit it stung that she seemed content without him all these months. He'd been miserable without her. He'd almost sent for her many times, but had refrained.

"I've sent word to have additional men from Montchester meet me on the way to Lyndon. And I thank you, Sire, for providing me with some of your troops as well."

"Finish them, Panther. I am weary of these constant uprisings."

"As am I."

His horse was brought before him and he mounted. With a nod to Edward, he wheeled Viking out of the bailey, followed by the king's men. As the sun rose over the land, his unease over the odd undertones in the messages grew. No matter how he tried, he could not reach a suitable conclusion to the dilemma. The long hours of riding stretched ahead of him. Surely he'd come to a resolution before he reached Lyndon.

Two days later, he still hadn't come up with anything to explain the strange letters. His frustration grew, and he'd slept little at night when they'd made camp. It didn't help that when he did finally manage to doze, his dreams had been filled with his pretty wife. Worry for Gillian mixed with the need to be with her again, to hold her, take her, remind her that she belonged to him. His possession. He laughed. She possessed him as surely as he did her. Aware of the men beside him casting sidelong glances, he grinned.

"At least the weather is holding," he said.

"Aye," said Leopold, the knight to his left. "Even the cold has abated."

"A good thing, to my thinking," Royce replied. "We should reach Lyndon day after tomorrow."

"What are the plans for the rebels?"

"I'll speak with Burke when we arrive. If all I've been told is true, the rebels have not dared another attack. The execution may have been enough to crush their uprising.

But we still must catch Godwin."

The next days passed quickly, and by the time they neared Lyndon, Royce's bones ached with weariness. Eagerness to see his wife kept him focused as they picked their way through the forest. Once they broke out of the trees, the keep should be in view.

As if sensing Royce's urgency, Viking picked up his step. Soon. The word rang through his thoughts like a mantra, with a rhythm that matched the horse's gait.

"Ho, Panther!"

Royce reined in the stallion, wheeling about to see Burke a short distance away. He guided his horse toward the captain, a broad grin breaking free.

"Burke! 'Tis good to see you!"

"I fear there is trouble," Burke said when Royce reached him.

Worry eradicated his good humor. "What's happened? Your last letter said all was well."

"It was. Until this morn. Godwin has captured your wife."

Rage tinged his vision red, his heart slamming against his chest.

"What? How in all that is holy did you allow this to happen?" His fingers clenched on the reins, and Viking danced nervously. One hand went to the hilt of his sword. "Where has he taken her?"

Burke shrugged; oddly calm considering the news he'd just shared. Alarm prickled along the back of his neck.

"She ventured beyond the gates and the rebels were laying in wait."

That made no sense. Through the fury a strange calm took over. "Why would she be so foolish? Where is Simon?"

"Back at the keep. He is readying additional men."

"'Twould seem I arrived just in time. How long ago was she taken?"

"Not long."

"They couldn't have gotten far. Come, we'll find them.

And if I know my wife, she'll likely have torn the bastard to shreds!"

His stomach rolled as he thought of how frightened Gillian must be. While she was as fierce as any knight, being in the hands of a brutal rebel had to be terrifying. He cursed himself for not arriving home sooner.

He searched every tree, every bush for any sign of the rebels or his wife. Nothing. His breath grew short. The need to hit something, someone, to swing out with his sword, nearly overpowering.

"There!" Burke pointed and Royce looked ahead.

Several men gathered in a clearing up ahead. Rebels. Royce let loose his war cry and unsheathed sword. Spurring Viking he raced toward the band. He pulled up short before the lead man. The outlaw, disheveled and dirty, brandished his own sword.

"By order of the king, I place you under arrest."

The man said something in Welsh, and the others laughed. Royce growled. He wanted nothing more than to charge into the band, but not just yet.

"Where is my wife?"

The man continued to speak in Welsh. Royce didn't understand a single word. The man gave a smug grin.

"Godwin!" Royce spat on the ground. "Finally I face you. And I will kill you."

More laughter. Royce turned to Burke. "Charge!"

Why didn't Burke obey? His captain watched him with a strange expression.

"He is not Godwin," Burke said.

"I don't care who he is. I want them all arrested."

Burke moved closer and unsheathed his own sword. "Nay, my lord. They are under my orders. And protection."

Royce blinked. Surely his fury and exhaustion had left him confused. What Burke said made no sense. Unless...

"Explain yourself."

An evil grin curved Burke's mouth. Royce noted the flick of his captain's hand, a moment before several more rebels dropped from the trees. Two tackled Royce from his saddle, disarming him. Several blows landed about his head and neck, kicks to his back and gut. When he broke free and attempted to rise, Burke's sword at his throat halted him.

"You never figured it out." His captain's eyes held a demented glow. "I am Godwin, the rebel leader you seek. I've been right before you all along."

Royce shook his head, ears ringing. Each breath burned through his chest.

"I don't understand." Even speaking hurt and when Burke landed another kick to his stomach, he coughed and retched.

"My mother was Welsh, but you never knew that. And when my father was executed, we returned to her family. My revenge is at hand."

"That was not my doing, nor Edward's."

Burke let loose a maniacal laugh. "His father destroyed me, and now I destroy the sons as well. And when your bastard is born, I will kill it, and then your wife."

Wait, did Burke just tell him Gillian was pregnant? Carried his child? He should be overjoyed, but helpless and caught, he could find no happiness in this news. He looked toward the king's men. They had been stripped of their weapons, their hands bound.

Royce now knew the reasons the letters had seemed odd to him. Before he could start to put all the pieces of truth together, a kick to his head sent him into darkness.

*** 

His head throbbed, his mouth was dry and as he opened his eyes, he realized one was swollen shut. He lifted his head and tried to rub his face. He could not move.

His arms were chained above his head, his feet barely brushing the floor. The position left his shoulders and wrists aching from the strain. He tugged against the restraints, but could not free himself. Where was he? As his eyes adjusted to the dim surroundings, he realized he stood in what appeared to be a crumbling building. He searched the chamber for more clues, finding none, but more than ever became convinced he was at Apshire. It had been years since he'd visited, but through the arrow slits, he could make out the unmistakable octagonal tower that was a symbol of the ruined keep. He wasn't very far from Lyndon.

Gillian. Was she safe? Hurt or... he didn't dare think the worst. Did she know of Burke's duplicity? Surely she must, for if Burke was truly Godwin, then he was Anne's lover. No doubt that viper proved dangerous, and if she had dared harm Gillian... He tugged against his bonds again, but he succeeded only in making a racket that slammed into his already aching head.

"The chains are quite strong. They will even hold a Panther."

The familiar voice reached him from across the darkened chamber. Burke. Or rather, Godwin. A surge of rage near gave him the strength to pull the chains right from the stone walls, but he remained captive.

The sound of footsteps grew louder, until finally, Burke stood before him, illuminated in the light streaming through the arrow slits. He met Burke's gaze, stunned by the depth of the hatred in the other man's eyes. Burke watched him closely, as if he contemplated carefully his next words.

"This has not been easy, you know, keeping myself above suspicion all this time," Burke said. "Keeping your wife under suspicion was much easier."

Royce closed his functioning eye and leaned his head back against the wall. Burke tapped his face with his glove, forcing Royce to look at him once more.

"I won't tolerate such disrespect. You are now no more than horse dung and I am the lord here. This is my home, though not for long. Soon, Lyndon and eventually the entire border will be mine. After that, the crown."

"Why?"

"Why?" Burke threw his head back and laughed, a high-pitched maniacal sound. Abruptly, he stopped and looked straight at Royce once more, his lip curled in a sneer. "Because in England, I am nothing. I have nothing and never will."

"Burke, we gave you Apshire. There would have been more eventually."

Burke spat on the ground. "A ruined manor, with few servants to work the land. It was a meager attempt to assuage Edward's guilt over his father's actions. I don't want your leftovers. I should have had as much, perhaps more than you. I fostered with both you and Edward. But no one came to my aid when I was cast from my home, named a criminal."

"Edward and I welcomed you back, restored you as much as we could."

Burke sneered. "He's the king. He could have returned me to my status, instead of leaving me to depend on your charity for a position in your garrison. Tell me why I should be grateful for that."

"I spoke up for you; you were there when I asked Edward to grant you a title and lands."

Royce's thoughts swam, too many to focus on any clearly. The one thing he did want to know was how he didn't see the signs of Burke's hatred ere now.

"And once he said no, you did nothing more, except hire me as your captain. I was no better than your horse."

Before Royce realized what Burke intended, the blow to his stomach left him breathless. Unable to bend over, defend himself, the next strike left him gasping for air. While he choked and tried to breathe, Burke crossed his arms and watched, obvious delight carved into his features.

"Once I've taken hold of the border, I'll take Edward down. The House of Llewellyn will once more hold the throne, not only of Wales, but of England. Edward wanted unity, and he shall have it."

Another punch to his jaw left Royce dazed, though he struggled to remain conscious. Still one more strike to his cheek shattered the light into blackness.

# chapter twenty-two

As she had done every day since her captivity began a month earlier, Gillian paced. It was all she could do. But today, her agitation seemed worse than normal. The babe kicked often, making it impossible to sleep away the day. The sense that today brought a change invoked a desperate need to somehow find a way free.

Her thoughts drifted to Simon, as they often did. She hadn't seen him since the day Burke took control of Lyndon. She feared for his safety and it maddened her not to have any word. Did Burke and his men torture him? Was he already dead? The sting of tears forced her thoughts in another direction. She could not give in to the urge to fall apart.

Shouts from the bailey drew her attention. She peered out of the arrow slit, but saw little. She turned away, halting mid-stride at the sound of the key in the lock. 'Twas too early. Why did Burke come now? Every day, he had been the one to deliver her evening meal, so he could taunt her with the fact that Royce would soon be dead. How she'd managed to contain her rage, she might never know. Fear for her child factored into her decision to ignore him best as she could. Knowing he wanted her to rant and rave, and that she didn't frustrated him, brought her one of the only pleasures she savored.

She held her breath, the sound of the bar sliding free seeming a roar. Her frayed nerves and racing heart left her trembling. She stood behind her chair, hoping her need for the support didn't reveal her weakness. A swift kick from the babe drew a startled gasp. She bit her lip, the door slowly creaking open.

A rush of joy nearly made her swoon. Simon stood in the doorway, his dark eyes hard with anger. His sword raised, she noticed the blood staining the steel. He held out a hand.

"Come."

She hurried to him, grabbing tight to his hand as he pulled her from the room and down the corridor. Screams and sounds of battle rose around her. She tugged, urging Simon to stop.

"Wait! My bow!"

Her brother shook his head. "No time. You're better off with your hawks."

Her eyes widened and she grinned. "You're right! I must get to the mews!"

Again, Simon refused. "We have an advantage; we must take it and flee."

"At least let me set them free." She winced at the sound of a bloodcurdling shriek. Another battle besieged Lyndon.

Simon studied her then gave a curt nod. "We must hurry." He stopped to bend over one of Burke's men, prying the sword from the dead rebel's hand. "Can you use this?"

Gillian took the offered sword. She'd not trained with the weapon, but she could manage the weight. The cries and shouts, wailing and weeping from below added to her determination. Her people needed her, now more than ever. She twisted her wrist, adjusting to the feel of the metal in her hands.

"I will."

"Let's go."

He pulled her behind him, blocking an attempt to stop them. Gillian kept her head down as best she could, the weapon in her hand held before her. Thankfully, few posed a threat, and those who did were easily dispatched by Simon's skill. He led her down the stairs and she gasped.

Chaos reigned in the hall. She recognized many of Lyndon's people fighting against the rebels. What had happened to change the balance of power?

"Burke has ridden out to meet your husband. While he and his men may be... Edward sent more troops on a secondary mission. Come on, we have to go now!"

He dragged her across the hall to the wide-open doors. In the bailey, the melee was even more frenzied. Simon wove through the bedlam, dragging Gillian with him. When one of Burke's men attacked, he released her, to fight his opponent. Gillian stood at his back, waving her sword before her to fend off another attacker. Still another rebel joined the fray and soon she and Simon were surrounded. She feared her escape would be cut short, in the worst possible way. For a moment, she wrapped a protective arm around her belly, then lifted her sword once again, ready to fight to the death if necessary.

A bellow of fury sounded nearby and she turned to see several of Lyndon's men coming to their aid. Her ears crackled with the screeching sounds of metal on metal, the war cries and the swearing as one by one, the rebels were cut down. Simon turned to Edgar.

"Defend Lyndon!" he ordered, once more grabbing Gillian's hand and pulling her behind him.

"Wait!" She broke free of his grip and ran toward the mews. Heart pounding, she could barely breathe as she entered. The sounds of the battle had the birds agitated, their wings fluttering as they pulled against their jesses. One by one, Gillian unhooded the birds, then released their tethers. She waved her arms, urging them to fly. All but one did as she wanted, quickly flying from their nests. She turned to see Ares sitting on his perch, watching her with golden eyes. Memories of Royce flooded her thoughts. He had to be safe.

She held out her arm to her favorite hawk. She'd had little time with him these past months, since her husband had found a falconer to see to their care. She winced as the bird settled on her arm, his sharp talons scratching her. She'd not thought to find her gauntlet, but then, there'd been no time.

"Come you silly bird, we have a home to defend!"

Ares gave her a soft coo, as if he understood. Gillian stepped out of the mews. The battle seemed to have calmed. Bodies littered the bailey, groans of pain and cries for help lingering in the air. The king's men had joined with Lyndon's loyal soldiers to defeat the rebels. But where was Burke?

She spotted Simon and waved. She raised her arm and Ares took flight. He would return, as would all of her beloved birds, she felt sure of it, but at least they were now away from the danger.

Simon ran over, grabbing her shoulders and studying her. "Are you all right?"

She nodded. "Unhurt. And... ow!"

She clutched her belly. That kick had been ferocious, seeming to jar her ribs loose. She stroked her belly, calming the babe.

"Where are Edward's men?"

"Robert, Earl of Harmenberry leads them. Come."

All around, soldiers wearing the king's coat of arms either gathered the uninjured rebels together, or finished off those who'd been wounded. Gillian strode past the disheveled bunch, surprised to find herself looking forward to their executions. When had she become so bloodthirsty?

"Lady Gillian, I am glad to see you safe." Harmenberry gave her a half bow. "Thank you for coming to Lyndon's aid. Have you subdued all of them?"

The earl nodded. "Edward knew your husband had misgivings about the letters he'd received from you. Our king feared he was riding into a trap. 'Tis why he sent us."

"I must send word thanking him immediately. Have you any news of my husband?"

Robert nodded. "He's been captured by Burke. One of the men with them managed to escape and met up with us last eve. Shortly we ride for Apshire."

Gillian couldn't breathe, try as she might. Her heart seemed to stop at hearing Royce had been captured. Her legs trembled, her knees buckling. Simon caught her before she fell. For several moments, the world seemed to spin about her, but she leaned into her brother. Slowly, strength seeped back into her limbs.

"Apshire? That's only a short way from here."

Robert nodded. "It's one of the Panther's holdings, but he and the king decided to give it to Burke when... we believe Burke has your husband there. And clearly he is in league with Godwin."

Gillian shook her head. "He is Godwin. And I know about Apshire. Royce told me before he left. We must ride south immediately!"

"Gilly, you are staying here."

"No, I must save my husband."

A loud scream from the top of the stairs drew their attention. Rage filled Gillian's senses at the sight of Anne, dressed in a fine gown of emerald velvet, fought off one of the earl's men. She was quickly subdued and led down the stairs. Gillian straightened and strode over to her former stepmother.

"Traitorous whore! You'll pay with your life for your attempt on mine!"

Anne laughed, even as she fought against the bonds holding her hands behind her back.

"You can't kill me, I am with child."

"Hiding behind your babe. No matter, once it's birthed, you will hang," Gillian vowed. She clenched her fingers, longing to strike the red-haired bitch, but held herself back. She turned to Simon. "She must be kept in a chamber above until the child is born. I will send a message to the king. Robert, would you have one of your men ride for London?"

"As you wish, my lady."

Gillian nodded. "Secure her above in the small chamber off the solar. She cannot escape, but place guards anyway."

"Gilly, mayhap you should rest." Simon drew her into his embrace.

She shook her head, pushing him away. "Nay, I must save my husband."

"I forbid you to join us."

Gillian laughed. "You can't forbid me. I am the

Panther's wife, and I will show I am as capable as he."

"But the babe —"

"Will be fine. He will one day tell the tale of how he and his mother saved his father."

Simon rolled his eyes. "Fine, but you heed my orders or the earl's."

Gillian nodded. "Of course." From the way he looked at her, she suspected her brother didn't believe her.

"Get me a horse."

*** 

The only sounds were those of the rats scurrying across the floor. Royce peered into the darkness, the last of the sunlight having disappeared hours ago. This room, while mostly intact, had still crumbled enough to allow a freezing wind to cut through. He shivered, hating feeling so weak.

His thoughts remained filled with a raven-haired vixen with violet eyes. He wished he had listened to her misgivings about Burke. How had he missed the signs and not known Burke was the same person as Godwin? He'd been a fool, never realizing where Burke's mother came from. Did Edward know Burke was distantly related to Llewellyn and Dafydd? Royce hadn't, and he thought he knew everything about the man he'd named his close friend and captain.

He groaned. By sending his captain to scout the lands of Apshire, he'd unwittingly aided the rebel. Over and over, he tried to find clues he'd missed, but nothing came to mind. Or maybe he was just too weak and exhausted to see it now.

Once more, his thoughts turned to his wife. Was she safe? Did she truly carry his child? He ached to see her, though feared if he did, 'twould mean the worst. He had to free himself before she ended up here, chained beside him.

The throbbing in his cheek and jaw had faded slightly, but Burke had cracked a rib, judging from the fire that burned his gut each time he inhaled.

Tugging on the chains once more, he knew there was no hope. Burke would kill him, would destroy him slowly.

He'd make Royce suffer first, as he believed he had suffered all these years. All because their fathers had made bad choices.

The door to the cell creaked open and Burke stepped inside, carrying a torch. He smiled as he neared Royce, holding the torch close enough so he could feel the heat on his bruised face.

"I hope you do not feel I am neglecting you. I have been busy making plans for my future as the Prince of Wales."

"You will not succeed. Wales is Edward's now."

"Edward will run like a beaten dog once he learns I have taken down his prized warrior." "Edward will crush you like an ant under his heel when he learns of this."

"I think not. I already have Lyndon, and this ruin. I'm well-equipped to take over the remaining border properties. With your men and Lyndon's combined, plus my loyal countrymen, I will be unstoppable. The Welsh shall have their revenge and will follow me as their new king."

"They followed Dafydd and he was put to death for his actions."

"Dafydd was an unfortunate incident. But now he cannot gainsay me. And when my queen bears my son, my succession will be secured."

"Your queen? Who would have you?"

"Lady Anne is my lover. It is my child she carries. As soon as I destroy Edward, we will wed in London."

"You're daft if you think you can defeat the king."

Burke laughed. The sound chilled Royce's blood. His captain had truly gone mad.

"I know I can. Look at how easily I took Lyndon from you. Once I claim Shrewsbury, I will set my sights on the king. He cannot hope to win."

"He'll kill you. If I don't first."

Another laugh. "I shall enjoy sharing word of your death with your wife. I am looking forward even more to sharing her bed. I suspect she's got quite a fire worth savoring."

"If you harm one hair on her head, I will see you suffer a fate worse than Dafydd's."

"You will be dead. Come the morrow, you will be hanged. And your head will rest on a pike outside Lyndon as word to all what happens when you try to crush the Welsh. And she will be mine."

The idea of Gillian helpless against this man consumed Royce. One of the things he loved most about her was her spirit. Burke would break her and...

*Jesu*, had he just admitted he loved her? Yes, yes, he had. A glimmer of joy poked through his rage, calming him. He loved her and somehow, he would return to her and keep her safe from this madman.

"You'll not succeed." A slight smile curved his lips. "Don't forget the panther is cunning and smart. And his mate is a wildcat who will strike you down."

"If it makes you feel better about your impending death, think what you will. But know this, the countryside will resound with cheers at your death."

"Never." The calm word shattered Burke's feeble composure. He landed three swift blows to Royce's stomach and left the cell, taking the torch and pitching the small chamber into darkness.

***

Scratching sounds and whispers reached through the half slumber that claimed Royce. Coming awake, he strained to listen.

"Down here!"

"Wait, let me go first. The walls of this place could collapse at any time."

"Hurry! Before he comes back."

Did he imagine Gillian's voice? He must have. She wasn't here. The hazy dreams fogging his brain lingered. He closed his eyes once more.

"This door, there's a lock!"

"God's bones, how will we find the key?"

Again, Royce swore he heard his wife's voice. He lifted his head, heart pounding. Surely he still slumbered.

The draft crossing his face told him he was indeed awake. A flash of light from under the door drew his focus.

"His arrogance is our advantage. The key hangs here!"

That voice, laced with excitement, also sounded familiar, but the ringing in his ears kept him from determining who spoke. This time a strange moan, like a choked sob, came in response.

More rustling, a key turning. The door creaked open. Two shadowy figures, one holding a torch, stepped into the chamber. Vision blurry, Royce didn't dare accept what he saw.

Then hands touched his face, small, soft, feminine hands. Gillian's hands. A bolt of joy filled him. She stood before him, smiling and weeping at the same time.

"You're alive!" Her hoarse words sounded as if they choked her.

"How... Gillian..."

She covered his mouth with her hand. "Don't speak, we must hurry. Simon, get him down!"

Her hands continued to move over him. Simon handed her the torch and within moments had managed to somehow unchain Royce's arms from the wall. But the metal cuffs remained around his wrists. At least he could walk, somewhat.

"We must leave now, the smith at Lyndon will remove the rest." Gillian's brother seemed older somehow. What had happened in the time Royce had been in London?

Chained, weakened and sore all over, Royce had no choice but to lean on Simon. The three made their way from the chamber to the corridor. Gillian held the torch, lighting their way as they moved through the ruined keep. Ere long, they'd reached the outer grounds, where several mounted knights waited.

"You must ride with Simon."

Gillian's order was sharp and steady. He smiled. Her strength and courage roused his pride. His Wildcat was a fitting mate for the Panther.

"Did you lead the men here?" he asked.

"Of course. They know I'm capable."

Unable to resist, he leaned over and pressed a firm kiss to her lips. She tasted of honey and spice and even in his weakened condition, he ached to take her. She responded eagerly, her hands cupping his face before pushing him away.

"We must go now!"

She turned away, mounting a horse while he allowed Simon to help him onto his stallion. He cursed his weakness, but didn't resist the assistance. When Simon climbed up behind him, he swore the other man chuckled. A moment later, as the group raced from the ruined keep, Royce gave thanks for Simon's aid.

The ride to Lyndon passed in a blur. His weakness increased as they rode and he could do no more than lean against his brother-in-law. He hated the feebleness holding him securely in its grip. Suddenly, they were in the bailey, and his men were carrying him to the smith's forge. Faces blurred before him, the heavy weight of hands holding him still bringing a moment of alarm. Soft hands once more stroked along his cheeks, calming him.

"It might hurt, but there's no other way."

His arms were once again dragged above his head and held in place. A moment later, shattering pain wrenched through his arms, the smith blasting his hammer to a spike laid against the iron cuffs. Though still weak as a babe, he struggled futilely against the men restraining him. At last, when the manacles fell away, the pain settled to a dull throbbing.

"Come. Fetch the physic."

Gillian's voice seemed a lifeline keeping him aware. He closed his eyes once more, saying nothing as he was lifted and carried into the keep. The comfort of his bed finally chased the remnants of worry. Aware of Gillian sitting beside him, holding his hand, filled him with peace. He wanted to open his eyes to look at her, wanted to tell her how he felt, but he had no strength to do more than breathe.

***

Gillian sat up, still unable to sleep. Royce slept heavily beside her, the herbs in the ale helping him get much needed rest. But she worried to see the bruises on his face, visible even through the beard that covered his jaw. His lip had been split and one eye had swollen shut. The physic had assured her in a few days' time, he would be well again, but she still fretted. She gazed at him, the sliver of moonlight shining down.

A sudden kick drew a chuckle. Her babe grew every day, hale and hearty judging from his movements. Did Royce know? She caressed her belly and the baby quieted.

Warmth slithered along her spine. She looked at Royce, surprised to find him awake and studying her.

"How are you feeling?"

"Like my horse trampled me."

"You'll be well soon. You must rest to recover your strength."

He smiled. He reached out to run his fingers through her hair. She shivered, even as the heat within climbed. The slightest touch could set her aflame. They had been too long apart, but she didn't dare give in to her wants. Royce needed to recover. Not only from the ordeal he'd suffered, but learning how deeply he'd been betrayed.

"And how do you fare?

She knew what he asked. She placed his hand over her burgeoning belly.

"Your son grows within me."

The babe chose that moment to kick and Gillian nearly laughed at the expression on her husband's face. Even battered and with one good eye, he appeared as amazed as she had been the first time she'd felt her child's movements.

"He is quite active."

"Strong."

She nodded. "Yes."

"When?"

"Likely the night we wed. Your seed took root immediately."

"Your illness, at Shrewsbury."

She nodded again. "I didn't know until after you had left for London."

"You should have written me, I would have returned immediately."

Gillian hesitated. She had fought with herself about what to tell Royce during his time in London. She'd made the worst decision, and it had almost cost her everything.

"I feared Edward would be angry if you left. And I didn't want you to worry. But if I had told you, mayhap Burke wouldn't have revealed himself."

"What did he do to you?"

"Nothing really. Locked me in here, and Simon below. He and Anne had free rein over the entire manor. Until Edward's men arrived and helped us restore Lyndon."

His hand moved to stroke through her hair. "I'm sorry I wasn't here to help you."

"How could you know what would happen?"

"Edward did."

She held back a smile. He sounded like a grumpy child, but doubted he would appreciate being told of that.

"No matter. It's over, for now. And I will kill Burke for what he's done to you. To us."

Royce smiled and ran his hand through her hair. "Nay, Wildcat, you will not. 'Tis my fight. I will see it finished."

"But..."

He placed a finger across her lips. "Have a care for the babe. You have been through enough and we are lucky he is safe. I won't risk you or him."

"But..."

"Don't argue. I am not in the mood to deal with your stubborn disobedience."

"I saved you. Had I not aided you, you would be...dead."

"And you took a foolish risk." He held up a hand when she started to protest. "I am proud of your bravery, but you should not have risked yourself. You could have been killed."

"As could you. In fact, you would now be swinging

from a noose if I hadn't saved you.

Again." She risked much reminding him of the day Lyndon had first been attacked. Flames rose within as she considered what he might do about her defiance.

"I thought you meant to kill me."

"But you trust me now."

He nodded. "I do."

He cupped her face in one large hand and she leaned her head into the caress. The simple touch sent the fire surging. She stifled a frustrated groan. Her husband was in no shape to make love to her now, no matter how much she wanted him to.

When he drew her head toward him, she didn't resist, needing his kiss. He devoured her, like he always did, and her heart raced with excitement. She let him continue for a few more moments, his tongue tangling with hers. Then she drew away.

"Where are you going?"

"You need your rest, much as I'd like..." Warmth flooded her cheeks.

He arched an eyebrow. "I've dreamed of being here with you over the last months. And now you refuse me?"

"Nay, but you need to recover. You've been wounded."

His gaze grew intense and he sat up. He reached for her and she went willingly into his arms. Being held like this could almost make her forget all the troubles that had passed between them.

"Not terribly, and I've rested enough. Do you know, I came to an important realization these past few months?"

"What is that?"

"How much I've come to care for you."

Joy sang in her heart, her grin and laughter impossible to contain. She'd longed to hear such words from him. Tears of happiness blurred her vision. A deep breath steadied her senses.

"These months of being apart weighed heavily on my heart. I missed you terribly."

He remained silent, his penetrating gaze sending

tendrils of heat through her veins. He cupped her face in his hands and drew her near. The soft kiss he placed on her lips wasn't what she really wanted, but she made no protest when he pulled away.

"I love you, Wildcat." His golden eyes, one still half-shut, held her as surely as if he'd bound her with his ropes.

She froze, afraid that what she'd dreamed was just that. "You...what?"

"I said I love you. Don't you have something to tell me in return?"

She laughed, recognizing the demand in his question. Even longing for his love didn't stand in comparison to the reality. Surely, she dreamed, this fierce and suspicious earl admitting his feelings had once seemed impossible.

"Royce, I love you, I do." Tears ran down her cheeks, too many emotions coming together in a crazed whirlwind. The gentle stroke of his fingers as he wiped her tears nearly set her to weeping anew.

"Why do you cry?"

"Because I'm happy. I've hoped you might care for me, but that you love me... it's my deepest wish and it's come true."

"'Tis the babe that makes you weepy."

"Mayhap. But know this, Royce Langley, you've made me happier than I thought possible."

She hugged him tight, but pulled back when he gasped in pain.

"What is it? Have I hurt you?"

"My ribs."

Despite herself a snarl escaped. "I want to kill him for what he did."

"He will die, no doubt. Leave that to me and Edward."

"I want to help.

He shook his head, and she recognized his stern demeanor taking over. "You are not to put yourself in any sort of danger. I will bind you and lock you in myself."

She knew he would carry through on the threat. Surely, there must be something she could do and said as much.

"You can lay here with me while I rest. I want to hold you, as I dreamed so many nights."

Her heart felt nearly full to bursting. That she would do, and anything else he asked, with great eagerness, and went into his embrace. He covered her mouth with his, a heated stroke of his tongue that soothed her rather than ignited her. She savored the comfort of his mouth and didn't protest when he drew away and settled her against his shoulder. Despite the gravity of the situation still to be resolved, Gillian thought she'd never been happier.

# chapter twenty·three

"My lady, 'tis Anne! The babe is coming!"

The maid blurted out her words then ran from the room. Gillian pushed herself from her chair, running a calming hand over her belly. The babe settled. She'd anticipated this day for weeks, but now that 'twas here, a strange apprehension rose. She strode to the hall, calling for Thomas. The steward appeared before her.

"Fetch the midwife. Anne births her child."

"I've already sent for her, my lady."

Gillian nodded and set herself to the preparations for the birth, ensuring the stool was brought in and plenty of blankets to swaddle the babe. By the time the midwife arrived, Anne screamed in pain.

"I cannot bear this agony!"

Anne's panicked shouts roused a responding alarm in Gillian's stomach. She leaned against the wall, a strange weakness seeping into her limbs. She closed her eyes against the sight of Anne's huge belly contracting and quivering under the strain of her labor. Anne continued to yell, her cries piercing Gillian's ears. At least this morn, she'd awoken without that great pressure on her lungs, making it difficult to breathe. She needed a clear head through this.

"Take deep breaths and pant like a dog, my lady," said the midwife, Maida. "'Twill help the pain."

Anne seemed not to hear, continually bawling and cursing. Gillian rubbed her belly, the child inside moving in fierce, agitated motions. For several hours, Anne cried out while Maida barked orders. Gillian seemed to feel each pain as it contracted through Anne's body, knowing that in a few short weeks, she would be facing the same agony. Fear rose up and despite her hatred for her former stepmother, Gillian shared more empathy with the woman than she'd ever imagined. She stepped still closer, surprised when Anne grabbed her hand, squeezing hard. *Jesu*, the woman had the strength of an ox!

A piercing wail from Anne and another order from Maida broke through Gillian's unfocused thoughts. Again, pain grabbed the red-haired woman and she squeezed Gillian's hand with such force, she thought her fingers had been broken.

"'Tis a boy!" Maida's triumphant cry preceded the infant's wail. Anne slumped weakly against the stool and closed her eyes as the midwife tended to the babe. His mewling cries drowned the sound of her stepmother's gasping breath.

"Give me my son." Anne weakly reached for the babe. Maida swaddled the child in clean cloths and handed him to his mother.

Maida set about cleaning up the afterbirth. Gillian remained silent, watching Anne with her child. Burke's child. The babe of a traitor. What would happen to him once his parents were tried and likely executed? Fearing Edward would be ruthless toward the helpless infant, Gillian already formulated a plan. Convincing Royce to support the notion would take some work, but she felt sure she could...

"My lady, take the babe!"

The panic in Maida's voice indicated something terrible. Gillian reached for the infant, alarmed at how pale Anne had grown. She looked at the floor, eyes widening to see copious amounts of blood pooling beneath the stool. Much more than there should be. As she drew the crying child away, Anne made a feeble attempt to hold onto him.

"My baby. I want my baby."

"Let Maida tend you," Gillian said, rocking the wailing baby. He was likely hungry but she could do nothing for him now. Had the wet nurse been summoned? All she knew was the distress in the room had grown palpable. She stepped away to let Maida and the others work, but with each passing second, realized whatever had gone wrong could not be fixed. Anne quickly lost consciousness, her limp body falling to the floor.

"Summon the physic," Maida ordered, sending one of her young assistants in search of the one person who might save Anne. A moment later, Maida shook her head and stood. "'Tis too late. She is gone, my lady."

Gillian gaped, unable to comprehend what had happened and how it occurred so quickly. Anne, dead? One look at the woman's waxy countenance and blankly staring eyes, and Gillian knew it to be true. Yet, what she'd so desperately longed for all these months seemed strangely unsatisfying. Sad. Near tragic.

As if he sensed his mother's death, the child's screams grew louder and more urgent. Gillian cooed to him and cuddled him close, but it wasn't enough to quiet him.

"Maida, send for my husband. And the wet nurse."

As she rocked the infant, a sharp pain stabbed into her belly. Breathless, she hurried to the bed, fearful she might drop the newborn in her arms. Something seemed wrong, or was it simply the sudden passing of Anne that sparked the pain?

"Maida, I think something is wrong with me."

The midwife carefully drew a blanket over Anne's unseeing face and studied Gillian. She folded her arms and shook her head.

"'Tis a bit early, but it looks as if your babe is anxious to be here as well, my lady."

Gillian shook her head. "Nay, 'tis impossible. I can't possibly be ready to..."

"Ready to what?"

Royce stood in the doorway, a scowl darkening his face. His stare moved from Gillian and the babe to Anne's body on the floor.

"What happened?"

"Anne birthed her son. Then she... died. There was so much blood, and –"

Another pain, a tightening of her belly, stole the rest of her words. She gasped and shook her head. 'Twas too soon.

The babe shouldn't be born for at least another month.

Royce was at her side in a moment, alarm gleaming in his golden eyes.

"What is wrong?"

"I think Maida might be right. Our babe comes as well."

"Are you sure?"

"No, but she knows better than I. Maida?"

The midwife took the baby from her arms and handed him off to another maid. Just as she was about to speak, a gush of liquid ran between Gillian's legs, soaking her, her gown and the bed.

"'Tis time, my lady. Your waters have broken and your baby is coming today."

Gillian grabbed hold of Royce's arm. "Nay, 'tis too soon. Make it stop!"

"Babes come when they are ready," Maida replied, her tone too calm for Gillian's liking.

"My lord, you must help me get her to your chamber where she can labor in comfort."

Gillian's protests went ignored as she was led from the chamber down the corridor. She looked around for the maid with the baby, but didn't see her.

"Where is the child?" Her panic made her voice weak and shaky.

"He will be well-cared for. The wet nurse has arrived and will feed him. Have a care for yourself."

Royce's tone bordered on a command but the urge to laugh at his worried expression vanished as another wave of pain gripped her back and abdomen. She bent forward, trying to ease the terrible cramping sensation, but it did little to soothe the discomfort.

Royce's gaze grew troubled, adding to Gillian's worry. He held her close by his side, moving carefully so as not to pain her further. But another slice of agony cut into her and she couldn't contain her cry. Royce bent and gathered her into his arms, cradling her bulky body. She clung to him trying to restrain her sobs.

Royce obeyed Maida's orders and laid Gillian in the bed. He sat beside her, taking her hands in his. His eyes never left her face, his concern feeding into her apprehension.

"Something is wrong." His tone sparked still more distress.

"Nonsense, 'tis the way of things," Maida said, bustling about the chamber. The door opened and a tub of hot water was brought in, just as had been done for Anne.

"She is in pain. Ease her suffering!"

Gillian might have laughed at Royce's order if she wasn't so afraid. She squeezed his hand.

"There is nothing to be done. It will stop when the babe comes." Maida busied herself arranging blankets and cloths, and instructing her assistants.

When Royce looked at Gillian with such deep concern, she almost wept. Recollections of the cold, hard warrior who had arrived so many months ago sprang up. Not even a year had passed and knowing this fierce man loved and protected her, possessed her, left her breathless.

"My lord, you must go now." Maida stood with fists on her hips, a disapproving scowl etched into her round face.

"I'm not leaving." He scowled at the woman. Somehow, a giggle escaped Gillian.

"But 'tis not proper!" Horror widened Maida's dark eyes.

"Madame, this is my home. I am lord here and will remain."

"'Tis all right," Gillian said. "I would like him to stay with –"

Her words dissolved into a strangled moan, this time the sensation of a knife twisting in her gut sucking the breath from her lungs. Maida's protests ceased and she set herself between Gillian's legs.

"Very good, my lady. There is plenty of time yet."

"Plenty of time? How long must my wife suffer?"

With the wave of agony behind her, Gillian squeezed

Royce's fingers, a weak attempt to calm him. His fierce expression did not soften.

"Several hours at least. 'Tis normal for a first child."

"Several hours? Not acceptable! I will seek someone else."

"My lord, forgive me, but there is nothing anyone can do now." Maida pressed on Gillian's belly. Shouldn't that hurt? Instead, it felt as though a great pressure eased inside.

"Royce, there's no one else!"

He glanced sharply at her. "I will not stand by and watch you suffer for hours!"

Another squeeze of her belly left her panting. "'Tis how a child is born."

One look into his face and he knew he shared her thoughts about how Anne had suddenly died moments after her son arrived. She held his stare, lifting her chin. It earned her an arched eyebrow and a scowl, but he said nothing more.

"Sit with me and hold my hand. I'll need to –"

The pain came on suddenly and more excruciating than before. She squeezed her eyes shut, willing herself to relax. Struggling against the agony seemed to make it worse. In her hand, Royce's fingers cracked under her fierce squeeze.

"My lord, sit up by her head. You are interfering."

Gillian gave a weak giggle at Maida's words. Royce still scowled, but remained silent. She realized his fear had grown. She held back a smile. Likely her fierce warrior husband wouldn't like knowing his apprehension showed to everyone in the room. To distract him, she took his arm and placed it around her shoulders, leaning back against his chest.

"You must hold me each time I –"

The scream erupted before she possessed the will to contain it. The pains now came closer together. Royce's embrace tightened as she trembled under the force of her labors.

Several hours later, she screamed with each twisting squeeze of her belly. Now Royce calmed her, whispering reassuring words in her ear, encouraging her to bear this agony.

"You bear it!" she shouted.

His chuckle only added to the tempest of emotions warring within her. God's bones, she wanted to cuff him soundly, but another great pain was upon her. His lips pressed against her sweaty cheek, and he gently mopped her brow, soothing her anger. The small sense of comfort gave her a moment to catch her breath before another contraction left her squirming in agony.

"Do you want the stool?"

Gillian shook her head, images of Anne's suffering now taking over her thoughts. She wanted no part of that evil contraption, even if Maida insisted it made the birth easier.

"She birthed her son that way. I cannot..."

She caught Royce's eye, knew he understood by the single nod he gave her. She squeezed his fingers, gently this time. Another wave of hurt came over her, but somehow this seemed different.

"Maida? Something's changed." She gasped the words out.

"Aye, my lady!" The midwife peered between Gillian's legs. "Yes, it's time to push."

As soon as the words left Maida's mouth. Gillian was overcome by the need to bear down. Royce held her up as she pushed with every muscle in her body, falling weakly back when the need passed. Over and over, her body strained, the pressure and pain changing with the need to expel the babe. Her hair clung to her face. As if sensing how it distressed her, Royce brushed it free.

"Just a little more," Royce whispered. "Our son is almost here."

She barely heard him over the roaring in her ears. Her heart threatened to burst free of her chest, and she panted and gasped for breath with each assault on her exhausted body.

"One more, my lady! I can see the head. The babe is

almost here."

Gillian sucked in a breath and once more bore down with all her strength. In moments, the babe slipped from her body, and the pain immediately receded.

"'Tis a girl child!"

She stared at her husband, his eyes wide in surprise. Then he let out a laugh of joy and gathered her close just as the babe began to cry, a strong wail that echoed in the chamber. Gillian leaned weakly against Royce, her heart now racing for another reason. Tears flowed freely down her cheeks as she reached for her baby.

Maida placed the swaddled bundle in her arms. Vision blurred by her tears, Gillian looked at her daughter for the first time. In wonder, she raised a finger and caressed the tiny pink cheek.

Lifting her head, she found Royce staring at the babe with the same awe in his eyes that rested in her soul.

"She is beautiful, just like her mother."

"She is perfect. Royce, look at how tiny she is!" Gillian could not prevent herself from touching every part of the child. Royce leaned over and pressed a finger against the babe's hand. His eyes widened in astonishment when the tiny fingers clutched his.

"She is strong," he whispered.

"Like her father."

Her husband hugged her and the babe to him, placing a soft kiss on her damp forehead. Never had she known such contentment. She settled against him, content to stare down at this child they had created.

"Her name should be Marissa."

Gillian's head snapped up. "Really? You would like to name her after my mother?"

"Your mother gave me a gift on the day she bore you. I would like to thank her in this way."

He covered her mouth with a heated kiss, expressing without words all the love he felt for her. Tendrils of warmth filled her, but exhaustion made her eyes heavy and unable to respond as she normally would. The yawn fought its way free. Royce drew back, watching her with amusement.

"Do my kisses bore you, Wildcat?" he asked.

"Nay, Royce, never. But I am so weary."

"Your lady wife must rest now." Maida shook a gnarled finger at Royce and reached for the baby. "Allow her some peace."

"Stay with me." Gillian clutched his hand. He nodded, drawing her against him. She snuggled closer, contentment and peace filling her.

She must have slept, for when she next opened her eyes, candles lit the now darkened room. She sat up, looking around, her gaze settling on the chair before the hearth.

Royce held his daughter in his lap, her tiny body settled amidst a soft blanket. Gillian remained silent, content to watch him as he studied the child, turning her and stroking her arms and legs, counting her fingers and toes. His large hands dwarfed the babe, but his touch was gentle, almost reverent.

"She is perfect."

He turned. "You're awake."

"Unless I'm dreaming now."

"'Tis no dream. She is perfect. And she will grow to be as beautiful as her mother."

He gathered his daughter close and strode over to Gillian, placing Marissa in her outstretched arms. She positioned her daughter carefully, and pulled the shift from her shoulder, exposing her breast.

"She must be hungry." Sure enough, the child easily found Gillian's nipple. The sensation of her daughter catching onto her breast stirred a strange set of emotions. When the baby's eyes opened, Gillian gasped.

"She has your eyes, Royce!"

Tawny eyes studied her from above and below. The stroke of her husband's hand along her hair brought a sense of peace.

"Edward arrives tomorrow."

His words shattered the calm. Without looking away from her daughter, she asked, "Why?"

"He was coming to await the birth of Anne's child and pass judgment on her. Now that she's died, he will assist in the search for Burke."

"And what of her babe?"

He looked away and didn't answer. She knew what Edward intended.

"Nay, he cannot! Please tell me he doesn't mean to..."

Royce met her gaze and the regret she found there left her heart lurching. She shook her head.

"He's just a babe, an innocent child!"

"He is the son of two traitors. Edward must decide based on that."

She shook her head, dislodging her daughter, who let out a protesting cry. She soothed the babe with soft whispers and eased her back to her chest. There must be some way.

"I know! We'll tell him Anne's baby died, and I birthed twins. Maida can spread the word throughout the manor. None have to know he isn't ours."

Royce shook his head. "Edward will not be fooled."

"Then I will convince him! I won't let him kill a baby!"

Royce's smile seemed full of regret. "If any can sway the king, I suspect 'twould be you. Very well, you may try. But I'll have your word you won't do anything foolish should Edward insist on ..."

"Not to worry. I will convince him 'tis the right thing to do."

# Chapter Twenty-four

The king rode into Lyndon accompanied by what seemed to be every soldier in England.

Gillian stood at the top of the steps beside Royce as the king dismounted in the inner bailey. She clutched her husband's hand, unable to quell the churning of her stomach. Exhaustion still had a firm grip on her, and her arms ached without her daughter, but before she could return to her chamber, she must convince the king of her plan. Royce assured her he would back her claim.

Edward wore a somber expression as he climbed the steps. Royce bowed, and Gillian attempted a curtsy, but her aching muscles made the movement ungraceful. She kept her head down to hide her grimace.

"I hear you are to be congratulated." Edward strode past them into the keep.

"Aye, sire. Our daughter was born yesterday."

"And the traitor's bastard." He stopped in the center of the hall and turned a piercing stare on Royce.

Gillian tugged her husband's hand, nodding to the crowd gathering in the hall. He reassured her with a squeeze of his hand.

"Sire, may we speak in private?"

Edward hesitated, studying them both closely. Gillian managed to remain upright on her trembling legs, her chin high. The king nodded.

"Aye."

Royce led the way to Thomas' chamber and closed the door. He turned to the king, still holding Gillian's hand.

"My wife has a request."

Edward held up his hand, his pale eyes cold and icy. Despite her determination to convince him to grant her boon, Gillian shivered.

"I suspect I know what you will ask Lady Gillian. But I

cannot –"

"Please, sire, he is an innocent child. He has nothing to do with the sins of his parents."

"That may be, but rebel blood courses in his veins. I'll not risk England."

Gillian pulled free of Royce's grip, stepping closer to the king. She clasped her hands before her.

"Please, Your Highness, Royce and I will raise him to be loyal to you. He will never know of his birth."

"And what if he does learn of it? What will he do, seek to avenge his parents' deaths?"

She shook her head. "Nay, he will not. Royce will train him, I will nurture him. He will be as one of our own."

"And how will you explain it?" Edward folded his arms and scratched his chin.

She glanced at Royce, smiling at his encouraging nod. She faced the king once more.

"We will tell him he is the twin of our daughter. Everyone else will be told Anne's baby died."

"All here at Lyndon already know."

"No, Maida, the midwife, and her girls have been sworn to secrecy. We have shared the truth with no one else."

Edward scowled. "I don't like it."

"I promise you, no one will ever know. We will raise them at Montchester and he will never be permitted near Lyndon. In time, anyone who suspects the truth of his birth will forget and no one else will discover the truth."

Edward began to pace, muttering under his breath. Finally, he turned to Gillian. She held her breath, her fingers twisting tightly together.

"Very well. But he may not be fostered." Edward faced Royce, his expression somber. "He cannot gain any of your lands, I will not have it."

"As you wish," said Royce.

"He, and many others, will wonder why your first-born son will not inherit."

"When the time comes, we will think of a reason."

Edward returned his fierce stare to Gillian. "And you will swear to keep this a secret."

Able to breathe again, Gillian grinned. She threw herself against Edward in a fierce hug.

"Thank you, Sire. I promise you will never regret this."

"Gillian!"

Her husband's voice sharpened her awareness. She gasped and released the king, who now bore an amused smile.

"Forgive me, Your Highness. I meant no disrespect."

"None taken." His expression sobered. "No one must ever learn of this."

"You have my vow and that of my husband." She looked to Royce, who nodded.

"Congratulations, Panther, not every man is lucky enough to have twin children!"

Gillian grinned, tears of joy blurring her vision. The tight fist around her heart eased and she breathed steadily once more.

"A feast has been prepared," said Royce. "We will celebrate your arrival and that of our children."

"I will fetch the babes." She hurried from the room, her breasts aching. In her chamber, the wet nurse and Maida looked after the infants. She hurried across, looking at the two cradles, side by side.

"They are beautiful babes, my lady," said Maida.

"Yes, they are. My husband and I are very lucky."

"The king granted your boon?" The older woman's eyes widened and she smiled.

Gillian nodded and bent to lift the boy into her arms. "He has. We will proclaim him our son at the feast. No one is ever to know."

"Gladys and I will take this to our graves." The midwife nodded to the younger girl who vowed her silence as well.

"I must give him a name." Gillian studied the babe, his tiny arms flailing as he began to cry.

She hushed him and began to rock, thinking of what

name would fit the son of the Panther.

"He'll be strong, like the rowan tree. That is what he shall be called. Rowan."

"It's a wonderful name, my lady. Now we must feed these children so you can attend the king."

\*\*\*

Gillian paced, the wailing Rowan in her arms. He simply would not quiet, no matter what she tried. Her head pounded from lack of sleep. Even with the wet nurse, the last days of tending two babes had left her utterly exhausted.

She shifted the boy, offering her breast once more. This time, he accepted and began to suckle. She sighed, relieved that his crying had stopped and the ache in her breasts now soothed.

"You are a greedy boy," she cooed, smiling for what seemed the first time in days. Her thoughts drifted to Royce, and guilt over falling asleep last night rose again. He'd sworn he wasn't angry, but she knew he wasn't pleased. The past weeks had left very little chance for intimacy and, even then, his tender and gentle lovemaking, while exhilarating, frustrated her. She wanted his fierce passion, the way he laid her across his lap to redden her arse. He'd refused during the time she carried Marissa and though she understood why, it didn't help her frustration. She'd been looking forward to last night. How could she have fallen asleep?

Rowan finished and Gillian laid him on her shoulder, patting his back. At that moment, Marissa awakened, crying, and Gillian groaned. Where had Gladys disappeared to? She rose to put Rowan in his cradle and stopped short to see Burke standing in the doorway.

"How did you get in here?"

Royce and the king had taken a group of men into the forest, seeking the traitor out. But plenty of knights and the household remained. How had the bastard snuck past them?

She tightened her hold on the baby, wishing a secret door had been built into this room as well.

Burke smiled, an evil leer that sent chills along her spine. "You forget, I know this manor as well as you and your husband."

He withdrew his sword and advanced on her. "Is that my son?"

She shook her head. "Nay, 'tis my babe. Your son... died with Anne."

His eyes narrowed and he shook his head, still moving closer. "I don't believe you."

"'Tis true. I bore Royce two children."

"You lie. Your wet nurse told me all before she...succumbed to her fall."

Gillian struggled to catch her breath. Gladys was dead? "Murderer! When Royce and the king return −"

"We will be long gone. I've come to claim my son, and you are coming with us."

She shook her head, backing away. In her cradle, Marissa still screamed. She fought the urge to look at her daughter, forcing her focus to remain on Burke.

"I'll kill her if you don't come with me now."

Her heart seemed to stop mid-beat. Rowan now squirmed against her tight grip. God's blood, what could she do? The sword pointed menacingly at Marissa's cradle. She had only one choice, and felt confident he would not harm his own child. Or her, since he needed her to care for Rowan. She didn't doubt Royce would find her soon enough.

She had to believe in all of that, otherwise, she feared she might very well lose herself to despair. Closing her eyes against the burn of tears, she nodded in acquiescence of Burke's command. He grabbed her arm and pulled her into the corridor, to her former chamber. He must have gotten in this way, she realized, noting the way the tapestry hung crooked. Pushing her ahead of him, he guided her to the stairs, but down, to the lower chambers, rather than up to the ramparts. The musty smell made her gag, and Rowan whimpered.

"Keep him from crying." Burke's menacing order

sounded beside her ear, an ominous background to their slow shuffling through the dim light.

She nodded, shushing the child. Soon enough a glimmer of light from outside grew brighter as they neared the end of the tunnel. She squinted as she stepped out into the field beyond the castle walls.

"This way." He pulled her into the woods, a horse tethered to a tree. He shoved her toward it. She stumbled, nearly falling, but his grip on her arm kept her upright.

"Get on the horse."

"But –"

He wrenched the child from her arms and she cried out in rage, stretching to take Rowan back. Burke held him out of reach.

"Get up. Now!"

With his sword pointed at her head, she had no choice but to obey. She mounted the horse, relieved when Burke handed the baby up to her. She'd barely considered jumping down and running, but he was behind her in a moment, securing her with a strong arm around her waist.

*Jesu*, how could she get free? None had seen him taking her away, would Royce know who'd kidnapped her? And what of Marissa? Her heart ached to think of her daughter still crying helplessly in her cradle. Would anyone hear and sound an alarm?

Burke spurred his mount and headed deeper into the forest. If someone didn't give chase soon... she shuddered to think what could happen.

"Where are you taking us?"

"Deep into Wales, where none will find us. You will care for my son until I tire of you."

"Royce will find you and you will pay for this! How could you risk harming your own child?"

"I thought he wasn't my son," he taunted.

She silently cursed her slip of the tongue. "He isn't. He's mine."

"He is Anne's son. My son. And you will all pay for killing her!"

Gillian shook her head. "We didn't kill her; she died birthing your babe."

"Lies, all of it! You'll all pay. When I return with more men, I'll destroy Edward and take the throne for myself. Anyone who dares to defy me will pay with their life."

"'Twill be you who pays with your life."

Royce's voice rang out through the forest. Joy bubbled through Gillian until she found the tip of Burke's sword poking at her throat. His arm around her waist tightened painfully, making it hard to breathe. Sensing her panic, Rowan began to cry.

She looked around, choking back a relieved cry to see Royce, Edward, Simon and several other knights surrounding them. Burke had nowhere to flee. She had to get off this horse. A trapped animal will fight its way out, to the death if necessary. And Burke was now a cornered animal.

"Release my wife and the child."

Burke let loose a maniacal laugh. "Can't do that, Royce. They're mine now and you will let us pass, or I will strike them down right here."

"If you harm a hair on either of them, you will be dead before they fall."

The sword lowered, Burke shifting behind her. She remained perfectly still as he assessed his chances of getting away.

"You would kill an innocent babe?" Gillian asked, thankful her voice remained steady and calm.

"And you as well, Lady Gillian."

There was an insult in his tone, but she ignored it, her gaze remaining firmly on Royce. He was here, he would save her! She must keep calm, for surely her opportunity to flee would come. If only she knew of some way to get off the horse without endangering Rowan. At that moment, the babe let out a wail that echoed through the forest.

The cries must have startled Burke, for he loosed his hold on her. Did she dare risk it? She had no choice. Holding the child securely in her arms, she jerked free of

Burke and hurled herself to the ground, away from his sword. As she fell, she twisted, hoping to land with the babe atop her. Shouts echoed around her, but she ignored them in her attempts to protect Rowan. Her son. When she landed hard on her back, the brief satisfaction at her success was chased by the breath forced from her lungs. Hands were upon her, and she struggled for a moment, until a familiar voice broke through her panic.

"Gilly, come with me." Simon helped her to her feet. Struggling to breathe, she accepted his assistance and hurried away before Burke could come after her again. She and Simon took up a position surrounded by the king's men. She rocked Rowan, thankful he finally quieted.

"There is no place to run, Burke. Surrender now." Royce dismounted and unsheathed his sword.

Burke shook his head. "I think not. You will have to kill me here and now."

Gillian held her breath, hating the sorrow that came into her husband's eyes. Even though Burke had betrayed them all, clearly Royce still mourned the loss of his friend.

"Very well, if that is how you choose to die, face me."

Burke gave another one of his mad grins and dismounted, sword at the ready. "Let us end this now."

\*\*\*

Royce circled his former captain, recognizing the madness in the other man's eyes. All these years, he had trusted his friend, while the entire time Burke had been planning to destroy them all. These last weeks, Royce had learned more of Burke's mother's family, and knew now how Burke had been able to amass enough men and weapons for the constant sieges that occurred along the border. And Royce had unwittingly helped, sending him to scout Apshire several times. He'd correct his mistakes now.

"What are you waiting for Panther?"

The taunt drew a few derisive shouts from the men surrounding them. Royce didn't dare take his eyes from his opponent.

"Your first mistake."

Burke's smile slipped, turning into a sneer. He charged, sword raised. Royce easily blocked the blow, the screech of the blades crackling in his ears. Shouts of encouragement came from the men, whistles and cheers sending any remaining animals of the forest fleeing.

"I'll kill you, you sanctimonious bastard!" Burke screamed, swinging wildly now.

"You can try," Royce drawled, evading another wild slash. Over the next several minutes, he merely evaded and blocked every move Burke made. The other man tired and grew more sloppy. He blocked another overhead blow and shoved, forcing Burke to stumble backward. He advanced.

The unexpected swing at his face startled him and he pulled back, but not before the tip of the blade sliced along his cheek, burning. A shrill scream filled the air. Gillian. He didn't dare look up, but the time for toying with his enemy ended now. Royce swung at Burke, but the captain sidestepped. Narrowing his eyes, he watched the other man, looking for any weakness.

There, his left side. His mail gapped. He thrust at Burke, a rain of blows that compelled Burke to retreat. Yet, with a ducking roll, the captain was now behind him. Before his thrust reached flesh, Royce turned and caught Burke's blade with his, immobilizing the steel. His free hand fisted and he slammed it into Burke's face, the satisfying crunch of bone accompanied by a howl of pain. Cheers and applause erupted among the men.

Burke collapsed, holding his face, blood dripping in rivulets to the ground. Royce strode over and lifted his blade, ready to finish the battle. At the last moment, Burke rolled away, somehow rising again to stand. Blood covered his face and tunic, and he swayed unsteadily.

"Surrender," Royce ordered. "Before the king and these witnesses."

Burke gave another one of his mad laughs. "I will never surrender."

Royce never expected the charge, and moved to sidestep, but Burke wheeled suddenly about, hooking his foot behind Royce's legs. Off-balance, Royce stumbled and fell. The clearing fell silent when Burke stood over Royce, sword raised.

"Now you die!"

Just as Royce lifted his blade, an arrow slammed into Burke's chest. Royce immediately rolled away and to his feet, staring in shock at the blood spilling over Burke's chest. The heavy sword fell from the captain's hands as he gaped at the arrow, his bloodied hands grabbing the shaft in an attempt to pull the arrow out.

Royce thrust his sword into Burke's gut, pulling it out and thrusting once more. One last tug jerked the blade free. He turned.

Gillian stood just inside the ring of men, bow in hand. He looked back at Burke at the very moment the man collapsed to the ground. Thunderous roars of exultation rang through the forest. Royce faced his wife.

Even now, she taunted him with a smug smile. While he could have easily blocked Burke and regained the upper hand, he refrained from saying so. He stalked over to her, stopping inches away.

"Whose is that?"

She shrugged. "I don't know his name." She searched the jumping and cheering crowd. "There, that's him."

Royce didn't look to see who she pointed at. He merely studied her, his gaze roving over her to ensure she was unharmed.

"He didn't hurt you?"

She shook her head. "He needed me. To take care of Rowan."

He said nothing for a few moments, too many thoughts racing through his head for him to be coherent about any one. Instead, he grabbed her shoulders and drew her near, taking her mouth in a hungry kiss. It seemed the only way to tell her what he felt. To his delight, she wrapped her arms around him, opening her mouth to him. His fingers caught in her hair, holding her still as he ravished her mouth.

When he drew away, she leaned weakly against him.

"Thank you." He buried his face into her hair, crushing her tightly against him.

"There is nothing to thank me for. I did what had to be done. That man and his lover caused me no end of trouble. I enjoyed it!"

He chuckled. "You are truly a Wildcat, in every way."

The sound of the babe crying had her stiffening in his arms. "Rowan!"

He released her. "Go."

"I wondered if you'd ever let her go."

Royce turned to Edward. The king grinned broadly, pulling Royce in for a boisterous hug. "Once I learned this was all his doing, I knew 'twould end this way." He sobered. "I am sorry it had to come to this."

"I had no idea he'd harbored such hatred. Madness." Royce stared at the body of his childhood friend. Hell, all of them had been close, growing up as they did. Before Edward was king, he'd been much more lighthearted. As boys, they'd shared everything, from pranks to training, even women. 'Twasn't often he thought back on those days and missed them. He heaved a deep breath.

"Sire, I would make a request."

"Anything. You have done England, me, a great service today."

"I wish to retire to Montchester."

"Of course."

"I don't want to return to London for some time." He held the king's gaze.

Edward gave a brief nod. "I see. I suppose it won't do any harm. I will, of course, be visiting sometime this summer."

"Of course, Sire. My home is open to you any time."

"Are you sure that's all you want?"

"I have another request I'd like to discuss, but not right now."

"Very well. Attend me later and we'll talk about it."

Gillian appeared beside him, the baby in her arms. A

burst of joy shot through him, and he slid his arm about her shoulders.

"With two children, we must be settled for some time. I'd rather they be more grown before we travel."

Edward grinned. "Of course. Now, let's return to Lyndon."

The king turned and mounted, his men following suit. Royce led Gillian to Viking. He took the baby as she mounted. Dark eyes stared up at him. Another glance at Burke's body and the question solidified. Mayhap Anne had lied to them all and the child wasn't truly Burke's. He contemplated the child again. No matter. This was his son, and he would protect him.

"Royce?"

The apprehension in Gillian's soft question drew his attention. He handed the child to her.

"He is our son."

His declaration drew wide eyes and a blinding grin.

"I feared you were angry... at him. You looked so fierce."

Royce climbed up behind his wife. He wrapped his arms around them both. Soon, they'd be back at Lyndon, where their daughter awaited. He almost laughed at the realization his eagerness for the next battle, political or otherwise, had utterly vanished.

"We will leave for Montchester after the planting."

His wife said nothing.

"I know you don't want to leave."

She shook her head. "It's not that. I know my home is with you, and our children. But..."

"Simon." He chuckled at the way she turned to look at him. "Yes, I have an idea and I think Edward will agree."

\*\*\*

Gillian gaped at her husband. He stared straight ahead. She slapped at his arm.

"Tell me your plan!"

"Do you think Simon would do well as baron?"

Did he mean it? When he caught her stare, she knew

he did. Each day, he gave her more reasons to love him.

"Thank you! Royce, that makes me so happy."

"Well, after he weds Lady Madelaine, he will need lands to provide for her. Her dowry is not inconsiderable, but he will still need wealth of his own."

"Edward knows?" She supposed she should thank the king for ordering her marriage. If he hadn't insisted, she wouldn't be here with this man, this Panther, who claimed her for his own.

"I've mentioned it. And now that this is all done, he is willing to grant me whatever I wish."

"Except that I stopped Burke before he could strike!"

Indignation rose. Did he not intend to give her any credit?

"Aye, you did. And I thanked you for it. I will do so again later."

He stole her breath when he covered her mouth with a bruising kiss. When he drew away, she could barely, her vision hazed with lust.

"I love you, Wildcat. I will forever."

Tears of joy burned her eyes. "As I love you."

His lips moved along her cheek, back toward her neck. Tendrils of heat wisped through her veins, and she must have clutched Rowan a little too tightly, for he let out a protesting whine. Royce's fingers sliding her hair from her neck, following the motion with his lips, soon had her forgetting anything else but the way fire scorched her skin.

"When we get back to Lyndon, you are to give both children to the wet nurse. For the night."

Her heart clenched at the thought of being away from the babies. "Gladys is dead. Burke killed her."

"He lied. Gladys is alive and well and able to care for the babes tonight."

"But –"

"You will be much too busy to even think of them."

She shivered. "Will you bind me?" Heat crept up her cheeks as she asked, even as the idea set her body to yearning for his.

His chuckle roared into her. "Only if I must."

"I see."

She squirmed, her sex swelling, the sensitive flesh soaked. She bit back a cry when he lifted her skirts and slid his hand along her thigh. She peered around him, but the other men had ridden on ahead. At the first touch of his fingers along her cleft, she moaned, her head falling back against him.

Then recalling his words, she shoved his hand away. "My lord, there are others about."

She tilted her head to look at him. He grinned and winked.

"Well, wife, I suppose you must be... punished."

She smiled, biting her lower lip. "'Twould seem that way."

He dipped her back, covering her mouth in an alluring kiss that promised wicked delight, yet also revealed how she possessed his heart. But being possessed by him, in every way possible, had given her all her heart wanted.

# The end

# Coming Soon:

**Warrior's Vengeance, Book 2 in the Medieval Warrior's Legends**
**Warrior's Wrath, Book 3 in the Medieval Warrior's Legends**
**Warrior's Witch, Book 4 in the Medieval Warrior's Legends**

Thank you for taking the time to read Warrior's Possession. I hope you enjoyed it, and if so, please consider telling your friends or perhaps you wouldn't mind posting a short review. Word of mouth is an author's best friend and more appreciated than you know.

# about the author:

I'm a proud born-and-bred Jersey Girl with Brooklyn roots. And I still live where it all started - I married my very own alpha male many eons ago, and have an amazing college-bound daughter and a 10 year old son who charms and frustrates me at every turn. Free time is always a luxury and I spend the bulk of what time I manage to scrounge up lost in the worlds of my own making. I love to read and write hot, sexy and emotional stories about people both glamorous and not-so-glamorous. Be warned - some of my characters are even downright un-heroic, which is part of what makes them so interestingly sexy, in my opinion!

On the rare occasions I'm not taking advantage of that valuable free time by writing, you can catch me poking around in my other favorite twisted historical worlds of Sleepy Hollow, Reign and the History Channel's Vikings. I'm also a huge fan of Harry Potter, Highlander, Charmed, and DragonBall Z! Yeah, a strange fandom medley, but each one features some of the sexiest villains ever. Did I mention I love villains? And of course, let's not forget my beloved NY Rangers.

**Find Gianna online:**

**"A Kinky Twist on History!"**
**"Magically Kinky!"**
**Website:** www.giannasimoneeroticromance.com
**Blog:** http://giannasimone.blogspot.com
**Twitter:** @Gianna_Simone
**Facebook:**
www.facebook.com/GiannaSimoneRomanceAutho
r
**Goodreads:**
https://www.goodreads.com/author/show/4493720.
Gianna_Simone
You can also find me on Pinterest, Google+,
LinkedIn!

**I love to hear from readers - don't hesitate to
reach out and say hi!**

# medieval warrior's legends

**WARRIOR'S VENGEANCE:** Near the Scottish border during the reign of Edward I, Marissa Langley, daughter of a powerful English earl is captured by a band of marauding Scotsmen. Completely at their mercy, she is desperate to escape. When the leader of the group saves her from certain rape, she believes she will be freed.

But Ian MacCallum is no savior. He takes her for his own, seduces her then makes her a submissive. Her collar and chains are part of his vengeance on her father—the man Ian claims is responsible for the death of his beloved wife and son.

But her immediate death is not Ian's plan. He subjects her to daily suffering and punishments and goes so far as sharing her with another clansman. Yet, her spirit will not be broken. He finds himself drawn to that core of strength within her; finding
it most exquisite as it cannot be violated.

When danger from within his clan threatens her, Ian protects her, discovering at the
same time that he does not want to lose her, ever.

Marissa makes her own discovery: she comes to

crave Ian's torturous touch. When she learns the source of his hatred, she is certain he is wrong. Her father would not commit atrocities. She waits for the moment when she can escape and prove her father's innocence. But that would mean leaving Ian when she is no longer sure she
wants to be free.

Featuring A Kinky Twist on History, including bondage, collars, spanking, multiple partners and so much more!

**WARRIOR'S WRATH:** In 14th century England, a long-kept secret devastates Rowan Langley. Anger sends him on a quest for truth. He trusts no one, keeping others away, except fellow knight Gerard.

Aeron Dawkyns, fleeing Wales and a charge of murder, lives on the street, pickpocketing. She steals Rowan's coin. Later, Rowan catches her attempting to steal his horse. She has a choice – serve them both with her body, or be handed over to be hanged. She chooses Rowan and Gerard.

Serving an angry Rowan has dark pleasures Aeron learns to crave. She feels safe, despite the knights' wicked games. When Rowan drags her back to Wales, she fears that safety will be destroyed.

Rowan learns Aeron's plight and vows to hunt down her enemies, promising to protect and keep her. Yet he worries he's no better than her enemy. Still, he craves his slave's touch, as much as he craves her heart.

Staying with Rowan becomes Aeron's heart's desire – but could mean her death.

Featuring a Kinky Twist on History! including bondage, spanking, multiple partners and so much more!

# The Norsemen Sagas

**NORSEMAN'S REVENGE:** Being kidnapped by a Viking raider on her wedding night might really be a blessing from the gods.

Geira Sorensdotter awaits her new husband, but she's filled with doubts about the man and the marriage. Those doubts are forgotten when the village is attacked, her husband is struck down and she is tied up and carried off amidst the raid.

Kori Thorfinnson has waited years to take revenge against the man who murdered his wife. But he soon finds the innocent young woman he's taken as his personal slave is not his enemy, despite her marriage to his foe. Her courage in defying him, her caring heart, and the fiery passion she shares stirs feelings Kori hasn't known since his wife died. Afraid to lose Geira, he binds her to him in many ways – not only with rope, but with his body, his collar and his brand.

Geira quickly learns just how despicable her husband was, and despite her difficult circumstances, grows to care deeply for Kori, her captor. Still, dreams of freedom linger. But once she finds herself with child, she must plan her escape, to save herself and her baby. However, Kori has plans of his own.

**NORSEMAN'S DECEPTION:** He saved her life – can the gods save her heart and soul from the mysterious loner's dark desires?

Fearing an arranged marriage, Thora Korisdotter flees her village, vowing never to return home. With her two pet wolves beside her, she is confident in her safety, and protected by the loyal animals. But when outlaws attack, wounding one of her beloved pets, she is thankful for the mysterious stranger who arrives just in time to save her. Now in his debt, she must repay him as he asks – with her body.

Ari Hugisson has wandered for years after being cast out of his clan as an outlaw. The time of his banishment is nearing its end, and Ari has the proof he needs to clear his name and unmask the real murderer – his brother. But when he comes across a beautiful woman under attack, he is compelled to step in and save her. He knows just the way to make her repay her debt, with the passion he senses lurking just under the surface of her fiery nature.

When Thora learns Ari has lied to her and knows well the man she was to wed – his brother – the betrayal cuts deep and she determines to leave him at the first opportunity. But the passion he stirs is unlike anything she has ever known, even if he sometimes insists on treating her as little more than a slave.

When he confronts those who would see him killed, will she stand beside him and defend him, even at the risk of losing her family?

The Norsemen Sagas contain explicit love scenes featuring A Kinky Twist on History, including bondage, spanking, multiple partners and more!

# The Bayou Magiste Chronicles

**CLAIMED BY THE DEVIL:** Helene Gaudet finds the perfect Dom in an internet chat room. It's as if he can read her mind – and he knows how to make her beg. When they agree to meet in the real world, Helene realizes why her Dom knows her so well – he is none other than Devlin Marchand, the same man who handed her over years ago to a dark sorcerer – to be killed.

She thought she was free from suffering – including a rageful ex-husband who cursed her, leaving her unable to bear children. She wants to forget the past – but her lust for Devlin is so intense after each tormenting, releasing encounter, she doesn't want to leave him.

Devlin wants to repair his past wrongs – but guilt over his past betrayal is multiplied when he learns the curse that has dogged Helene for years comes from the trove of magic created by his very own family. Devlin fears the tentative relationship they've built will be destroyed – and he cannot allow that.

Can they overcome the past to have a future together?

** Contains lots of explicit Magically Kinky! love scenes of the paranormal kind, including magical sex toys, potions, bondage, spanking and more!

**CLAIMED BY THE MAGE:** Lily Prentiss wishes she could ignore her inborn healing magic so she can live life on her terms, not follow the path her Magiste family chose for her. But when she stumbles across Aidan Marchand in the excruciating throes of evolving into a Mage, her touch is all that stops his pain and she can no longer deny her powers. When the sexy Dom seduces her into willing submission, she finds she doesn't want to resist and actually enjoys giving up control.

Aidan has more to worry about than just his rapidly maturing powers – his business partner is blackmailing him into funding a venture that involves kidnapping young girls both magical and mortal, and selling them as sex slaves. Even as Lily's touch eases Aidan's pain, he knows staying with her puts her in danger from his enemies. But the gift of her sexual submission helps him even more than her healing magic...so how can he let her go?

** Contains lots of explicit Magically Kinky! love scenes of the paranormal kind, including magical sex toys, potions, bondage, spanking and more!

**CLAIMED BY THE ENCHANTER:** Regine

Marchand loves being in control – and the role of domme is the perfect way for her to exert that control. An accomplished equestrian, she has her goals of championship in sight and no one will get in her way. Her life and future are in her hands, she doesn't need to depend on anyone for success and happiness.

Cameron McIntyre is fascinated by the cool façade Regine displays, but he senses the depth of her passion lurking under the surface. Despite her protests to the contrary, he recognizes in her a desire to submit and be dominated. But when he is forced to suspend her from competition due to performance enhancement spells used on her horse, he worries he may drive her away, instead of back into his arms. Believing her innocent of the charges, he vows to help her uncover who set her up while convincing her that submission to him is what she truly wants and needs. Submitting to the tall Irishman brings a new level of pleasure Regine has never known, at the same time making her question everything she knew about herself.

Regine is unaware an enemy from her past has targeted her for revenge. Together she and Cameron must discover who wants to knock her out of competition for good, possibly killing her in the process.

** Contains lots of explicit Magically Kinky! love scenes of the paranormal kind, including magical sex toys, potions, bondage, spanking and more!

**CLAIMED BY THE ZYNDEVINE:** In 13th century France, attacked by those carrying out the Papal Inquisition, *Magiste* Enchantress Chantal Belliveau is thankful for rescue from certain torture and death. But she never expected it to be at the hands of Henri Marchand, one of a powerful pureblooded line of ancient *Magiste*, the Zyndevines. Henri holds the key to her survival, but the danger he poses to her heart and soul could turn out to be even more perilous.

Henri is part of *Il Resistasse*, a handful of powerful *Magiste* fighting the atrocities the Catholic Church inflicts on their race. Saving Chantal becomes more than a simple rescue - the innocent young woman with half-trained powers enchants him more than he has ever been before. That she enjoys the dark side of pleasure he inflicts on her makes him question his determination to never give another his heart.

Chantal is horrified when Henri invokes an ancient spell, the *Possede Puissant*. The incantation leaves her little more than his possession. While she finds herself enjoying his dark and wicked sensual delights, she determines to free herself. Still, the security she finds with Henri encourages her to stay by his side, claiming spell or not.

Resentment toward her from Henri's family convinces Chantal she must ultimately break free of Henri's possession. But when the Inquisitioners attack, Henri convinces Chantal to embark on a journey to a new land, a journey that may well mean the survival of the entire *Magiste* race but the loss of her freedom forever.

\*\* Contains lots of explicit Magically Kinky! love scenes of the paranormal kind, including magical sex toys, potions, bondage, spanking and more!